Praise for

ETCHED IN STONE

"A fascinating, intriguing and suspenseful coming-of-age story with a witchcraft twist. A unique combo that will keep you on the edge of your seat until the very last page!"
—Natacha Belair, Award-Winning Author,
A Stellar Purpose trilogy

Etched in Stone
by Sarah Alserhaid

© Copyright 2024 Sarah Alserhaid

ISBN 979-8-88824-346-6

All rights reserved. No part of this publication may be reproduced, stored in a retrieval system, or transmitted in any form or by any means—electronic, mechanical, photocopy, recording, or any other—except for brief quotations in printed reviews, without the prior written permission of the author.

This is a work of fiction. All the characters in this book are fictitious, and any resemblance to actual persons, living or dead, is purely coincidental. The names, incidents, dialogue, and opinions expressed are products of the author's imagination and are not to be construed as real.

Published by

◀ köehlerbooks™

3705 Shore Drive
Virginia Beach, VA 23455
800-435-4811
www.koehlerbooks.com

Etched in Stone

Etched in Stone

Sarah Alserhaid

VIRGINIA BEACH
CAPE CHARLES

To my fellow Elliot witch, thank you for being the sister you are. The pranks, tears, and laughs are things we will carry for the rest of our lives, and to me, they are more powerful than any witch, wizard, or book.

To the Daniel I met later in life, your continued support means more than words can describe and more than anything that can be measured.

Prologue

"Becoming a mother changes you," the woman whispered to the infant in her arms as she drifted into the dark blanket of trees. Peering around the haunting forest, she sighed. "Though some may argue that it's a burden, I look deep into your eyes and know that you're nothing short of a blessing."

And she stepped further into the abyss of what might be her doom.

She could have easily avoided danger by staying indoors or around family. But this young lady was not like other people. She had a secret. A secret so grave that she played out her days in complete denial of what she possessed. But the secret had potentially been exposed.

So she set out to meet the ominous person who had threatened to reveal her. Usually, she would ignore such an accusation. Surely no one had proof. But things had changed. She had a little one to worry about. The mere allegation would endanger the helpless child she held so tightly in her arms.

As she cooed to her fragile infant, she explained why she had stepped foot into such a place, on such a night, during such an hour—promising that even though she had grown up alone, her baby would not. She spoke with conviction and confidence, and the child remained calm in her arms.

Then she heard faint steps and froze in place.

As the steps grew closer, a faint light appeared: a lantern. The shimmer grew brighter and brighter until the moment arrived—when the person who had been sending subtle hints for weeks appeared before her, ending the passive torment.

The hooded individual stood in silence.

This person was unafraid of her; otherwise, this quiet and secluded meeting would not have taken place. They wanted something from her, an absurd demand in exchange for their silence.

Paralyzed with fear, the new mother looked down at her child and summoned the courage to speak. She asked what they wanted. Rather than reply, the mysterious person lifted their hood.

The shock of seeing one of her closest friends left her aghast. This person who was as close as family, who was practically an older brother, stood before her, grinning maliciously.

"I ask again," she announced, riddled with the pain of betrayal yet determined not to show it, "what is it you want from me?"

"Your power has grown remarkably well for a young, untrained witch. Now, after so many years of merely watching, I'm here to take it," the man gloated.

Memories flashed through the witch's mind: of this friend helping her find her way, find her husband, find her calling. But she understood now that he had never accepted nor loved her. The greed hidden for years had surfaced. The witch gazed down at her child and affirmed that—friend or foe—she would protect her family with all the strength she possessed.

Her not-so-friendly friend seemed to expect nothing less and threw his lantern to the ground. Grasping a small sack of herbs, he echoed an old chant—one known to strip witches of their power. He repeated the chant over and over, its effect cumulative.

Unfazed, the witch stood calmly.

She had planned for such an event. Although she never foresaw her comrade as the one to seek out her demise, she was nonetheless ready for it. And in this battle, there were two witches, not one. Although the baby's innate power had not manifested, it was very much present.

The witch confidently fended off the mediocre power of the chant, the spell to halt its effect falling effortlessly from her lips. She smiled.

"You have come underprepared, and your lack of knowledge in witchcraft will be your undoing. You were not born a witch. No matter what chant you use, we can stop it, and we will." She tightened her hold on the bundle in her arms.

Her friend growled. Clearly, he had not planned on the child's power.

The witch hesitated for only a second. She could not drum up the anger to harm the man, regardless of the betrayal, but she could not allow him to leave. The words formed in her mind—a spell to erase memories. She hoped it would suffice.

Before she could unleash her magic, her friend threw the herb sack to the ground and hummed a rhyme as a cloud of smoke engulfed the young mother. She fell to her knees under the consuming power of an invisible force, never losing hold of her child.

"You may have the advantage with power and magic, but you are not immune to a curse."

The witch, shaken, held the baby close as the smoke disappeared. Tugging the hood back over his head, the envious creature slowly backed away.

"I curse you with a confinement in your power . . ."

With her free hand, the witch urgently dug through her bag for the scroll containing the magic she had collected over the years. Finding it, she squinted at the scribbles.

The witch's new nemesis stretched out his arm.

"With my curse, I take your power and place it in a totem, that scroll in your hand. Your power will, from this moment and forever, live in that scroll; and without that scroll, your precious power will be gone."

With an evil snicker, the man continued, "Next, I curse your child and your entire bloodline. Only a sixth daughter shall control the totem's power. Without a sixth daughter in every generation, your bloodline's power will end. And should she die before the next sixth daughter, your family's power—no matter how great it grows—will be lost, forever."

The hooded horror then disappeared into the void of night.

With flooded eyes, the witch recalled what she knew about curses. She slumped on the ground, clutching her daughter, tears gliding down her cheeks. She thought through everything she had ever read and every rule she'd learned as a young witch. She could not break the curse.

And then, an idea came to her mind. A solution. She could not break the curse—but there was one thing she could do.

Chapter One

"**MADEMOISELLE.**" The eccentric man peeped up from his camera. "Zee tassel, move zee tassel, s'il vous plaît."

Unsure what he was referring to, Amber tilted her head, thinking the tassel hanging from her graduation cap had come too close to her face.

"Non!" he barked as he drew closer. After barely touching the threads, he returned to the *X* on the mat. She waited for a sign that he was about to snap a picture, knowing he would provide no direction. After a flash, he sighed at his camera once more.

She was uncomfortable with the stool he had her sitting on, and her patience with his lack of professionalism was wearing thin. Still, her sister had recommended this photographer, and she wanted to give him the benefit of the doubt.

"Mademoiselle, none of these pictures I like," he huffed, glaring around as if to blame a noisy audience.

"Perhaps you could tell me when you're going to take the picture," Amber cordially suggested. "I have posed for portraits before."

"Non!" he shouted. "I know what it is I do not like." He threw one hand in the air while the other clutched his camera. "It is zee necklace," he proclaimed. "Remove it for zee pictures. Yes, it is my wish that you remove zee necklace."

Amber's last nerve had been severed.

"No." She stood abruptly, hiding the ache in her back. "It is my wish that I leave here with at least a few decent pictures with my necklace on."

The strange man with the clearly inauthentic French accent had crossed a line. Never in Amber's twenty-two years of living had she been so annoyed by a single person. Her oval, orange citrine necklace was her most treasured possession, given to her by her parents just before her tenth birthday, and it was one of the last things she received from them before they died.

As a little girl, Amber had disliked her birthstone. Orange was a uniquely unforgiving color, and disappointment filled her when she first opened the velvety black box wrapped with a thick orange ribbon. But she'd hidden her feelings as well as a young girl could, thanking her parents politely. Her mother placed it around her neck, and then Amber and her father walked hand in hand along the soft, crumbly sand of the beach, flicking sand with every step.

Her father had glanced over to the fading sunset, and she followed his gaze, finding the sight magnificent. The sun's rays warmed their faces. He described the masterpiece as a vision that precious few appreciated.

Then he compared the glorious sunset to her necklace, drawing her attention back to it, but this time with a fresh perspective on what made a thing beautiful. She moved her little fingers over the heavy gem and the platinum panel marked with her initials and birthdate. In that moment, a moment perhaps too mature for such a young girl, she saw what her father meant and smiled up at him in genuine gratitude. He flung her up in the air as he often did, and laughter returned to the sullen little girl.

Now, for this monumental turning point in her life, she would have one of the few physical symbols of her late parents' love with her, regardless of some flighty photographer's distaste for it.

Albeit with slight ferocity, the man finally managed to snap a few pictures that delighted Amber. She grabbed her phone, noting the time. She had a reservation for drinks with a few people she dared call her friends, and she had long ago determined to always be ready on time and to arrive early at any event or appointment.

She had met her closest and most trusted companion, Oscar, after her parents' accident. The other three classmates, Liotta, Leon, and Charlotte, were the few who had passed her friendship test. Amber had learned to be wary of people claiming to be her friends; many people, she knew, befriended her for her wealth and connections.

The faux Frenchman professed a wish for better images, but Amber was adamant.

"I arrived at this session on time, and I *will* arrive at my other engagement on time as well," she said firmly, retrieving her coat from the rack by the door and draping it over the graduation gown already on her arm. "We can set up another appointment if these pictures are not up to standard."

Not waiting for a reply, she strode out of the studio and down the hall with her graduation cap in one hand, texting with the other.

She stepped into the restroom briefly to redo her hair, allowing her black locks to fall casually about her shoulders. She smiled in the mirror as she freshened her blush, then fluffed the curtain bangs framing her face.

Her makeup had remained intact throughout the session, but true to form, she inspected her mascara to ensure it hadn't smudged. Then she gathered her belongings and headed down the hall. Humming to herself, she peeked through the glass door, waiting for her car to pull up.

Chapter Two

JADE CAUTIOUSLY WAVED to her younger sister as the car door opened, trying to decode Amber's scrunched expression and body language.

Amber was vibrating with annoyance and frustration when she jumped into the back seat. Al, their driver, gently shut the door, then placed Amber's gown on the passenger seat beside him before climbing in and rolling out of the parking lot.

"He wanted me to take off my necklace!" Amber spat.

"What on earth for?" Jade demanded.

"It was his *wish* that I do so," Amber mocked as she rolled her eyes. "Did you hear him speak?"

"Obviously," Jade replied with a chuckle. "I don't think he'll stop with that accent until he's confronted by someone who's actually French."

"I'd like to see that go down." With a smirk, Amber pulled her phone out.

Jade tugged a divine-smelling paper bag from behind her legs, giving Amber a generous grin. Handing it over, she congratulated Amber on graduating college. The younger Parker sister, who adored any type of dessert, graciously accepted the treats. She asked once more if Jade wanted to accompany her for drinks, insisting it would not be a bother.

"Oscar is going to be there."

Jade politely declined. She preferred to return to Syndicate, the company that had instigated the opening of this next chapter in their lives. Tomorrow, Amber would officially take ownership of her portion of the pharmaceutical company their late parents had founded.

Syndicate was their parents' legacy, a culmination of everything they had worked for. Although Jade had gone over the details with their family lawyer and father's closest friend, Mr. Porter, she wanted to review it one more time. One could never be too thorough, not with such a massive shift in leadership and control over the reputable company. But also, deep down, Jade wanted to revel in the fact that her sister was joining her, and together, they would lead Syndicate as their parents intended.

ॐ

Jade waved as Amber scampered off to meet her friends, past the quaint businesses surrounding the restaurant. Amber radiated elation as she approached her friends.

Syndicate was housed in one of Solas's most prestigious downtown buildings. The city Jade called home was nothing compared to Boston, the closest well-known metropolitan area, but was nonetheless elegant, with a robust population.

Al accepted Jade's offer of a chocolate chip cookie as he drove, and she relaxed back into the seat, staring out at the people bustling through the brightly lit downtown district. She absently patted her heart-shaped emerald necklace. It was a habit she and Amber shared when they were deep in thought, and as she contemplated the photographer's strange request of Amber to remove hers, she resonated with her sister's strong refusal.

Jade played back the night she'd received her necklace.

With a warm smile, her mother had explained that receiving a gemstone on the tenth birthday was a family tradition. Each daughter had helped plan their own milestone celebration. When Amber's turn came, she announced that she wanted a picnic on the beach. Their parents arranged an early celebration so that everyone could enjoy the day while the weather was mild.

Jade, on the other hand, wanted her tenth birthday to be an event of sophistication. She requested a silky black dress with a white sash around the waist but absolutely no bows. She insisted that whatever dress her sister wore also have no bows—a statement that made her parents burst out laughing.

On the night of Jade's birthday, their father walked her down the staircase to the grand dining room, which was immaculately decorated with hunter-green balloons and white streamers. After a few less-than-perfect dances with each parent before dinner, Jade's mother pulled out a red jewelry box with a vibrant green ribbon wrapped around it—with absolutely no bow.

Jade squealed when her mother opened the box to reveal the stunning emerald gem, its silvery platinum backing etched with JEP and her birthdate on the back. Her father had the honor of fastening the piece around her neck before calling the staff to serve dinner. Amber had gawked at the sparkling stone.

As perfect an evening as ever, Jade thought as the car slowed to pull into the drop-off lane of the Syndicate building.

"Al," Jade said as he held the door for her, "I think it might be better to pick up Amber, then come get me."

"Then I'd better hurry, Miss Jade," he chuckled. "We know how she is about being on time."

Jade laughed, adding that she herself was in no hurry.

She slowly climbed the smooth steps lined on either side by tiny lights. Her badge was ready as she pushed through the main entrance and greeted the night security team before crossing the lobby, her steps echoing.

She peered at the directory next to the elevator bank, at the names of the other companies occupying the extensive luxury building. The most notable were three law firms serving international clients and a logistics company with some substantial government contracts.

Syndicate comprised the twenty-fourth and twenty-fifth floors. When Jade's parents founded Syndicate during her toddlerhood, it was a small company helping patients receive the proper medication regardless of economic status. It grew to include research divisions and acquired many smaller start-up companies that shared the goal of advancing pharmaceutical research.

"A pharmaceutical company with a heart" was the phrase associated with the company that had made her family one of the wealthiest in the country. She loved her parents for showing her how to manage a growing career while prioritizing family.

As the numbers lit with every passing floor, she ruminated over her time at Syndicate. Unlike her sister, who had majored in business from the beginning, Jade had studied psychology during her undergraduate years, fascinated by the complicated connections between the mind and the biology of the brain.

A stipulation in their parents' will and estate plan required Jade and Amber to complete degrees in either business or pharmacology to claim ownership of the company, so Jade entered an MBA program soon after graduating with her BA. Throughout her graduate studies, Jade worked at Syndicate in a fairly insignificant position—her parents' contingency should the incentives for ownership not be met. But she had completed the MBA program right as Amber received her undergraduate degree.

Having signed for her own portion of Syndicate earlier that day in her eagerness to get started, she made her way to her new office on the twenty-fourth floor. She pushed open the glass door and flicked on the lights, showcasing the spacious room. Three offices would have easily fit inside.

She passed two long black sofas with a gorgeous glass coffee table between them and made her way to her wide, dark desk. The glossed surface added the perfect touch; Jade immensely disliked rough or uneven textures.

Jade picked up the folder displaying her sister's name, noting the door behind the desk was open; the cleaning crew must have already been there to stock the toiletries in her personal restroom.

She hummed as she approached the expansive window to observe the busy city below. The constant movement always captivated her. No one seemed to notice anyone else. She stood lost in thought until a light tap at the open door called her back to reality.

"How ya doing, kiddo?" Mr. Porter asked, smiling as he stepped into her office. "Enjoying the view?"

"Enjoying the space," Jade giggled, walking over to meet him. They sat together on one of the sofas.

For her roughly two years as an employee, Jade had neither a desk nor chair to use, forced to rely on a swivel stool and an open shelf for her belongings. When plans commenced for her takeover, she'd proudly restructured the layout of this floor to accommodate two sizable offices for herself and Amber.

"What has you worried?" Mr. Porter asked, hearing what she did not say, as always.

Jade avoided his eyes. "I'm not worried."

"Okay, so why are you all alone in a barely lit room, clutching Amber's folder and your necklace and staring out at the world?"

"Well," Jade chuckled, "I'm not worried."

Mr. Porter implored her to continue.

"I'm not, Mr. Porter, really. You went through everything, so I know it's okay." She sighed and added, "Lately, things have . . . I think I just have too many ideas bouncing around my head."

"Are you happy Amber is joining you?"

"Thrilled!" Jade exhaled. "Relieved. There's so much that needs fixing here, and she's the business-savvy one, not me."

"Hey, kiddo," Mr. Porter said softly, "I know you don't want to celebrate your MBA. I saw how hard it's been for you, working here. And I have one thing to say."

"Mr. Porter, did you bring cake?" Jade teased.

He beamed, ignoring her attempt to deflect. "I am so incredibly proud of you, Jade."

Jade could not speak. She gazed at her father's closest friend—who had stepped up to help take care of her and Amber after the horrible fire—with a grateful heart and tears in her eyes.

"You grew up to be a woman that I respect, a woman I care about, and a woman who makes me the best *I* can be." He held her hand, squeezing it. "Proud doesn't seem to cover it, little gem. I am that and so much more."

The pair locked Jade's office and were padding down the hall of the quiet floor when they spotted a single light illuminating a side room in the board members' suite. Jade knew exactly who was working long after the rest of Syndicate's employees had gone home. Sighing, she asked Mr. Porter to accompany her.

Jade had recently begun to suspect something was wrong with Amy. She had interviewed the young college student almost a year ago for the position of assistant to one of the board members, and a work friendship soon developed. However, something was off. Amy never lied, not really. But Jade always sensed a secret lurking beneath the surface.

Yesterday's Jade would have left Syndicate and gone home to prepare for her sister's graduation dinner. She would have left the issue for Mr. Reynolds, the horrible board member Amy worked under.

But today, Jade was part owner of Syndicate, and Amy was now her employee, her responsibility.

Jolting from her seat at their entrance and scattering the notes on her desk, Amy profusely apologized. She wiped tears from her eyes, begging Jade not to fire her for trying to study in peace. Jade took a few steps into the small room and bent to scoop some papers off the floor. When she straightened, she shot a look at a bewildered Mr. Porter and absently fondled her necklace.

"Amy, are you safe at home?" Jade asked gently.

Stammering as she stuffed her documents into her bag, Amy replied without eye contact, "Why wouldn't I be safe, Miss Jade?"

"Amy, you are not in any trouble. I just want to know."

"Everything is fine, Miss Jade," Amy responded with a slight shiver. "I didn't realize how late it got. I promise, it won't happen again."

"Is he hurting you?" Jade pressed a little harder.

"Miss Jade, I don't know what—"

"Your husband," Jade remarked, gesturing to Amy's wedding band.

"I can't talk right now," Amy replied, hurriedly grabbing her phone from the table and glancing at Mr. Porter.

"Amy, Mr. Porter is a close family friend. We talked about him being more like my uncle, right?" After hesitating, Amy nodded. "You are perfectly safe to answer me. Is he hurting you?"

After brief hesitation, the nervous woman replied, "Only when I do things he doesn't like. That's why I study here. I distract him at home."

"Do you want to leave him?" Jade asked as though inquiring about the weather.

"I, I . . ."

"Amy, I have the resources to help you. You don't need to worry about the finances or the legal help. I just need to know if you want to leave him."

"He knows people, Miss Jade," Amy whispered in defeat. "He'll come after you, too."

"Oh, I wouldn't worry too much about that. Right, Mr. Porter?"

"We will help you in every way you need, and his people won't be an issue," Mr. Porter agreed.

"I just want to go home, to my family," Amy confessed.

"That's all I need to hear." Jade turned to Mr. Porter. "I'll come find you tomorrow, after I get more information on how we should proceed."

"Miss Jade, he gets so angry. I don't want you to get hurt," Amy begged as they left the room in a group.

Insisting that the matter would go smoothly, Jade escorted Amy to the lobby, and they waited along with Mr. Porter until she was on the bus. Mr. Porter headed back to the garage elevator, explaining that he needed to make a few calls before Amber's party.

Joy filled Jade as she took her first step as the owner of Syndicate. Not every decision would be this easy, nor every choice this clear. Smiling at Al, who graciously opened the car door, Jade accepted that this was how things were meant to be. Hopefully the struggles of the past and the crippling pressure would now ease as she took on what she believed to be her destiny.

Chapter Three

The drive was full of merriment as Amber recounted her evening at the restaurant. Jade eagerly listened to every word, glad to be with her sister. When Amber finished, Jade joked that managing work with a social life would get more challenging after Amber took her share of the company.

Amber grinned. "Are you preparing me or warning me?"

Jade laughed, not answering. Pointing out how her life had drastically changed when she accepted the menial position at Syndicate, she explained the cruel reality of working at such a successful company.

Amber did not actually know any of Jade's friends, while Jade knew all of hers. This was in part due to a huge fight between the sisters nearly two years ago.

After matriculating in college, Amber drifted away from her family. In fact, she was nonexistent in the Parker household by her sophomore year as Jade prepared to complete her bachelor's degree. Amber had befriended a large group of people and busied herself with attaining good grades, building connections, and paving her own path, thereby distancing herself from the strings attached to being a Parker.

Jade initially accepted her sister's behavior at the request of their housekeeper, Kacey, who had raised them after their parents' death. Kacey suggested Jade let Amber explore the world; however, this came at a price. Jade had to assume all the pressure of representing the family.

The argument erupted when the final straw broke Jade's back. Jade had been overwhelmed and overworked with finishing her undergraduate degree and preparing to start her MBA program, all while working under Syndicate's insufferable board members. Amber agreed to help carry the load by giving a keynote speech at a benefit in their late parents' memory.

When Jade's calls went unanswered on the night in question, she was left in the lurch. Short and fragile were the words that unraveled on a cocktail napkin. The room of people waiting for her to fail was dire enough, but the burden of speaking about her parents' legacy compounded the situation. Out in the world, the Parker sisters never, ever talked about their parents as human beings. To the public they were the extraordinary James and Annalise Parker. Jade needed to keep up that image.

And that was it. Jade had had her fill of unanswered messages and phone calls. She'd had enough of setting up meetings with Amber as though she were a business contact.

They fought as most sisters did, but this fateful quarrel was louder and more vindictive than any before. Jade called out Amber's behaviors, mocking how Amber's standards forced everyone around her to accommodate them. She used one example in particular: Amber's punctuality. That one habit started as a funny quirk but grew in intensity, leading to more complex idiosyncrasies.

With anger fueling her, Jade railed that she had made allowance after allowance for Amber's rebelliousness but was sick of being the target. Amber was as much a Parker as Jade was, and it was time she shared the responsibility.

It often felt like the argument was only a few weeks in the past. But Jade and Amber had ultimately agreed to mend their bond and admit their individual contributions to the strained relationship, and they'd actively worked on it ever since.

"I'm not saying that you'll lose your friends," Jade calmly added, "just that it'll get harder to keep everyone happy and run the company."

Jade worried her warning was too abstract, but Amber would learn soon enough.

"Can I tell you something?" Amber asked, moving on from the conversation.

Jade nodded.

"Oscar was talking about his restaurant and how excited he is about it."

"He'd better be excited," Jade laughed, pulling bottles of water from the refrigerated compartment between them. "Both of us invested in his business."

"Yeah, but that's not it," Amber said. "And Leon was talking about taking time off to relax after school. His parents are helping him take a six-month break. Liotta wants to do the same, but she has an offer waiting for her."

"Aren't they twins?" Jade asked.

"Yeah," Amber replied. "Meanwhile, Charlotte is struggling to find a position even though she's been using every trick in the book."

"Okay?" Jade said, confused by the rundown.

"My friends are following their passions, or they're trying to figure out what their passion is. I'm lucky to know mine. I know you said that I'll probably be too busy at Syndicate, but I *want* to be busy." Amber paused to sip her water. "I've been working for this moment since I was like sixteen, ya know? I want to take over Syndicate and make it my own—still Mom and Dad's flame but my flare."

Jade grinned. "I can't wait to walk in there and take over. I mean, really take over."

She mentioned the head of the board, Mr. Reynolds, and that she'd enjoyed watching him grieve the money train he had been riding for twelve years when she signed for her portion of Syndicate. Seeing that Amber looked a little disturbed by her characterization of the board chair, Jade didn't elaborate. She didn't want to spoil the moment.

Instead, Jade smiled at Amber, letting thoughts of looking to the future and keeping the past in the rearview mirror take over.

As they neared home, Amber pulled up a blue paper bag with a white box inside. She blushed as she handed it over.

"I saw this blouse while I was walking around after drinks and thought you'd like it. I could practically see you wearing it."

Thrilled at her sister's thoughtfulness, Jade insisted it was Amber they would be celebrating that evening but thanked her nonetheless.

Chapter Four

As the car pulled into the driveway, the hum of the closing gate faded behind them, and Al forked right to roll around the back of the property, where the Parker girls preferred to enter and exit the grand house.

Al parked on the concrete between the back door and the three-car garage and stepped out of the car, first opening the door for Amber, then Jade. Amber was rambling about Oscar's restaurant and her promise to attend opening night. Just as Al handed Jade her bags, he paused, his eyes darting to the far side of the yard. Jade glanced in the same direction, staring at the storage shed beside the garage.

Initially, she thought Al had forgotten to lock up his quarters, but she suddenly worried that something else had distressed him. She whipped her gaze back toward Amber, who was now walking toward the house, rambling about the menu with her back facing the world, vulnerable.

Al hurried across the paved ground and stood behind Amber, bringing her to a stop near the back door.

"Miss Jade," Al whisper-called, "please come here."

Jade casually jogged to meet the group, and Al warned her not to open the door in case someone intended to barge in. He had the girls remain by the door to sound the alarm if anything should happen, then cautiously approached the shed.

"Jade, what's going on?" Amber asked, then gasped when she saw Al stumble out from behind the shed, dragging a frail person from the shadows by the arm.

"Miss Jade, Miss Amber, it's fine," he announced.

The unfamiliar woman's unruly blond hair was thrown in a lopsided ponytail, and her discolored and torn clothes smelled like they'd come from a barn. Al announced that he would call the police, declaring it was safe for Jade and Amber to enter the house.

The young woman sobbed and begged, "No, please don't call the cops, please!"

She wailed, trying to free her arm from Al's grip and failing miserably.

"It was wrong to hide behind your house, but I need to talk to you! You don't meet anyone without an appointment, and . . ." She trailed off helplessly, staring at Jade.

Jade and Amber exchanged looks before Jade asked the strange girl, "Who are you, and why do you want to talk to me?"

"And more importantly, why did you think hiding behind the shed was gonna help?" Amber added, looking the girl up and down.

"I'm Lucy," she sniffled. "I was hoping you would help me." She wiped her face with the sleeve of her crusty hoodie. The rough fabric begged for a washing machine, and Jade shivered at the sight of the material touching Lucy's face.

"What do you need help with, exactly?"

"My brother, Daniel, talked about you."

Jade's eyes went wide, her breath stilling. She abruptly faced Al.

"Thank you for getting her, Al. I don't think the police are needed; she'll be joining us inside."

Looking uneasy, Amber opened the door, allowing Lucy to enter first. Al placed a hand on Jade's arm and asked her to reach out if anything seemed off. He declared he could be there within two minutes; he had timed it and done drills.

The aroma of a fine meal greeted them as they removed their shoes and placed them in the cupboard by the door, hanging their coats. Amber left her sister with Lucy in the mudroom and greeted Kacey. When Lucy followed Jade into the bright kitchen, the happy chatter ended.

"Are we having company for your dinner tonight, Amber?" Kacey asked, regarding Lucy with a practiced gracious smile. The housekeeper pulled her loose, light-brown hair around the top of her head, wrapping it into a neat bun.

"If we are, it's a surprise guest," Amber teased, turning to Jade.

"Jade, is this your guest?"

"This is Lucy, Aunt Kacey," Jade announced, moving to the side. "She's Daniel's sister and needs some help. I'll take her to the guest room so we can talk before dinner. It won't be long."

"Oh, Daniel's sister!" Kacey exclaimed.

Amber looked flabbergasted, but Jade didn't have the energy to get into her history with Daniel right now.

The housekeeper cheerfully continued, "Oh, I'll make us some tea. I have a new Earl Grey I've been dying to try."

Amber gave her sister a grave stare as they turned toward Lucy, who had been perusing the kitchen.

The small table in the kitchen was set for dinner. The appliances sparkled under the bright white lights above. Fish swam about on small screens embedded in the fridge and freezer nestled amid the stove and ovens in the cooking nook.

The grayscale marble counters paired pleasantly with the white cabinet doors and matte-black handles. Adjacent to the cooking nook was a marble island with a large sink on one side and two dishwashers on the other, making the space ideal for quick meals and conversations. Elaborate crystal chandeliers added to the sophistication of the room. Behind the island, glass-front cabinets showcased a collection of glassware. The last corner of the kitchen led to a formal dining area.

Having been to Lucy's home, Jade determined that the girl's admiration must result from having no current accommodations, which was disturbing.

She subtly gestured for Lucy to follow her and Amber out of the kitchen. As they passed through the house's official entry and rounded the staircase by the black front door, Amber glibly whispered, "She's getting her tea, Jade!"

"I know, I know." Jade smiled, desperately hoping Kacey wouldn't chatter at Lucy.

Leaving the front door behind them, they arrived at a white door with a round black knob.

"Be it ever so humble," Amber said, opening the door to the guest room. "We have it cleaned weekly, so it's not dusty."

Preoccupied with her phone, Jade let Amber play host.

୨୧

"It's perfect. Thank you. I feel so terrible invading like this," Lucy stuttered.

"Oh, it's the least we can do for someone behind the shed. Now, if you'd chosen the garage or even Al's place, you may have gotten a room upstairs."

Lucy chuckled with a grateful expression and excused herself to the bathroom to freshen up. When she emerged looking slightly less disheveled, Jade finally looked up from her phone.

"Um, there are some clothes in the drawer. I think they'll fit you, but if they don't, I can run up and get something from my room."

Amber glared at her sister. She knew Jade was aware that anything of Amber's would not comfortably fit the thin and frail Lucy—although it would surely cover her. Not as well endowed as her younger sister, Jade was closer in size to their visitor, though both sisters were taller. They left the room to afford Lucy privacy.

"Okay, *who* is this person?" Amber whispered.

"She's not lying," Jade replied, looking back at her phone. "I figured she wouldn't lie about who she was, but I just got confirmation."

"Who is she?" Amber insisted.

"She's the half sister of a friend of mine."

"You don't have friends," Amber blurted. Her sister had always been happy to have many acquaintances but few friends.

"I don't have *many* friends," Jade corrected, glancing up. "Daniel and I were in college together."

"Are you in the habit of taking in friends' siblings who seem to be having a rough time?"

"No, which is why I think friendship is a weird concept, but I guess every rule has an exception."

"Jade," Amber hissed as Lucy stirred behind the door, which stood ajar. "You realize how crazy this looks, right?"

"I'm sorry I don't have the time to go over everything now," Jade said. "I want to speak candidly with Lucy before Aunt Kacey joins."

"Speak candidly," Amber repeated, contemplating her sister's choice of words.

Jade's phone buzzed, and she excused herself and paced down the hall.

Beyond curious, Amber knocked, then reentered the guest room. Lucy had washed her face and changed her clothes. Amber could not bring herself to mention discarding Lucy's old clothes, but she eyed the pile on the floor with distaste.

Lucy settled on the edge of the bed and explained that she was a journalism major at the same university Amber and Jade had graduated from. She had gotten involved with the wrong sort of people, which changed the trajectory of her life.

"Who were these people?" Amber asked. "I went to the same school. I might know—"

"Drugs," Lucy interrupted. "The kind of people that will give you anything and everything to get you hooked. I was the perfect client, rich and lonely."

"I'm rich and didn't meet these people," Amber confessed, studying Lucy.

The girl rubbed her arm. "You must be a good judge of character then."

Amber stared at the glossy wood floor, not as keen about people's hidden intentions as her sister was.

"You said rich," Amber continued. "How rich? Do we know your family?"

"You should. I'm Lucy Prescott," Lucy nervously said.

"Oh, sweet banana bread!" Amber exclaimed. "Yup, you're a good one, alright."

"My dad's last name tends to be the first thing anyone notices about me," Lucy said somberly. "Generational wealth and an entrepreneurial genius meant more and more attention."

Amber related to what Lucy described but remained wary. On a level she could not explain nor describe, she did not trust this girl.

Jade entered the room, softly closed the door behind her, then turned.

"Lucy, I must speak with you before our housekeeper comes, so let me do you the favor of being curt."

Amber took a few steps back from the foot of the bed in response to Jade's changed demeanor.

"I spoke to Daniel," Jade stated. Lucy's forehead wrinkled, and her eyes shifted. She fidgeted on the bed as Jade continued, "He told me everything."

Lucy stood and walked to the window, turning to reveal a sorrowful face.

"You were kicked out of your home when your father found a concoction of pills and I'm assuming cocaine," Jade announced.

"What?" Amber exclaimed. "That's not just college drugs."

"Apparently she was a repeat customer from before she was a college student," Jade revealed. "When Lucy refused to go into rehab, her father refused to support her lifestyle. That's why you're in this 'rough' state. You've been living on the streets and know my name from when Daniel and I were in school together."

"Look, I know how this seems," Lucy cajoled.

Jade turned to her sister briefly. "Amber, did you know that Daniel and I started a foundation to help cancer patients?"

"Um, that's nice, but how does—"

"That's when I met your mother, Lucy," Jade said, sternly redirecting her words to their guest. "Daniel saw how hard it was on her and wanted to use your family's good fortune to help other people who suffered. Your mother was our inspiration."

"Please, stop," Lucy cried.

"Your mother, who passed away just months ago, while you . . ." Jade paused. "You weren't there." Amber detected a hidden pain in her sister, surprising her further.

"Do you think I like that?" Lucy suddenly screamed. "Do you think I liked coming home to beg for money only to see an ambulance on the property? Do you think I like not being there for her last words?"

"You sneak into my house hoping to gain something from me and thinking you could play me?" Jade demanded.

"I don't even know what I was going to ask. I just needed—"

"You needed a sympathetic ear," Jade said flatly. "And I *will* help you. Not because of your little act but because I value your brother's friendship and, more importantly, to honor your mother, who was gracious to me."

Amber knew when her sister was being honest and when she was putting on a show. In that moment, she knew Mrs. Prescott's passing deeply saddened Jade.

"Aunt Kacey will come in if we don't head out, so we're all going to be *civilized* while I think of the next step," Jade announced, opening the door and waiting for confirmation from Lucy.

Once again, Amber led the way, wondering how one could be civilized after such a revelation.

Chapter Five

"JADE, AMBER, there you are!" Kacey called the girls from the hall, inviting everyone back to the kitchen. "The tea is ready."

Accommodating their housekeeper's love for tea, the girls went around the island, sitting on the bar stools and grabbing the cups and saucers stacked there.

"Lucy, I do apologize for not being able to offer dinner in the formal dining area," Kacey said, pointing to the small table across from her. "There's just not enough time to prepare the room properly."

"Oh, please," Lucy said with flushed cheeks, "don't go to any trouble on my account."

Before Kacey could continue, Jade lifted the cup of pungent tea and said, "Lucy was just telling us how she found her way to our home, Aunt Kacey."

Kacey sat beside the younger women, eager to learn more.

"Aunt Kacey," Jade whispered, reaching for Kacey's hand, "Mrs. Prescott passed away a few months ago. Daniel just told me."

A sorrowful Kacey offered her condolences to Lucy. Lucy nodded uncomfortably and thanked her before taking a sip of tea.

"Ms. Parker," Lucy began with a hesitant whisper.

"My dear," Kacey laughed, "my last name isn't Parker."

"Oh, Jade called you Aunt—"

"Aunt Kacey was the only one who stayed after our parents' accident," Amber said, pushing into the conversation. "We call her 'Aunt' to show our appreciation."

"And respect," Jade added with a proud smile.

"Oh, girls," Kacey chuckled, blushing. "Lucy, you may call me Kacey."

"I went to the same university Jade and Amber did," Lucy told her. "Unlike them, I came across the wrong group of people and got involved with, um, controlled substances." Her demeanor shifted, giving her tense shoulders and fidgety fingers. "I thought I had it under control."

"You thought you had using 'controlled substances' under control?" Amber scoffed, flinching at Kacey's sharp glance.

"It was foolish. I'll admit that."

Lucy explained how videos of her illicit activities began circulating on different media platforms. Her father's company had borne the consequences of her actions.

"It wasn't fair to my dad, dealing with all that, and my mom . . . she was sick."

Although Jade detected genuine guilt in her tone, she could not say she found Lucy to be regretful. Lucy seemed to know that others had suffered because of her poor choices, yet not once did she express remorse.

"My dad sent me away for rehab, but I left. I wasn't welcome back home at that point because, uh . . ."

"You had drugs inside the house, didn't you?" Jade asked.

"How did you know?"

"I met your father, on several occasions," Jade revealed, ignoring Amber's bewilderment. "I think that would be the only reason he'd limit your access to the house."

"He wasn't wrong," Lucy admitted. "My mom was sick."

Jade inferred that even though she did not disagree with her father, Lucy didn't think it was right either.

"I couldn't make it on my own," Lucy continued. "I went home to beg for another chance. When I saw the ambulance in the driveway, I knew it was her. What hurts is that she asked for me and asked my dad to take it easy on me up until her last breath."

Lucy cleared her throat before explaining that her father made the hard rule of only accepting her apology if she committed to rehab. She tried to explain her disdain for rehab as her reason for not wanting to return, but the scent of a poor excuse was strong.

Turning to Jade, Lucy continued, "I haven't used any type of stimulant in two months. I want to show my dad I can do this, but he won't listen."

"And you thought Jade could help?" Amber interjected.

"I just need to show him I'm serious about getting a job and being sober."

"How do you think I'm going to help you?" Jade asked with a neutral tone.

"I really don't know, but I'd do anything you ask. My dad knows you and would believe I'm ready to come back if he knew you agreed to help."

"Are you looking for Jade's help getting a job at Syndicate?" Kacey asked.

Lucy gave a shy grin. "I didn't graduate, but I'd like to use the skills I learned in journalism."

Leaning back on the bar stool as an idea occurred to her, Jade smiled thinly, then hopped out of her seat.

"Aunt Kacey, I'd like to talk to Lucy before Mr. Porter comes, if that's okay." Before Kacey replied, Jade turned to Lucy. "Mr. Porter is our family lawyer, coming to celebrate Amber's big day, and I think it would be best if we spoke before he arrives."

Upon returning to the guest room, Jade closed the door behind her.

"Lucy, I don't have much time," she said, looking at her phone as she received a message from Mr. Porter.

Lucy nodded, taking a step back and sitting on the bed.

"I *will* help you. I don't want to, because I see a plethora of red flags here, but instead of walking away like I should, I will offer you this," Jade stated, trying to calculate the next few steps.

Clearing her throat, she announced that she knew why Lucy was there. The help she so cluelessly wanted was in fact an interview. Lucy did not deny this claim. Reluctantly, Jade agreed to a short interview the following day at her company, which Lucy could potentially use to shop around for employment. Lucy looked stunned.

"I want to make a few things perfectly clear, Lucy," Jade said, crossing her arms. "I will only agree to this interview after I speak to Daniel tomorrow and he corroborates that you have returned home. You need to speak to your father about your sobriety and make amends."

After a short exhale, she continued, "Then we can talk. I'll allow you to record the interview if you want, and I will be willing to talk about"—she sighed—"my personal life. Your mom was incredibly kind to me. I'm doing this in her honor and memory."

Lucy thanked her, and Jade plastered on a small, forced smile. Then she mentioned the graduation celebration and requested privacy; this event was exclusively for family.

Lucy insisted she wanted an early night's rest anyway before meeting with her father, agreeing to a car service taking her home in the morning.

"Who is Daniel?" Amber demanded once the other two had left.

Kacey laughed, "Oh, Amber, surely you're joking?"

"Apparently everyone but me knows him," Amber whined, crossing her arms.

"Well, he *has* met everyone, even Al."

"Seriously?"

"Oh, you know Al. He wanted to tag along with Jade when Jade studied on campus."

"Who is this man, Aunt Kacey?"

"Daniel is Jade's friend," Katherine replied matter-of-factly. "So far, the only one that accepts her unusual habits. Her direct manner." She laughed. "Oh, but he's nice, and his mother was lovely with Jade."

"I think my point isn't coming across, so I'll try again. How is it that everyone knows him, and he somehow manages to hide from me? Why haven't I met him if he's so nice?"

"Well, Amber," Kacey reluctantly replied, "you weren't here."

Flashing back to the time of estrangement, Amber felt her stomach drop.

"I'm sorry, dear. Did I upset you?" Kacey asked softly and knowingly.

"You mean Jade got a friend when I wasn't around? She replaced me?"

"Oh, heavens no!" Kacey exclaimed. "How did that idea even—"

"Then what, Aunt Kacey?"

"I think I must rip off the proverbial Band-Aid." Kacey leaned over the marble countertop and quietly explained how Jade and Daniel had been classmates and how Jade often spoke of the intellectual challenge he offered.

Jade avoided declaring a major for as long as possible, wanting to find her place in the world. However, eventually, she needed to either officially declare a business or pharmacology-related major and slightly delay her graduation date or follow her heart as an undergrad and leave the business and pharmacology for graduate school, thereby taking on more years of study. Jade was caught between doing what her parents chose for her and choosing what made sense to her. Jade sought out her sister's advice. When Amber did not return her attempts to connect, she postponed the inevitable.

Mr. Porter and Kacey's efforts to ease the pressure were not particularly helpful, as they did not wish to persuade Jade either way. Jade continued to reach out to her sister, begging for guidance from the one person who understood her.

"It was on that night, the night of the benefit, that she had to choose," Kacey said.

"Choose what?" Amber asked.

"Jade was going to graduate that year, remember?" Kacey said, awaiting Amber's nod. "The university had been more than accommodating. You know your sister, though. She never truly liked either option, and psychology was a good match for her."

"It's like she can get into my head," Amber agreed with a stifled chuckle.

"That was the night she needed to inform Syndicate's board of her major so they would know she was in line to meet with the incentives of your parents' will."

Doubting she'd made the right choice, Jade contacted Mr. Porter, stating that she would graduate as a psychology student and pursue an MBA.

"That's kinda weird."

"Law is Mr. Porter's forte, I'll admit," Kacey stated. "I know Jade doesn't like talking about it—not since the, uh, fight. But it all worked out. She graduated with a degree she is proud of, got her MBA in time to take over Syndicate with you, you and she made amends. It was a bumpy road, but everyone arrived safely."

Amber vaguely remembered the stipulations in the will but hadn't bothered with the details as she'd already known what she wanted to do with her life.

"That's why helping Daniel is important?" Amber muttered. "Because he was there when I wasn't."

"Personally, I think it was their similarities that allowed a friendship to blossom. Daniel's biological father was murdered when he was a young boy."

Chapter Six

"Mr. Porter is here!" Jade squealed, skidding across the sparkling waxed floor and trotting out the back. She returned with him beside her, their arms locked. The family convened around the table as Jade explained Lucy would not be joining them.

Amber sat, brimming with joy, and poured coffee. Meanwhile, Jade and Kacey briefly disappeared into the dark dining room and emerged carrying a large white box. Amber gasped at the sight and tried to guess what might be under the cardboard.

"Is it cake?" Amber demanded.

"It has cake," Jade hinted.

Amber bounced in her seat. "Oh, honey roasted peanuts, did you get a cake that looks like me?"

Mr. Porter laughed, and Kacey ended the torture, tugging the bright-blue ribbon—Amber's favorite color—attached to the top of the box so that the four sides collapsed outward on the table.

Raising her hands to her lips, Amber leaned close to marvel at the exquisite three-tiered dessert tray.

The circular ceramic layers of the display were topped by a pristine silver handle for carrying. The bottom of each plate was a vibrant cobalt speckled with glitter. The tops showcased clean white backgrounds with miniature pictures scattered across. The photos were of herself, Jade, Kacey, Mr. Porter, and her parents.

She brushed her fingers over the smooth, cold surface encapsulating her loved ones over the years. In the spaces between the photographs, miniature portions of some of Amber's favorite desserts awaited. She spotted the chocolate stamp of a bakery she adored on one of the raspberry pastries, then tearfully thanked Jade. Kacey offered a warm hug, whispering congratulations to Amber and reiterating how proud she was of her.

Jade smiled a few steps away, standing beside Mr. Porter. Respecting her sister's distaste for physical affection, Amber laughed, wiping her teary face, and only murmured to her, "You're the best."

Amber served everyone decadent desserts from her gift. Taking his plate, Mr. Porter asked Amber for a moment to present his gift before she sat down.

"Now, I'd like to prepare you," he chuckled, pulling a box from under his coat and placing it on the kitchen island. The white box was wrapped with another bright-blue ribbon and a bow on top. "I tried to find a gift that held sentimental value, but after learning about the masterpiece Jade planned and with Kacey finding the designer, I don't think I stand a chance."

The box fit neatly in his hands, no larger than a small notebook. Amber tried to be proper and calm, but she was brimming with curiosity. Eyeing the big bow, she smirked at her older sister. Jade smiled back.

Amber thanked Mr. Porter, taking the box from him. It was heavier than she expected. "Definitely not a book," she noted. She pulled the ribbon and slowly opened the flimsy white box. She took in the gift wordlessly, overcome by emotion.

Her eyes feasted on a photo of herself, Jade, Kacey, and Mr. Porter on Amber's first day of college. Surrounding their smiling faces in the picture frame, metal branches and vines intertwined, scattered with miniature roses bearing the names of her family, including her parents.

"Oh, Mr. Porter," she exclaimed, rubbing her fingertips along the velvet backing, also a vibrant blue. Her eyes filled with tears once again, shifting between the images of her broken yet perfectly wonderful family and the family itself.

She set the frame down and lunged toward Mr. Porter's seat to give him an affectionate squeeze, thanking him for moving her soul.

"Yeah, but can you stack cakes and cookies on it?" Jade teased, passing the picture to Kacey.

"I don't think anything can compete with cakes and cookies," Mr. Porter said merrily.

Amber returned to her seat, thanking everyone once again for their thoughtfulness.

ꙮ

The evening chugged along, shifting to conversations about Amber taking her place at Syndicate. Jade admired Amber's certainty about what she wanted to do with her life. Meanwhile, Jade had struggled academically, unsure of her path until she was forced to step into the unknown. She had not graduated business school with the same excitement that Amber now expressed.

"I've learned my life lessons—well, for that part of my life—and I want to start the next part right away," Amber announced around a bite of cake.

One commonality between the two sisters was that they did not truly fit in with their respective social groups. While Jade made it a habit to avoid people who found her unusual, not bothering to adapt or assimilate to their expectations of her, Amber tried to conform to whatever situation or group she was in. Neither had many friends. Jade welcomed this state of affairs; it saved her from heartache. She often philosophized with Kacey and Mr. Porter on what truly made one a friend.

Family was the one thing Jade felt had substance to it. She often described friendship as a mutual agreement until there was no longer a need, albeit always noting that avoiding loneliness was a substantial benefit.

Daniel Prescott presented a challenge to this principle. At first, he was merely her partner in public speaking class during the first semester of undergrad. He was also in her introduction to psychology. They worked well together; he never asked Jade to explain her choices or how she conducted her affairs.

Enjoying the exception to a rule she believed to be true, she welcomed his presence at school, leading to a friendship that extended beyond her graduation.

Amber, on the other hand, was the more sociable and amicable Parker sister, though she reserved her most honest thoughts for her family and for her dearest friend, Oscar Davis. She learned this lesson the hard way.

After a few months as a freshman, Amber decided she needed to find new friends and make the connections that would set her up for success. She came to regret this decision two years later when she overheard her so-called friends discussing her, outing themselves as selfish, greedy jerks. Realizing that she had been wrong to exchange family for friends, she returned home with wounded pride.

None of these issues were discussed during this night of celebration.

After taking his coat and bidding the family good evening, Mr. Porter prodded Jade one last time about celebrating her graduate degree.

She politely declined. "Thank you, Mr. Porter. I only got that degree because I had to. Nothing about it was fun. I'd rather just move on."

"I feel it's my fault that you took the MBA, Jade," Mr. Porter said as he grasped the handle of his car door. "I encouraged you to do what worked for you, but it added more pressure."

"Oh, no," Jade protested. "Looking back, it was hard, really hard. But I think everything turned out fine."

Chapter Seven

COMFORTABLE IN HER NIGHTGOWN and securely tucked in bed, Jade heard a light tap on her bedroom door. Amber bounded in, jumping and landing headfirst into the pillows. Jade laughed at her sister's familiar habit.

"Just wanted to pop in and say good night," Amber said, holding a stuffed bear Jade had appropriately named Theo. Amber brushed her hair from her face, smiling.

"That's mighty thoughtful," Jade chuckled.

"Can I ask a question, Jade?"

"Sure. Can't promise an answer, though."

"Daniel, your friend," Amber began hesitantly. "How much of a friend is he?"

"So far, he's the only one. I don't think a lot of people tolerate me very well." Jade laughed wryly at the harsh truth.

"Like Oscar and me?"

"Yeah, excluding the shorter duration of time I've known him. Why do you ask?"

"Lucy," Amber answered, playing with Theo's ears. "Something about her, it just bothers me, ya know. Like, I want to help. I even arranged for a refurbished laptop to be dropped off at Syndicate for her since she's a 'journalist,' but I can't shake this feeling."

"I'm glad it's not just me," Jade admitted.

"Really?"

"Yeah, I'm only helping because . . . 'cause I feel awful. After graduation, Daniel and I were close, but once I started classes again and started working at Syndicate, I didn't stay in touch."

"If he's a friend like Oscar . . ." Amber twisted her mouth in thought. "Is that what you meant in the car about Syndicate taking over my time?"

Jade nodded. "His mother passed away, and I didn't even know. He probably didn't want to distract me from school and work, but still, friendship should be a two-way street."

"So, we both agree that Lucy is something to worry about?" Amber confirmed.

"Yeah, Mr. Porter thought it was weird that I offered an interview, but when I told him about Daniel's mother—"

"What interview?" Amber interrupted.

"Tomorrow, I'm letting Lucy interview me and use that to prove herself as a journalist."

Amber stated the obvious, concerned her sister might have forgotten or simply chosen to ignore. "We never give interviews, not unless we have to."

Jade agreed but mentioned the usefulness of a publicity article marking the leadership changeover. Still looking hesitant, Amber silently nodded.

"I'm nervous about tomorrow," Amber finally said. She mentioned being worried about the board members after Jade's comment earlier that day.

Jade rolled her eyes and gave Amber a more thorough heads-up, sharing that Mr. Reynolds, the presumed head of the board, had a special way of getting under her skin. The elderly man was a business veteran, and characters like him made her loathe the profession. She despised the way the board members spoke of her parents and how it was never acceptable for Jade to discuss them because showing any distress would be viewed as womanly weakness.

"Isn't death a universal form of distress?" Amber griped.

Jade rolled her eyes again before assuring her sister there were many great things about the job as well. She shared how she often had lunch with the building staff. In particular, JJ was a security officer she had grown fond of, and she'd helped his son find an appropriate tutor after a dyslexia diagnosis.

"That's when I started our outreach program at Syndicate," Jade explained. After first joining Syndicate, Jade found little to do in the way of executive tasks, so she began a new division focused on Syndicate's community service responsibilities.

Beaming, she described the benefit this program could bring the world. She'd first discovered a burning desire to help as an undergrad when she worked with Daniel to establish their humble cancer foundation.

"We wanted to help cancer patients fully understand and explore all their options."

"Don't people fighting cancer have one goal: to beat the cancer?" Amber asked.

"It's a main goal, but not the only goal," Jade replied. She explained that some patients refused care because it was too expensive; they feared dying anyway and leaving their families with the heavy burden of debt. Some had long, exhausting arguments with insurance companies that hid behind policies designed to make money rather than help the ill.

What started as a means for Jade to help a few people turned into a position that Daniel left school to pursue full-time. Daniel was not born a Prescott but accepted his stepfather's last name and the benefits it brought, including the massive wealth. He went to school for the experience and left because he'd found his calling.

Moved by the story, Amber felt distraught that this was her first time hearing it.

She desperately wanted to ask why Daniel hadn't been introduced to her but then caught sight of the bottle on Jade's nightstand.

Jade only used medication when absolutely necessary, and even then, she had to be cajoled, so the sight of a botanical sleeping aid concerned Amber. Pointing at the bottle when she stood up to leave, she asked, "Having trouble sleeping?"

Jade quickly replied she only used them in extreme situations when she couldn't sleep after a hectic day at work.

When Amber finally left, she couldn't help but feel distressed at Jade's nonchalance—about sleeping poorly, her struggles at work, and her refusal to celebrate her own recent achievements.

☙❧

Jade awoke the next morning with several tasks on her list for the day, but she needed to handle Lucy first. Rushing out of her room, she nearly crashed into her sister in the short little hall leading to her suite.

"Amber! Hey, I have a few things to take care of with an employee at Syndicate today. It means I'll be busy during your signing ceremony with the board."

"Oh, that's fine. I know you hate pretending things are cool around those guys. Is everything okay?"

"I hope it will be," Jade replied reluctantly. "I suspected for a while that Amy, Mr. Reynolds's assistant, was an abuse victim. She acknowledged it yesterday, and I'm helping her out."

Amber murmured her sympathy and understanding as they approached the main hall near the staircase.

"Jade," Amber whispered, gesturing to the lower floor. Kacey's humming drifted up to them. "I really don't feel right about this interview with Lucy."

"What do you mean?" Jade asked, more defensively than she meant to sound.

"I know we want to help her, but an interview is risky. What if she writes something bad? And with today already a big press day—"

Jade sighed heavily. "I appreciate your concern, but I'll be fine."

"This doesn't only affect you," Amber pushed. "Beyond me, there's Syndicate. I know she's your friend's sister, but isn't there—"

"You and I don't, for lack of a better word, trust Lucy," Jade interrupted, crossing her arms.

Amber nodded.

"Then trust me. I would never put you in harm's way and bring scrutiny on Syndicate for the sake of a friend's estranged half sister."

◈

When Amber entered the kitchen, she learned that Lucy had already eaten. Moments later, Jade joined her, cheerfully announcing that Lucy had just left. Kacey peered through one of the front kitchen windows, watching the car drive off, the gate closing behind it.

The delectable aroma of freshly baked goods did not go unnoticed by Amber. She quickly spied the careful arrangement of frosted cupcakes packed in pink boxes with clear panels showcasing their glory.

"Is there a bake sale?" Amber asked, taking a bite of the pancakes Kacey placed in front of her.

"Jade made them."

Jade looked away. "I woke up early this morning and, well, baking helps clear my head." She stirred the coffee in her mug, taking a pancake from the stack and spooning fresh berries on top, avoiding the sweet syrup.

"Were there any extra?" Amber asked casually.

"Oh, I believe they're all accounted for," Kacey declared. "I'm taking them to the senior center today. There is a ceremony kicking off the teenage and not-so-teenage collaboration."

Jade joked about Amber's greediness, and Amber took it graciously from the only person allowed to tease her about her love of snacks.

Grabbing their work bags and coats, prepared for the unpredictable coastal spring weather, the two sisters marched together through the back door. Amber passed her bag to Al. At the last second before they slid into the car, Jade handed a generously sized blue box to her younger sister with a grin. Kacey stood near as though waiting for a special moment.

Inside the box were four red velvet cupcakes, each embossed with AMBER'S CUPCAKE in red letters over cream cheese frosting. In her childlike but never childish manner, Amber shrieked and thanked her sister, giving her a small side hug.

"I wouldn't dream of keeping my cupcakes from you," Jade laughed as the sisters hopped into the car and buckled up.

"Have a lovely first day, girls." Kacey grinned, pulling one of her many volunteer badges out of her purse and pinning it her blouse. "I can't wait to hear all about it when you get back tonight."

Al declined his employers' gracious offer of a cupcake, leaving Amber to nibble as Jade reviewed her morning calendar.

Recalling the bottle beside Jade's bed, Amber maintained a suspicion that Jade had not woken up early that morning but in fact had never gone to sleep. Though she desperately wanted to know what was keeping Jade awake, she hoped her sister would share when she was ready.

Chapter Eight

JADE AND AMBER hurried through the underground garage, their steps echoing in the humid, salty air. Since the building held several establishments requiring the utmost security, the garage elevator had one route. Access to the remainder of the building required a visit to the security desk or an access card. As the doors opened to the magnificently busy reception area, Jade showed Amber an electronic card, explaining how Amber would receive a similar one

She then left Amber in JJ's care.

Amber was cheerfully chatting with the security guard when a timid young man cleared his throat, following up with a barely discernible squeak of her name. She turned and smiled.

"Ms. Parker," he said once again with a faint grin, "please follow me."

Amber didn't budge. "Excuse me. Eric, is it?" she asked, peering at his Syndicate name tag. When he nodded, she continued, "I was under the impression that I would be meeting Mr. Porter."

His eyes darted to the side. "I, I was told to come down and take you to your office, miss. Your access cards and packet are waiting for you there."

She reluctantly followed him onto the elevator.

The elevator chimed on the twenty-fourth floor, and the doors slid open. Eric walked ahead, taking a slight left toward a hall leading to two rooms. The entrance to the suites boasted a large bouquet of roses on a small table.

Her office was the first. In a magnificent show of design, the office wall lining the hall was made of glass. Amber peered through, impressed by the sophistication. The hallway blinds in Jade's office down the hall were pulled down.

Eric stopped by the glass door. A black plaque beside it was etched with Amber's name. Before entering, she peeked again at Jade's office and spotted an identical plaque.

She strode into her office, expecting to find Mr. Porter waiting for her. Instead, another man sat in her desk chair. The older man with the salt-and-pepper hair rocked back and forth while she waited for him to say something. He stared far too intently for her liking. She had only met this man a handful of times, but having heard how he treated her sister, she disliked him immensely. She'd heard Kacey talk about his indecent comments and unsolicited advice in the face of polite rejection. He never ceased until he was either the last to speak or everyone agreed.

Mr. Reynolds was sending an unmistakable message by carelessly occupying her chair and eyeing her as a predator would prey.

She knew to be cautious but was not about to be intimidated by such juvenile tactics. She let her shoulder bag slide down her arm, catching it in her hand, and sidestepped to place it on one of the long, navy-blue couches.

Watching him twirl in her chair, she crossed her arms and shifted her weight to one leg. The conceited man stood and came around the sizable dark-wood desk, striding toward her.

"Ms. Parker," Mr. Reynolds said, "it's a pleasure to finally be here on this day."

"Here in my office?" Amber emphasized.

"Well, yes. In this fine and uniquely decorated office of yours." He smirked. "I've watched you all these years, and it's an honor to have you take over your father's company."

"I have trouble remembering your presence through *all those years*, but you're right. It is an honor for me to take over my parents' company." She smirked back. "Where's Mr. Porter? I was expecting him."

Mr. Reynolds smiled and scanned her body. Her skin prickled with irritation.

"You know Porter, always forgetting things. Getting old gets to us all."

"Interesting." Amber held her index finger to her lips in thought. "I don't seem to recall him forgetting any events before. It must be something that only happens around you."

Mr. Reynolds grimaced at her candor, his nostrils flaring.

"Oh well, that's not a problem, Mr. Reynolds," she continued. "I'll just call him and see where he is."

At that moment, Mr. Porter rushed into the office, out of breath.

"Amber, there you are." He straightened, acknowledging the other man with a nod but not addressing him. "Everything is ready for you, but I'd like to walk you through a few things first."

"Of course, Mr. Porter." Amber picked up her bag and asked her lawyer to join her on the sofa. "Mr. Reynolds, is there anything else you need, other than testing my chair and noting the décor?"

The man did not reply, instead marching out. Mr. Porter gently shut the glass door and explained he had just returned from the lobby after he couldn't find her. JJ had alerted him to some mischief.

"I don't think there is anything those men can do to stop you today, Amber," Mr. Porter said, sitting beside her in front of the wide window, which displayed a cloud-saturated sky above the busy downtown. "But I wouldn't put it past them to try something nefarious."

"He was twirling in my chair, Mr. Porter," Amber harrumphed, "like it was his place, and I was visiting."

"I'd also be careful with anything you entrust the assistants with. At least, until you build a relationship with them."

"Mr. Porter," Amber whispered, "I have a question I really want to ask, but I'm worried I'll get into trouble if I do."

"You came to the right person, kiddo," Mr. Porter chuckled. "You'll never be in trouble with me."

"Why did Jade accept this guy acting like that? I mean, I heard her talk about how terrible he was. Why did she tolerate it? Is it 'cause Mom and Dad handpicked the board?"

Mr. Porter goggled at Amber as though she had sprouted a second head. His confusion agitated her.

"What? What's wrong? Does that man have something on Jade?"

"Amber, Jade tolerated his behavior because she was his subordinate. Well, she was until yesterday."

"What?"

"Jade worked here while she got her MBA because her degree was not in business or pharmacology."

"No, you fixed that right before she—"

"Don't you remember this, Amber? I spoke to both of you when Jade was preparing to apply to college."

Admitting she had no recollection of the details, she humbly asked to be reminded. He again explained the will stipulations.

"In the event that you or Jade did not get your degrees in the specified programs, you would be offered a position here at Syndicate, but without the executive authority to do anything," Mr. Porter said.

Piecing the puzzle together, Amber realized why Jade constantly asked her for help and made appointments for uninterrupted sister time. Jade had desperately wanted to study what she found intriguing but did not want to turn her back on her parents and their last wishes. The result was a life of stress and divided attention.

"Jade worked under him?" Amber asked with disgust.

"Oh, kiddo," Mr. Porter said somberly, "it wasn't easy on her, but she found a way to get by until you both could take over together."

"Is it just me, or does that sound weird?" Amber pondered.

"What sounds weird?"

"The will, the estate plan," Amber said, squinting at her lawyer. "I don't think I have ever heard of those provisions with a company or an inherited estate."

"Your parents had their own way of doing things," Mr. Porter confessed. "It's how they built this place."

Taken aback by how the decisions she had made years before affected her sister even now, Amber tried to focus on the task at hand and keep her thoughts under control. She apologized for not remembering the details, but her forgetfulness seemed to matter very little to the kindhearted Mr. Porter.

They stood and prepared to leave her office for the official ceremony to become Syndicate's co-owner.

Chapter Nine

Armored with **Mr. Porter,** Amber made her way to one of the conference rooms on the same floor as her office. Mr. Porter explained that the floor above consisted of cubicles and smaller conference rooms intended for internal use.

Amber marched into a space chock-full of what society would call middle-aged men, but they were much older than that, given the average lifespan of a person. They gawked from a cluster around Mr. Reynolds as she and Mr. Porter sat side by side, then adopted emotionless expressions. She counted twelve men in addition to the board chair.

She smelled a clash of various foods and concluded that a buffet must be waiting on the opposite side of the closed panels behind Mr. Reynolds. The well-lit room had conference phones lined up on the table. The blinds of the wide windows to the side were up, and she calmed herself with the view of a gorgeous sky filled with dark, swirling rain clouds. A thunderstorm was expected for the day, and she welcomed the delight of spring showers.

Mr. Reynolds pursed his lips, but a quick hand pat from Mr. Porter distracted Amber from the venom seeping from the air.

"And at last, Ms. Parker joins us," Mr. Reynolds announced, inciting the rest of his minions to swarm away, searching for their chairs along the long, black oval table like birds flocking together.

When everyone had fallen still, Mr. Reynolds spoke once again.

"Gentlemen, today Syndicate returns to being a Parker-run company."

A small, stunted round of applause followed, then ended when he raised one hand. None of the thirteen men attempted to hide their sour feelings. She glanced at each board member, at their pinched lips and squinty eyes, and wondered why her parents chose such men to lead their company if they could not.

Through the window to the hall, Amber caught sight of her sister walking briskly beside a young woman. Jade was on her phone, and the other woman stared at the floor, clearly distressed. As they headed toward Jade's office, Amber assumed this was Amy.

"I remember it like it was yesterday," Mr. Reynolds said with a grin that sent shivers down her spine. "When my dear friend James asked me to be an investor in a revolutionary pharmaceutical company, I agreed instantly, oh, a little over thirteen years ago."

It rattled her brain that such a man had somehow earned her parents' respect.

"Amber, I tell ya," Mr. Reynolds announced, "your father was a genius, and it was a work of art to see him in action. He built this company, his legacy, and he did it regardless of everyone telling him it would fail."

Sick to her stomach, Amber seethed. This man had been no friend of her father. James would never have ignored Annalise's contributions. He never referred to Syndicate as his own but as the product of their joint work and dedication.

Amber stared at the man who claimed friendship with the great James Parker and saw everything Jade had described. She saw the mediocre, self-absorbed, manipulative man hiding behind facts he contorted to fit his narrative, confident no one would call him out. She saw a man who represented the complete antithesis of her parents' stance against companies that kept patients sick to make a profit.

James and Annalise wanted to change the world through health and medication. They passed this goal down to their daughters.

The challenges of parenting two children and running a progressive company were numerous, but they kept Jade and Amber involved with every aspect of their lives.

"I remember the day we all agreed to be his investors and his backup plan for Syndicate," Mr. Reynolds continued, "a short-lived victory, as a year after that we lost dear James and his wife to a household fire."

Livid at how this man continued to disregard her mother, Amber furiously twirled her pen between two fingers.

"But thankfully, his daughters were unharmed."

Mr. Porter's hand nudged her pen, and he passed her a glass of water and a sympathetic look following the callous recitation of events.

"While we grieve his loss to this very day, we are all so very pleased that Amber has finally met the last incentives of the will and can now take over his company and follow in his steps."

Finally? Amber took offense. She had not "finally" finished her studies; she had finished on time and without delay. All Mr. Reynolds needed were two large fangs to complete the appearance of a complete snake.

"We were all thrilled when Jade Parker accepted her position at Syndicate two years ago," Mr. Reynolds said with a slight twitch of his lip. "She chose to study a field not in line with what James wanted, which delayed her taking ownership, but she, too, finally accepted her portion of Syndicate yesterday."

On the verge of erupting, Amber looked at Mr. Porter, who subtly gestured for her to take long, deep breaths. Although Mr. Reynolds had taken over the meeting, he would soon leave the room, losing something Amber had gained.

"Now, let us all join in signing these documents," he said, placing a red plastic folder on the table. Reaching for a pen, Mr. Reynolds signed the page before passing it on to the man beside him.

The folder arrived in front of Amber with an empty line awaiting her signature. She raised her pen, but Mr. Porter slid the folder across the glossy tabletop and took it in his hands.

He winked, shaking the folder. "Since this process is merely a formality and the official documents are to be signed by a notary, I'll look over this one for any typos. Okay, Reynolds?"

"You were James's lawyer and now his daughters' lawyer, Porter. Isn't that a conflict of interest?" Mr. Reynolds spat.

"Hardly. But I'll note your comments on the record when we all sign the official documents shortly. Let's not keep our associates waiting for that wonderfully catered breakfast you arranged," Mr. Porter tactfully replied.

Mr. Reynolds cleared his throat petulantly, gesturing for the board members to enter the adjacent room through the doors behind him, then inviting the rest of the employees to join.

Amber rose from her seat, and Mr. Porter guided her back to her office, suggesting that she order her own breakfast if she wanted to avoid conversations with the board members. While she agreed that she'd rather enjoy a second breakfast with Jade, she also wanted to spend time with the employees and properly introduce herself after she signed the necessary papers.

Amber complained about how Mr. Reynolds's overbearing speech had neglected her mother. Mr. Porter warned her that as a group, the board members had spent twelve years spreading their own version of Annalise's contributions.

She collapsed on the couch with a long exhale, and Mr. Porter reminded her of the final steps. He reviewed the document in the red folder, encouraging Amber not to sign it; the only valid one requiring her signature was a mere step away.

Chapter Ten

Once **Mr. Porter** had left, Amber let out a breath of relief and circled her office, making her way to the desk Mr. Reynolds had so blatantly appropriated. Gazing around, she saw Jade's touch painted across the canvas.

The stand for her laptop had a small flag on one of the legs embroidered with Amber's stand on Amber Land. She giggled and noticed three holders for writing utensils: the pen holder displayed pens of various colors; a smaller cup held the black pen Amber swore was the best pen ever made; and the smallest cup held four mechanical pencils and a small pouch for the lead.

Reaching for a colorful pen topped with an adorable gray tiger-striped cat, Amber warmed at her sister's thoughtfulness. Amber had found a gray cat days after their parents' deaths and grown fond of it.

She plopped down to twirl in the ever-so-comfortable chair, then leaned forward to peek underneath the enormous desk, spotting a few labeled storage boxes with extra pillows and blankets and one with dry pantry snacks. To her left, nestled in the corner of the cave her desk provided, was a miniature refrigerator etched with Amber's name in large bold letters.

The key to the office was hanging in the door lock, and Amber pieced together that Jade must have left it when she came up ahead of her—further proving that Mr. Reynolds had been lurking about, waiting to enter her office once Jade was gone.

She stood to investigate the door standing ajar in the corner of the room. She had only noticed it by the light shining along the crack, as the door was camouflaged with the same dark gray that coated the walls. Her jaw dropped when she nudged it open.

It was a small restroom complete with a shower. Amber also eyed the small closet, suddenly worried about the reason for such an accommodation. *Will I have to live here?* she wondered.

Amber's thoughts were interrupted by a forced cough. She turned to find Eric accompanied by two young ladies. All three stood with notepads in hand, awaiting her command.

"Hello, ma'am." He gave a small wave. "I'm Eric. We met downstairs. I'm one of your assistants." His use of the word "ma'am" troubled her with the reminder that regardless of their proximity in the age, she was his superior. She did not enjoy the idea of a strict hierarchy.

Still, she was now company co-owner; she had responsibilities and expectations to live up to. She would not be granted grace and peace to be her unique and fun-driven self. She would need to stake her place and make it known that while she was not a harsh leader, she would not be a weak one either.

"Ma'am?" Eric said, looking at her.

"Oh, my apologies," she murmured. "You are *my* assistants, correct?"

"Yes, ma'am," Eric replied.

"Do you mind me asking who hired you?"

"Miss Jade was the one to oversee the process, ma'am," one of the girls shyly replied.

"Good," Amber proclaimed, clapping her hands together. "You call her Miss Jade. That's a good start. I'll be Miss Amber, then. Please shut the door and have a seat."

The trio complied eagerly, eyeing her.

"Okay, so, I have a confession to make," Amber said conspiratorially. "Since we're gonna be working together, I feel we need to be on the same page." She leaned back against her desk and gestured vaguely. "I am absolutely terrible with names. I can tell you all the tricks I use to help me remember people, but I don't think that would work here. So, I'd like to ask you all, what's your favorite color?"

The three assistants glanced at each other in confusion, but they each listed their colors, with Eric's being green and the other two assistants chiming in with "Blue!" and "Purple."

"Great, so you," she said, pointing at Eric, "you're Green, as in that's what I'll call you. And you're Blue and Purple. When you come in, all I ask is that you have something on your person that corresponds to your color, so I know who is who." Amber noticed their dazed expressions. "Does that offend you? I don't mean that your names aren't important."

The three assistants leaned forward as one, shaking their heads and professing they had no issue with being referred to as colors.

"I can make the effort to learn your names, but trust me, it'll mean I don't talk until I can see your name tag, which you'd have to wear all the time, and then I'll stop and try to etch it into my memory and . . ."

Amber realized she was making excuses and sighed.

"I think this would be an easier way for me to learn who is who. *But* if it makes you uncomfortable . . ."

Once again, they shook their heads and agreed to wear the colors she assigned. They happily accepted when she invited them to attend the breakfast planned for the company while she went to talk with her sister.

"Please, take your time." Amber waved to them as they left, then sprang to grab her phone.

She merrily skipped out of her office, locking it behind her with the key, and was immediately startled to find Mr. Reynolds standing behind her when she turned. But she recovered in seconds.

He looked at her intently, then made a roguish remark about how she had flounced out of her office, glancing at her flowy, knee-length skirt. His eyes lingered around her chest, and she recalled Jade's frustration with him sending pictures depicting what he considered appropriate attire for women.

She refused to respond to his attempt to rattle her and cheerfully mentioned that she was going to her sister's office. Amber dangled her agenda in front of his face—the notebook plastered with stickers of various comical animals.

"Ms. Parker," he sighed, shaking his head, "I'm sure you can agree that while this is a family-run business, one should never allow family matters to interrupt the workday." He placed his hand on the back of her shoulder. "The other Ms. Parker, when she is in this building, she is not your sister. She's the owner of Syndicate and has a packed schedule." He patted her shoulder, moving his hand lower. "Maybe it's best that you leave your little chat and gossip for when you're home."

Amber's temper flared, and she felt her face heat. To talk about them being the owners and then belittle them in the same conversation was beyond presumptuous.

She cleared her throat and moved away a step, dropping his hand off her back. Flicking her head back, she deliberately crossed her arms over her chest, waiting until his eyes moved from there.

"Mr. Reynolds," she enunciated, "I thank you for your unnecessary remarks, truly. However, how I or my sister choose to spend our time as the owners of this company is none of your business." She opened her arms as she prepared to walk off. "Now, I will be going to see my sister regardless of her packed schedule—to chat and gossip as I see fit."

Amber did not whisper, she did not shy away, and she was not careful with her tone. She spoke loudly for all to hear, if they were close enough, then strode away without a care for what Mr. Reynolds did.

She grinned at all three of her assistants, who stood by the elevator. While they had not been directly in the trajectory of the conversation, their expressions showed that they had witnessed the encounter.

Chapter Eleven

"Oh, that man!" Amber exclaimed, attempting to slam Jade's office door before realizing glass doors had built-in precautions preventing such displays.

Jade was on her desk phone, exasperated.

"Joel, Joel, yeah, I need you to hold." She placed her hand over the mouthpiece. "Is this something I need to address, or do you got it?"

"No, I got it." Amber pouted, walking over to the desk and settling in a chair.

"Okay, Joel, I'm back," Jade said. "Joel, I know this is a big deal. Yeah, I am the owner, but trust me, crying is not going to help. I want the hard copies of all, *all* of Syndicate's business deals, offers, transactions, statements—everything."

She nodded as though he could see. "Yes, print out anything online. I want them as soon as possible, please. Thank you, Joel." Just as Jade was about to place the phone down, she pulled it back to her ear. "Joel, I don't need Mr. Reynolds's approval. I'm the . . . Yes. If he asks, tell him to talk to me."

Jade hung up, sighing loudly, then asked which man had Amber demolishing the treats in Jade's candy dish.

"Who's Joel?" Amber asked, circling to the cart behind one of the couches. While she would most certainly make an appearance at the breakfast buffet, she preferred her sister's company and the breakfast pastries Jade ordered.

"Joel is a project manager upstairs, and I requested hardcopies of everything Syndicate has been involved with in the past twelve years," Jade announced, lifting the metal lids off three plates on a cart behind the couch.

After hearing about Mr. Reynolds's comments, she reminded Amber that the vile creature had been rendered powerless.

"I can't tell you how many times those dolts planned things just to ruffle my feathers," Jade concluded.

"Jade," Amber quietly said, huffing the delectable aroma of quiche, "why did you stay here while you got your MBA? Why didn't you, like, take those years off?"

"I think it's what Mom and Dad would have wanted since they had a position offered, but . . ."

"But?" Amber prodded.

"But when I found out the board members could do whatever they wanted, I *wanted* to be here, watching. Sure, I had no authority, but they knew I was paying attention, getting ready for today."

"What about today?"

Jade placed her plate on the coffee table and sat beside her sister before matter-of-factly sharing her suspicions that the board members were embezzling money from Syndicate. Syndicate had closed most of its production sites and ended all research contracts, leaving Jade to wonder what the company did these days. It threw benefits and fundraisers galore, but no science went on behind the scenes.

She walked around listening, watching, and learning but could never get a legitimate answer. Jade's suspicions only grew when she began preparing for the sisters to take ownership a few months prior and could not locate their birth certificates. As paranoia sank in, Jade hired an investigator to track down the documents she assumed had been lost in the fire.

"Wait, I thought Mom and Dad's suite wasn't damaged in the fire. How could our birth certificates be lost? Didn't they have a safe in their closet?"

"They did, and Aunt Kacey showed us. I don't remember taking them."

"Did you ask her?"

"Yeah," Jade sarcastically replied, "Can you imagine me saying, 'Hey, Aunt Kacey. Things don't seem to add up at Syndicate, and when I got an investigator to find out more, I eventually found out that our entire family's records are sealed by court order, and I haven't found a single person to reverse that order.'"

"What!" Amber gasped.

Jade revealed that while she initially thought there was something questionable about the board members, in the end their own family records were equally dubious. Even the police report of the fire that left them orphans had vanished. Jade had kept this burden to herself, fearing it would distract Amber in her last semester at school.

"Do you really think our parents lied about Syndicate? That doesn't make sense. They helped so many people."

"Amber, their will is ludicrous!" Jade burst out. "I don't even know how it was accepted. There are so many questions—"

"Questions need answers," Amber interrupted her sister. "I agree, and I think we should find them. But let's not think the worst until we have to, okay?"

Jade simply nodded.

Amber laid her hand on Jade's arm. "I know you've been dealing with a lot here. And even though I only now understand how stressed you've been, I'm here to share that stress. Let me take some of it."

Jade nodded absently, avoiding a response.

"Really," Amber insisted. "I'll help go through those boxes when Joel brings them, and if we have to, we can have an office sleepover. Let's do this our way."

Jade finally gave a genuine smile, not one of appeasement. She admitted to suffering from insomnia over the recent months. On the nights she managed to sleep, she had dreams about their parents, riddling her with fear that she would be the cause of their company's demise.

Amber added that she too had been having dreams, but about the many trips they'd taken as a family. None of her dreams kept her from sleeping comfortably. While she brushed the disturbance off as nerves as she finally fulfilled her goals, Amber expressed concern about the worry weighing on her sister.

"I'm just happy we're in this together now," Jade said simply.

The Parker sisters sat together in the kingdom they had rightfully claimed, eager for the responsibility that came with their positions. The girls each took in a breath filled with hope, joy, promise, and, finally, purpose.

Chapter Twelve

*A*LONE NOW, Jade prepared for the conversation ahead. Giving open-ended interviews was nerve-wracking. Coupled with a stranger asking unknown questions, the whole exercise left her feeling anxious. Yet she also felt compelled to do it.

She paced behind her desk, thinking about the possible outcomes. Her fingers floated unconsciously to her emerald necklace, holding it gently. Glancing at her reflection in the mirror, she noted her hair was mussed. The smooth brown stands were only slightly loose, but a professional appearance was imperative.

In the comfort of her private restroom, she pulled out the high bun and allowed her hair to fall down her back. Checking her neutral makeup for mishaps, she then studied her reflection in a way she didn't often do. She saw a glimpse of her mother, and a faint memory of Annalise braiding her hair sprang to mind. The memory soothed her troubled spirit as she combed her hair.

Jade flicked the light switch off before leaving with a slight smile, flinging the French braid off her shoulder. She thought now of Daniel and his recently deceased mother.

This interview was the least she could offer as an apology to him for failing to be a good friend. She valued his friendship immensely. She could be herself around him and be honest about her boundaries and idiosyncrasies. Connecting to the pain and hurt of losing her own parents, she knew nothing she did could ease that agony, which deepened her sense of guilt.

Mr. Porter sent a text urging her to record the conversation herself and think about each answer for ten seconds before answering, as he had always instructed. Her hands trembled around her phone as she waited for one of her assistants to knock on the door and announce Lucy.

Glancing at the mirror by the bathroom door, she caught herself fidgeting. She gathered her thoughts and exhaled a long, therapeutic breath, followed by two short inhales to reset her mind and body.

She would be in control. She would lead her own path. She would reject any question she did not wish to answer. There was no need for jitters.

At a light knock, the glass door opened, and Blue poked her head inside. Lucy stood waiting behind her.

"Ms. Prescott is here, Miss Jade. She has her badge like you requested."

Jade smiled, thanking her dedicated assistant. Approaching the coffee table with two mugs positioned on opposite sides, Jade welcomed Lucy.

Her request to have a badge made had been a formality. She explained to Lucy that if she wanted to become a journalist, she ought to expect certain aspects of the job. However, Jade had another reason. While there was no way of guaranteeing the interview would have no negative consequences, she felt it prudent to document her professionalism in case legal action became necessary.

As Lucy joined her, she seemed like a completely different person. She told Jade her father was pleased with her attempts to get better.

"He really didn't believe me until I said you were going to help," she happily admitted, which alarmed Jade, though she hid it. "He said he'll give me a chance without needing rehab."

Tilting her head, Jade pondered a question. She poured the hot cocoa into each cup; she refused to serve Lucy any type of stimulant, no matter how benign caffeine might seem.

"What was the name of the facility you once tried for your rehabilitation?" Jade asked, removing the translucent cover from the platter of baked goods between them and setting a plate in front of Lucy.

"Master's Reform," Lucy said casually, taking a cookie and enjoying a mouthful.

Jade smiled at her guest, noting the improved appearance and heightened spirits. Placing her phone on the table to indicate she was recording the interview, Jade eyed the pack beside Lucy, which confirmed that she had claimed the laptop Amber arranged for her. Second Circuits gathered discarded electronics to refurbish and eventually donated the pieces to anyone needing help.

"Okay, Lucy," Jade began. "We agreed this morning that I would be answering questions that I usually turn down to help you put an article together, but I will not answer should we veer too far from the goal of this talk."

Lucy nodded, finishing up her cookie. "Of course."

"I'm glad to hear that." Sliding a folder with some papers across the table, Jade smiled. "Please look over these and sign them if you agree. It's a standard agreement my lawyer has for all interviews. I have already signed both copies. I'll wait for you to read—"

"No need!" Lucy said, eagerly leaning over to sign the documents, then passing them back to Jade, not taking her copy. "I really appreciate your doing this, Jade. I wouldn't hurt a friend."

Silently taking in the choice of words, Jade accepted the folder, crossed her ankles, and leaned back on the couch, asking Lucy to begin.

Lucy cleared her throat. "From the information everyone knows about you, the beginning is Syndicate." She briefly went over the company's history. "Your parents, like you and Amber, were very private. They went to great lengths to keep you both away from the public eye." After a slight pause, she asked, "How did that work as a child?"

"How did what work as a child?" Jade said, making eye contact, pushing Lucy to elaborate on her questions.

"How did your parents explain their work to you?"

"My parents were always direct with us, gentle and accommodating for our growing minds but still always direct," Jade said, thinking back. "I learned later on that they had a rule that one of them must be present with us for school events and other activities. Since they split the work between themselves, they also split family time."

"Split how? Like fifty-fifty?"

"Well, I won't say everything was equal. If anything, I recall my mother explaining the obvious difference between equal and fair."

"Did you ever have time as a whole family if their time with you was split?" Lucy asked with a hint of emotion. Having no intention of building a connection with Lucy, Jade tried to keep the focus on the interview.

"When I say split, I mean that was how they worked it out between each other. As a child, I knew very little of this. When I wanted or needed them, I had them there. Yeah, there were days when they worked, but I knew it was temporary."

Lucy stared down at her notepad. "Um, they were private. Did you feel safe?"

Regretting her decision more by the second, Jade cleared her throat. Lucy was asking questions that she related to and not ones that would benefit her with a well-written article about one of the mysterious Parker sisters.

"Safe? I don't understand the reason for that question."

"What about the fire?" Lucy blurted. "Can you tell me about the fire?"

"Can I tell you about the fire?"

"Oh," Lucy chuckled oddly, "the day of the fire, how did it start?"

"On the day of the fire," Jade said, taking a deep breath and struggling to give the girl the benefit of the doubt, "my sister and I had an appointment to tour another school my parents were considering moving us to."

Memories of the past came flooding back. Jade had grown tired of making new connections with people who found her strange, direct, and headstrong, and she'd been arguing with her mother about moving to yet another new school.

Stirring batter for red velvet cupcakes, Annalise sighed at her older daughter's fervent refusal.

"Jade, that school is not safe. Now, they may need something to happen to a student before they take action. I, on the other hand, will not risk that something being my girls."

The adolescent Jade huffed in defeat, but her mother lovingly handed her a wooden spoon to share in the beauty of baking. Although she resisted at first, Jade gave in and scooped the batter into the lined tins. She winked at her sister, then nudged Amber to find their father. By the time the tins were full and ready for the oven, Amber had returned, shaking her drooping head; she had failed to convince their father.

"Amber always had the baby-sister charm and could sweet-talk my parents into almost anything," Jade admitted with a smile, staring off into space. "I tended to beg and argue and be silly."

"Why wasn't the school safe?" Lucy asked, drawing Jade back to reality.

"A suspicious man was lurking about, and the kids all knew it. But the school officials said there was little they could do since he hadn't approached anyone."

"How was the new school?"

"It was alright." Jade sighed with a half smile. "In retrospect, it was even better."

When the girls and Kayce had left for the tour, Jade stormed out of the house, later texting her parents that she was okay. She apologized and calmed their worried hearts by complimenting the school. When they replied that she and Amber were the reason they did anything and everything and told her they loved her, she responded with the same love.

Her smile fading, Jade refocused on Lucy. "The ride home was fun. Our housekeeper had gotten us our new uniforms, and we picked up some ice cream. We were eating it when the first fire engine rushed past us. I remember seeing this enormous cloud of black smoke in the sky, and I had no idea where it came from."

She squinted as the images played in her mind—of the car pulling over when there was nowhere left to drive, emergency vehicles scattered everywhere. One ambulance had its lights on but stayed parked on the crowded street. Police officers held back the people gathering around, including Jade and Amber.

Amber sobbed until Kacey came out of the crowd, chastising the officer for handling her roughly. Jade released her sister's hand and darted up the enormous mansion's driveway, screaming for her parents. Firefighters prevented her from getting any closer as toxic fumes filled the air.

She texted her parents. She cried, staring at the screen, begging them to answer as a firefighter pulled her out of the way. She ignored his remonstrations and crumpled into the fetal position. Kacey eventually appeared out of a group of men who had gathered over Jade as she screamed for her parents over and over. Kacey held out her hand, calling Jade's name until the girl snapped out of her frenzy.

Jade refused to go with her, pointing to the house, begging for help to find her parents, screaming that they needed her.

"Come with me, Jade!" Kacey finally yelled.

Amber ran to Jade, crying, and held her tightly.

After a few more moments of chaos, the girls gave in and took Kacey's hands, following her to the car. They drove off—the sisters had no idea where. Amber peered through the back window with tears running down her dirty face, whimpering for their parents. Jade sat in her seat, now frozen in shock.

An exhausted Amber curled up by her sister as Kacey called to Jade. She looked up at her housekeeper in the rearview mirror with bloodshot eyes.

"They were in the fire, right?" Jade said.

"I . . ." Kacey trailed off.

"They're dead," Jade proclaimed, which seemed to freeze the car in silence. Amber stopped whimpering. Finally, with a strained voice, Jade stated, "My mom and dad would never hear me crying like that and not come, Kacey. They're dead."

Chapter Thirteen

T HE "BOXES OF DOCUMENTS" Joel sent down turned out to be one standard-sized file box.

In the dusty compartment, all Amber found were the financial forms relating to Syndicate's business contracts, where they claimed heavy losses and many tax deductions.

Perplexed with how Syndicate was being managed, she pored through the less-than-believable forms, shaken by the fact that the company had never been audited. *How has no one followed up on these?* Joel mentioned archived files online that he would print, but they all preceded the year of the fire.

Amber recalled Jade's concerns about the company and the board members who had run it since their parents' deaths. Were Jade's worries justified? Amber's guilt compounded when she realized that Jade had been seeing these red flags but hadn't said a thing, which likely caused her sleepless nights—all so that Amber could live out her school days in peace.

"Well, that was unpleasant!" Jade sighed, letting the glass door shut behind her. With a cheeky grin, she asked Amber about the opened box tossed to the side.

"Blurgh," Amber grunted, gesturing to the mess surrounding her. "But how was your thing?"

"I knew it was going to go down that road," Jade admitted. "I knew she was going to talk about Mom and Dad."

Amber rolled her eyes. "Doesn't everybody?"

"Not like that," Jade said. "Like, to relate to me, like our dead mothers were this struggle we would bond over—like she wanted to be friends because of that single fact."

"Ew. She said that?"

"No, it's just this feeling, and then her unorganized questions validated it."

"How much damage could she do if she twisted what you said?" Amber asked, trying not to sound too confrontational.

"The usual mess, if I'm being honest." Jade glanced at the four manila folders and asked if Joel was bringing more.

"This is the whole thing!" Amber proclaimed as she pantomimed the nonexistent enormous pile in front of her.

"This is twelve years of pharmaceutical business?"

"Those aren't even enough for a proper tax review," Amber scoffed. "Jade, what happened?"

Jade clawed at the air in frustration and explained she had never been granted permission to investigate. Her credentials had been similar to Amy's, who was Mr. Reynolds's second assistant.

"They kept everything away because I chose to study something else and wasn't an owner," Jade griped as she fell onto the couch.

"What did Mr. Porter say?"

"He said legally they were right, but I could challenge them when I finished my MBA."

"This is bad."

The Parker sisters needed time to figure out the next step—hopefully before criminal charges were made against their inherited company. Jade suggested giving the entire company the remainder of the week off.

"It's only a few days, and we can pass it off as a celebratory thing for you."

"Can I come to work in my pajamas?" Amber asked, quirking her lips.

Jade laughed. "You can come to work in pajamas every day."

She volunteered to send the emails to the HR department and the rest of the employees while Amber remained in her office, going over the lonely box.

Pausing by the door, Jade looked at Amber. "We should bring this up to Aunt Kacey and Mr. Porter. They may know something we don't, especially about the sealed records." She then muttered, "I think we might need to prepare ourselves for some hard-to-swallow truths."

Chapter Fourteen

Taking the sisters' bags, Al stood by the rear passenger door as they entered the car at the street entrance. He placed their bags in the passenger seat, then drove cautiously through a flock of photographers. Unalarmed by the crowd, Jade thanked him and grabbed a warm cup of coffee, passing the other to her sister.

The conversation about their parents' will continued, and Al respectfully raised the privacy panel with a mechanical whirr.

Amber expressed surprise that anyone would have agreed to be a minor investor in a company with the minute possibility of being a board member later on. There was little to be sure of, excluding the restrictions and incentives for the sisters' takeover.

The topic of their birth certificates having rekindled, Jade walked through her efforts to gain access to them, all to no avail.

"I used an old friend of Dad's." She went on to explain what Mr. Hough charmingly referred to as his "street smarts" and suggested Amber meet him at some point.

"Jade, I know I'm late to the party, but I want to take over the whole will and birth certificates thing. Just throw it on me. One less thing to think about."

Jade turned to Amber with relief. She saw her sister's earnest concern and graciously and gratefully accepted the help she was notorious for never requesting.

"I think having a new perspective and mindset is the right choice."

Moving to a more scintillating topic, Jade told her sister how Mr. Hough had initially crossed paths with their parents.

As fixtures in pharmaceutical research, Annalise and James were on the list for every fundraiser. At one of those events, James caught Mr. Hough trying to sneak into the hotel kitchen. Sensing an urgency in the interloper, James avoided calling the security team. Instead, he trusted his instincts and listened to the man's story.

Mr. Hough knew that these shindigs always wasted food. His salary was insufficient to support a family that had recently expanded by three identical babies, so a young Mr. Hough was forced to find other ways to make do without losing face or submitting his family to more hardship. He told Jade that he had gotten exceptionally good at concealing his identity and sneaking in to offer help as additional staff. Such positions always had last-minute call-outs, and if one knew what to do, they'd get away with doing it.

For months, Mr. Hough took food destined for the dumpster and spread any excess among struggling neighbors.

James was all too familiar with the concept of food waste and had long encouraged the donation of leftover stock. Jade learned that Mr. Hough's family had inspired one of her parents' smaller collaborations. James and Annalise provided aid to anyone who needed it, and they took on the added challenge; after all, proper nutrition was a critical factor in health, and health was a driving force for Syndicate.

Mr. Hough's street smarts earned him more money. James and Annalise hired him to be their personal investigator and were his only clients.

The car pulled behind the house, and Al quickly exited to check the perimeter. As the girls emerged, Amber shared that she felt conflicted after hearing the story of Mr. Hough and her parents. How could she and her sister question their parents' actions regarding the will and the suspicious history of Syndicate but also hold them in such high regard at the same moment?

Jade shared Amber's feelings and warned that the sisters would need to be delicate through the next steps with Kacey and Mr. Porter, for fear of hurting their parents' reputation—or worse, their memory.

Chapter Fifteen

Jade and Amber filled up the dishwasher as they summarized their day for Kacey. They discussed Lucy and giving their company the week off, not acknowledging the elephant in the room. Jade's attention shifted as the conversation died down.

"Aunt Kacey," Jade asked, handing Amber the last glass before Amber looked for the tablets under the sink, "can I ask you about that day?"

Kacey caught on immediately. "The day of the fire?"

Jade nodded, strolling with Kacey out of the kitchen as Amber turned on the dishwasher. Amber followed soon after, passing the entrance hall and crossing to the sunroom where the family often convened.

Kacey sat up as Amber joined them.

"That day is seared into my memory in a way I wish it weren't."

"I bet no one ever told you that taking Mom and Dad's position would be permanent," Amber teased, curling up on a chair beside the couch where her sister and surrogate mother sat.

"Oh, Amber," Kacey chuckled, "no one can ever prepare you for life's, well, dramatic turns. Certainly nothing prepared me for that day." She let out a deep breath. "That was the day I took you girls to tour your new school. Oh, you hated the idea of moving a second time and tried your best to convince your parents to let you stay."

"Dad said the old school wasn't safe," Amber recalled.

"Yes, dear. When you two came home saying you saw that strange man waiting for you and he tried to talk to Amber, that was the final straw."

Kacey explained how someone had also broken into their previous school to take pictures of the students on campus. That was the first time their parents had transferred them.

Kacey spoke softly, her eyes distant. "Your parents had important plans the day before the fire. They asked me to tour the new school and take you two along. They had a lot going on that day, but what mattered was keeping you safe while at school."

"I don't remember that," Jade murmured.

"They never told you," Kacey said. "Your old school saw their concerns as, well, they didn't agree that there was any real harm."

"I remember the tour with you," Amber said, steering the conversation back.

"It wasn't a bad option. I recall you liking it as well, Jade," Kacey said with a teasing smile. "I was hopeful for a pleasant conversation when we returned. I hoped your parents would see that you weren't as upset and things would be less intense."

Kacey paused, staring at the carpet as the memory unfolded.

"I remember the smoke in the sky as we drove to the house. The sirens were blaring, and I was worried, of course, but it didn't strike me yet what I needed to worry about."

She lifted her gaze back up to the girls, gently brushing loose hairs from her eyes.

"When the driver stopped because the emergency vehicles were blocking the road leading to the house, that's when it hit me. I wasn't looking at a passing fire engine and feeling sorry for someone I didn't know. I was anxious for your parents."

The silence filling the room had a gravity to it, leaving everyone unable to move or speak. Jade and Amber had never asked about that night, afraid it would bring up past emotions no one felt ready for, even after twelve years. But Jade's desire to make sense of what had become of Syndicate pushed them past the barrier at last.

"We stepped out of the car, and you two shot away from me so fast that I didn't know which one to chase. Amber's cries were louder because an officer caught her, so I ran to her. I held you, Amber, looking for Jade, scanning the area, hoping and praying that your parents would emerge unharmed.

"I heard a firefighter telling someone to get a social worker for the children, and I snapped out of my foggy daze. I needed to protect you until I had more information. I found Jade and dragged you both to the car and drove to a hotel for the night. I didn't know what to do, so I called Mr. Porter."

"I remember staying there for a while," Amber said, looking thoughtful.

"A month, right?" Jade replied.

Kacey nodded with sorrow.

Jade leaned closer to Kacey and asked about the will, explaining how it made very little sense: it followed no known laws about inheritance, yet it was never challenged and never contested.

"Who would challenge the estate your parents left for you?" Kacey ask, looking bewildered.

The fact that Annalise and James had no known surviving relatives only enhanced the oddness of the circumstances surrounding how the Parker family managed their wealth.

"Aunt Kacey, I said the will was weird back when the board members were hassling me for a declared major," Jade added. "But now that Amber has taken over, there are so many more things that just don't add up."

Kacey's somber expression disappeared. She glanced over to Amber, who was watching her intently, looking for answers to questions no one dared ask.

"What exactly are you girls asking me?"

Jade began citing the nonexistent work at Syndicate. She'd observed the lack of business while studying her MBA, but it was confirmed when Amber took over Syndicate.

"I was never given the chance to see proof of any actual work, and let me tell you, Aunt Kacey, I bugged them day and night!" Jade huffed. "They gave me the community service program to shut me up, I guess, but I never saw real progress."

Amber then explained that the documented trail for Syndicate's research efforts ended the year their parents died.

"I can't understand how Syndicate hasn't been audited," she exhaled, finally voicing her primary concern as she moved her bangs to the side.

"Aunt Kacey," Jade whispered, pulling herself closer to the motherly housekeeper, "is Syndicate a front for some criminal organization? Is our entire life a fraud?"

"Jade Elliot Parker!" Kacey exclaimed.

"Aunt Kacey, please!" Amber pleaded. "We just want to know what's going on so we can take over Syndicate the way Mom and Dad intended. We know they ran a legit company, but there's no proof of anything since the fire."

"I see," Kacey said calmly, picking up her phone. "You simply want to know what your parents' company was about, where their wealth came from—your past?"

They both nodded enthusiastically.

"I can see why you would want me to explain it," Kacey said, standing abruptly. "Unfortunately, I must leave."

"Leave?" Jade demanded, jerking back as Kacey moved about. She darted a glance over to Amber, who was loosening her braid, allowing her black hair to fall freely.

"Yes, I completely forgot that I promised an old friend something, and I'm incredibly late as it is. Can we discuss this when I get back?"

Kacey zipped through the door, not waiting for a reply.

A very odd hush fell in her wake.

"Did that just happen?" Amber finally asked her sister.

Peeking at her watch, Jade whispered, "Aunt Kacey has old friends? That she runs off to at eleven at night?"

"Okay, I'm gonna call it," Amber announced. "Mom and Dad were killed in what was meant to look like an accident because they made crazy agreements with nefarious people to cover up this grand scheme for helping people get affordable health care."

Jade laughed, tossing a pillow at her sister as the two tried to make light of the misinformation. While left unspoken, they wanted so desperately to know the truth. Agreeing to move on with their plan and report to work alone, they determined to search for more clues about Syndicate and their parents' legacy.

Chapter Sixteen

The following workday, technically her first full day as owner, was especially joyous for Amber, who wore her formal nightwear to work. With the employees taking the rest of the week off, she reveled in being her quirky self.

On the elevator, Jade reminded Amber that Mr. Hough would visit that morning. Amber welcomed the task of looking into their unobtainable birth certificates.

The sisters parted ways with a witty comment from Jade about Amber's attire under her trench coat. Accepting the tease, Amber laughed, cheekily flashed her sister, then entered her office.

Welcoming the day with a smile and trying desperately to ignore Kacey's strange behavior, Amber laid her snack bag on one of the couches and shuffled to her desk to work through the day's agenda.

A knock caught her off guard. She whipped around to find a young man standing by the open door, awaiting her permission to enter.

Expecting only Mr. Hough, she mentally tried to add up the years since her father allegedly met him. She was thrown off by the fact that he looked closer to her age than her father's. His face was clean shaven, and his hair was sleek and black without a hint of gray.

Amber gestured for him to enter. "Please, come in."

She picked up her snack bag to return to her desk, smiling down at her pajamas, unashamed.

"I just need to grab a notepad, and we can go over everything. Please, have a seat, or help yourself to the coffee bar."

"I'm quite alright. I was looking for Miss Parker," the young man cordially said, not moving.

She studied his casually expensive clothing. The subtle designer brands made her suspicious of this man who had built such a reputation working with her father. She noticed him studying her as well but was not bothered; that surely was par for the course with an investigator.

"Okay, let's get the formalities out of the way," Amber announced. "Hi, I'm Miss Parker. I wasn't expecting you this early, but since I haven't started on anything today, let's make this the first thing I check off my list."

The man regarded her oddly as he sat, and his reticent behavior began to annoy her.

"Is this how you treat all your contacts?" she demanded.

"Excuse me?" he said. "I worked with Jade Parker a—"

"Yeah, I know," Amber interrupted. "Who do you think referred me to you?"

He stuttered, then shot an obvious glance at her clothing.

"Oh," she gushed, "yeah, as you can see, it's pretty quiet here today, and since it's just us, I came to work in something a little more comfortable." She cleared her throat. "I know it's a bit unorthodox, but you've met my sister. Unorthodox is how we do it here."

"You're Amber?" the man said.

"Yup! In the flesh." She grinned. "My sister told me everything you did for her, but I was thinking of starting over with a fresh perspective. You know, try to see something that was missed."

"I didn't work for Jade. We worked together," he stated.

"Um." Amber paused. "What do you mean you worked together? I thought she hired you."

"Not really."

"You can't not really hire someone. You either do or you don't."

"She didn't hire me," he said, pulling himself closer to the edge of the seat, clearly under pressure but showing composure. "I mean, yeah, it was her idea, but both of us did the work."

"And how is your investigating people my sister's idea?" she asked.

"What?" He looked utterly bewildered. "We didn't investigate anyone."

"Aha!" Amber said triumphantly, then frowned. "Wait, what? You didn't investigate for her?"

"No." He again looked at her strangely. "We started a foundation to help cancer patients."

Her cheeks flushed as she shot to her feet. "Who are you?"

The young man smiled, standing and stretching out his hand.

"I'm Daniel Prescott." She shook his hand. "I met your sister in college. The way she talked about you made me wish I had a sister like you." He pulled back and slid his hands in his pockets. "It's a pleasure to finally meet you."

"Talked about me?" Amber whispered, uncertain of what to think.

Daniel nodded. "She described having you in her life like that song 'Better Place' by Rachel Platten."

This almost invisible detail, Jade expressing her feelings in relation to songs, was something not many people knew about. Amber only knew of three people who did.

She imploded with embarrassment. She'd made a fool of herself to someone she'd wanted to have a firm standing with on their first meeting. Clearing her throat, she tried to think of something to save the moment.

"Mr. Prescott, in the future it may be beneficial—and, honestly, it would just save time—if you introduced yourself first."

"I'm sorry about that," he admitted, bringing his hands out of his pockets to settle nervously in front of him. "I'm kinda lost. The front desk said Miss Parker's office was in front of the elevator, and here it is, but you aren't Jade." He glanced at her necklace with a smile. "I noticed your necklace. Jade told me about them."

Amber eyed him awkwardly, her arms slowly crossing over her waist with one hand then rising toward her necklace.

"It's your birthstone, right? With your initials and birthday etched on the back," Daniel said, not waiting for an answer. "I always thought that was an awesome family tradition."

Amber smiled briefly, then cleared her throat. "Jade's office is down this hall that doesn't look like a hall. I only joined the company this week. The front desk may not be up to date. My apologies for any confusion."

"Oh, nothing to be sorry about," Daniel chuckled. "I guess we both caught each other off guard. To be honest, I wanted to give you a better first impression."

"Huh?" was her inelegant response.

"Anyone who knows Jade knows how important you are to her, and I never had the chance to meet you. I promise, next time, I'll be less whatever this was." He gestured at himself charmingly. Amber didn't want to release her suspicions immediately, though.

"Does she know you're coming today? She didn't mention it this morning."

"No, I came to return something after her talk with Lucy. Thank you, by the way, for the computer," he said with a nod. "She mentioned you helped her get one."

"My pleasure," Amber muttered, still feeling foolish. "If you'll excuse me, I must prepare for my meeting with the *real* investigator."

"Oh, of course." He moved to the door. "It was a pleasure to meet you. See you around."

He walked down the hall, waving through the window, and she reciprocated, dumbfounded by what had occurred.

She wanted to hear about what Daniel had come to give Jade, but she had not lied about needing to prepare for Mr. Hough—and for the challenge the past would present.

Jade was deep in thought when a light knock on the open door startled her. Jerking her head up, she happily stood to greet her friend.

Daniel was gushing with excitement but respected Jade's boundaries with physical touch, offering their usual side hug when she invited him in. After getting refreshments, the two friends conversed about everything that had happened since they last saw each other.

"I can't believe it's been a year," Jade professed, sitting beside him, "but one could argue that it doesn't count if it was for work."

"Eh, it was a corporate dinner," Daniel said. "I'll take that over any other workday."

"I bet. Things can get crazy, especially with classes, but gladly," she sighed with relief, "that's *all* over!"

"I met Amber."

"Oh really?" Jade snickered.

"Yeah, I don't think I came across as well as I wanted."

"Oh no! Did you touch her chocolates without asking?"

"Never! I remember the cardinal rule about her treats," he joked. "But I thought her office was yours and didn't really introduce myself, so she thought I was someone else."

Jade burst into laughter, imagining how the conversation must have gone. "You asked for Miss Parker, not Jade, didn't you?"

He promised to make a better second impression.

"Looks like things are working out," he said, looking around her office. "I know it was pretty hard at one point, but I'm glad you're both in charge. I hope things won't be as hectic."

Jade thanked him, asking about his visit.

"Can't a guy just visit his friend who took over her parents' company and watch her do all the great things she said she would?"

Jade smiled devilishly. "A guy can, but you're just as busy as I am."

Unable to disagree, he pulled a box out of his jacket pocket.

"I came by to personally give you this."

She opened it to reveal a small tape. It looked like a tape from an old recorder, and she quickly recognized it. "Is this Lucy's?"

"Yes," Daniel confirmed. "I hope you don't mind, but I heard it. As in, she played it for me and my stepfather."

"Why are you returning this?"

"Officially, I don't think it's safe to leave something like that with Lucy. It could tempt her," he said.

"Tempt her? What does that mean?"

"I honestly don't know," he admitted, "but I've been to enough meetings with lawyers and police officers to know she's a magnet for, uh, misunderstandings."

"Unofficially?" she asked.

"I think you offered that interview because you feel guilty for not knowing Mom died."

"I do. I should have been there, Daniel."

"I didn't tell you, Jade," he said. "I saw how you hid your exhaustion every time we met or had an event. I didn't know how hard things were with grad school, but I knew that you not talking about it meant it was too much, so I chose not to tell you. I *chose* not to add more stress."

"Still, Daniel, your mom died."

"She knew she was going to go when she asked to stop treatment," he said warmly. "There wasn't anything anyone could do." He handed the tape to her. "I don't think you would have ever spoken about that day if you didn't feel guilty, and so I came to tell you there is nothing to feel guilty about. Mom wanted to go without anyone fussing over her. Even her funeral was small."

"I'm sorry she isn't with you anymore, Daniel," she finally said with a pain they both shared.

"Me too," he whispered, glancing to the ground.

Studying the tape in her hand, she was relieved. He was right; she had never felt comfortable telling anyone about the day she lost her parents, and while Lucy didn't seem like she could do much harm, Jade held that tape tightly, grateful it was no longer in the girl's possession.

"My publicist always tells me people are hunting for my secrets."

"I think there's a fine line between privacy and secrecy," Daniel quoted her with a grin.

"Thanks for bringing this, Daniel. I know the foundation keeps you busy," she said admiringly. Many described him as a genius for taking a simple idea and building a national group that assisted so many people, and she fully agreed.

He waved away her thanks and stood, making his way to the door. "No problem. It seemed important to keep it from falling into the wrong hands." He bid her a good day and promised a non-work-related meeting in the near future.

She waited until he was out of sight to grab a heavy crystal paperweight from her desk. Dropping the tape on the floor, Jade smashed the capsule, then ripped apart the thin black tape before tossing it all in the trash.

Chapter Seventeen

After watching Daniel enter Jade's office, Amber swung back around the doorframe and paced around her own space. This Daniel character was not terrible at all. She wondered why she had assumed that the one person Jade found suitable as a friend would be less than likable. But then, why had she not met him before? *Sure, I wasn't around at first, but why not after Jade and I reconciled?*

She paused by the door when she heard the elevator ding and the doors open.

A man near Mr. Porter's age emerged into the bright entryway of the twenty-fourth floor, peering side to side. His mostly gray hair was combed back, and his rugged, short beard was sprinkled with silver. He wore worn-out black boots and jeans that looked like they had seen a few adventures. He situated his denim jacket in front of the wide mirror on the wall.

Then he spotted Amber eyeing him. Glancing at his right pocket, she saw the visitor's badge and surmised that this was Mr. Hough. She briskly headed down the hall to greet him.

"You must be the investigator, Mr. Hough?" she asked with a welcoming smile.

"Yeah, miss," he said, a raspy whistle in his voice. "It's a pleasure to make yur acquaintance." Tilting his head down, he shook her hand.

"The pleasure is all mine," Amber said, leading him to her office and gesturing for him to enter ahead of her. "Can I interest you in a beverage, Mr. Hough?"

She crossed to the coffee bar as he sat on the couch.

"Urm, a coffee, cream only, miss."

"Certainly," Amber said, pushing a button on the shiny machine. A whirring sound accompanied the shunting of whole coffee beans from a compartment on the side. She pulled out a drawer holding an array of different creamers and carried them to him. Mr. Hough pointed at the milk-based cream, thanking her again.

"May I order you something from the café, Mr. Hough?"

"I'll take anythin' you say is good, miss," he said with a nod after a sip of his coffee. He scanned his surroundings nonchalantly. "Don't reckon I'll be here long, though."

Tapping on her phone, Amber asked, "Why not?"

"On 'count I don' have much to tell ya, miss."

"I see," Amber said, placing her phone down. She tried to pinpoint the origin of his peculiar dialect but found it hard to trace. It sounded intentionally Southern but vague. "Well, I'd like to assure my sister that I have done a thorough job. Would you walk me through everything?"

"How far do ya wanna go?" Mr. Hough asked, taking another sip.

"Let's go way back. Why did you start investigating privately?"

Mr. Hough chuckled as he explained that he wasn't an official private investigator. He only had one client prior to Jade: James Parker. While Annalise was always present, he primarily worked with James.

"No, miss. I ain't no investigator. I, how'd ya say it, I have my way of getting things from folks in a way they don' know thur telling me. 'Street smarts.'" He pointed to his forehead pridefully.

"Oh, I see," Amber said, checking her phone.

"Yes, ma'am. Most people don' pay attention to me. Yur father saw ma special gift. So, whenever he needed some 'street smarts,' he'd call."

"I understand you and my father met at a benefit?"

"Yup," he laughed. "My street smarts wasn't so good back then." Mr. Hough looked down to the ground, then back to her. "After that, he showed me how to use my street smarts in a better way. Let's jus' say, now I get paid for m'work."

Amber smiled. "Anyone who has earned my father's respect has earned mine."

"I remember the last job he gave me, before the accident." He slowly shook his head.

"What was that job, exactly?" Amber asked, standing to retrieve the meal when a café worker appeared at her door.

"Background checks," Mr. Hough announced and accepted the plate she handed him. "He wanted to know a whole lot about these board fellers before doing a business deal with 'em. His buddy Porter told me after the fire that he agreed to workin' with 'em."

"You didn't approve?" Amber inquired, spreading butter over a warm piece of toast.

Mr. Hough scoffed, not answering her.

"Mr. Hough, it is perfectly fine for you to have a differing opinion."

"No," he stated. "I won' be speaking ill of him, miss. You just be careful around that Bradley Reynolds."

"I definitely will," Amber noted. She pressed on, asking about the work Jade requested of him.

Mr. Hough had nothing of substance to show and seemed dismayed to admit it. He explained how all family records were sealed by a court order. Jade was told she needed a judge to release her own birth certificate.

"I still can' believe she couldn' get it, miss."

"Did Jade pursue the matter?"

"Beggin' yur pardon?" he asked, his brow wrinkling.

Amber repeated her question.

Mr. Hough shook his head. "I don' think she wanted a judge lookin' and askin' questions." He went on to explain that he'd also obtained the original copy of their parents' will. "I told yur sister that the will yur mom and dad made wasn't, uh . . ."

"Usual?" Amber said, completing his sentence.

"Nope, it was definitely unusual," Mr. Hough confirmed. "She didn' want other lawyers to start looking through it"—he paused for a moment—"until you took yur share of the company."

"In case someone wanted to challenge it?"

"Well, I'm no expert on that, but I told 'er that havin' a judge look at the birth certificates would get 'em lookin' in other places too."

"Mr. Hough," Amber blurted, "what about my parents' death certificates?"

"Sealed too, miss." He shook his head. "Even the police report about the fire."

No wonder Jade felt so helpless, Amber lamented. She observed him studying her after he finished his meal and realized her fingers were anxiously rubbing her necklace.

"Mr. Hough, can *I* ask for your services?"

"Anythin', Miss Parker."

"I'd like to get a new perspective on this, but from a less formal approach."

She wanted him to view the matter as a cold case, to interview and speak to people close to her parents around the time of the fatal accidents—former staff members or old friends. The goal was to find someone James and Annalise had spoken to regarding their daughters' birth certificates and their will.

"You think whoever put the seal on their death certificates is the same person who put it on your birth certificates?" he conjectured.

"Yes," Amber said. "My parents definitely didn't seal their death certificates, so I'm hoping someone remembers something from all those years ago. It makes sense, doesn't it?" She paused, then continued, "The unconventional will, the sealed birth certificates, and the records about the accident and their deaths are surely connected."

When Mr. Hough stood to take his leave, he agreed to search for the information she requested without alerting anyone to the purpose behind her inquisition. Walking him to the door, Amber thanked him and his street smarts.

Chapter Eighteen

"Amber, what's wrong?" Jade gasped when she spotted her sister on the floor. When Amber messaged about snooping through the board members' open cabinets for proof that Syndicate was an operational company, Jade had expected a larger pile of papers.

Dazed, Amber looked at her sister. "Jade, we're in so much trouble."

Passing a stack of papers to Jade, Amber explained the box she had found in Mr. Reynolds's office.

"I walked in, and something was off, which is weird 'cause I've never been there, so why did I feel like something was out of place?" Amber climbed to her feet as her sister settled on the couch's armrest. "It was like I could see him walking around the room, like the functionality of the office wasn't right." She dropped her voice to a whisper. "It was a box with these papers."

"These?" Jade asked, pointing to the floor.

Amber nodded. "It was kinda genius, hiding it in plain view. I don't know how I noticed. I just pictured him walking around and it being in the way."

The box contained an array of documents. The first pile showed how each board member had benefited from Syndicate.

"Jade, these stock portfolios don't make sense. They don't even look real, but they are."

"But Syndicate didn't go public," Jade commented.

"Exactly," Amber exclaimed. "How can they do that? How can two conflicting pieces of information be true?"

Jade pointed to papers behind her sister. "What's the next group?"

"That's a copy of Mom and Dad's will!" Amber proclaimed.

Based on the notes Amber had uncovered, Mr. Reynolds suspected that Jade would not honor the incentives her parents put in place to take over the company. That notion grew with every passing semester when Jade postponed her major selection. It appeared that he was preparing to seek claim to Syndicate before Amber could take the entire company.

"He was worried that I would take over everything, even if you didn't," Amber surmised. "Based on his notes, I don't think he liked Mr. Porter presenting a roadblock to him doing what he wanted."

When Mr. Porter announced that Jade had begun her MBA studies and accepted the nonexecutive position at Syndicate, the deception should have ended. Yet Mr. Reynolds kept the documents hidden away.

"Amber," Jade hesitantly asked, "does that sound right to you?"

Shaking her head, Amber eyed the last pile beside Jade. Jade sank to the floor in bewilderment.

"Mr. Hough said he did background checks on Mr. Reynolds and the other board members," Amber said.

"Yeah, he told me that too. He said he had no idea why our parents would willingly work with those people."

"Jade, that pile there is a signed agreement between them and Mom and Dad," Amber said with a hitch in her voice. "It's an agreement that while Mom and Dad were alive, the so-called board members would receive a fee, for doing *nothing*. But should they die before we could take over the company, the board members would run Syndicate until we graduated college in either business or pharmacology, and then we take it back, and they get nothing."

Jade stared at her sister, wondering why Amber was emphasizing something they already knew. "Is this legally binding?"

"That's not the point, Jade!" Amber shouted. "Look at the date! That agreement was signed a few months before the fire. What if they killed them to make more money?"

"By the looks of these financial statements, they made much more than the agreed-upon fee—like fifty times more."

"Jade, what if they killed them?" Amber repeated, her lips trembling.

"We need *all* the facts," Jade firmly replied.

"There are no facts!" Amber snapped back. "Mom and Dad had this great company, but since they died, Syndicate has produced nothing—yet it still reports huge profits. The board members are these creepy, greedy old men making money hand over fist." Amber was frantic as she rambled, "Oh, and if anyone finds out, we're the ones who have to deal with it!"

"How could Mr. Porter be on board with this?" Jade asked, pointing out that he was a witness to the will and the nonsense agreement. And with Aunt Kacey still not answering their messages or calls, they had no one trustworthy to turn to.

Jade implored her sister to return the documents after making copies. It was of vital importance that they pretend ignorance until they learned more. Then she announced that she would call Mr. Porter and Kacey to make dinner plans so as not to make anyone suspicious of what they'd found.

"We have to just keep up this charade until we figure out what's going on," Jade assured her sister.

Chapter Nineteen

THE GIRLS ARRIVED home exhausted after taking Amy to get a new phone number and other essential items. Amy had met up with the domestic violence advocates Jade connected her to and received a brief explanation of the process ahead. She should be safe with the new phone under Jade's name, and the supplies were purchased with Jade's credit card. Unless Amy contacted her husband, he would not find her.

"I'm really glad we're helping her," Amber announced as they exited the car, thinking back to the dark energy Amy's husband exuded in the photo in Amy's office. "I really didn't like the look of that man."

Jade frowned and opened her mouth to say something but was interrupted by Al opening the door at the house, informing them that Kacey had not yet returned from her trip. Jade wandered across the first floor, seeming a little lost.

Amber recalled how Jade always got restless when exams and assignments were due, as if carrying an unspoken burden. Amber hesitantly asked again about her sleepless nights. As usual, Jade brushed it off as overexcited nerves, claiming that when life regained some semblance of balance, she'd finally have her restful nights back. She presumed her dreams about their parents had been prompted by her search into their past and the questions surrounding Syndicate.

Watching her sister drag her body up the stairs, Amber ached for her. It was unfair that Jade lived this way. Amber offered to bring a glass of warm milk to help calm Jade's nerves, which Jade graciously accepted.

Unbeknownst to her sister, Amber added an herbal sleeping aid. While they had playfully argued about whether taking medicine was a sign of weakness, now was not the time for a debate. Following through on her executive decision, Amber headed upstairs and handed her exhausted sister the warm drink, promising to lock up, and wished Jade a pleasant night.

Amber felt guilty but convinced herself that sometimes others could not see how much help they needed, and Jade simply would not ask for it.

Her mind wandered between Jade's restless nights and Kacey's disappearing without a word of comfort or confirmation after a mere hint of their suspicions. She held on to Penny the fluffy penguin, a gift Oscar had won for her as a teenager, and sighed, trying to still her worried mind.

With darkness surrounding her, she took rhythmic breaths. Her mind returned to Penny, and she grinned at the memory of the theme park. Coming now to thoughts of Daniel, she concluded that Jade had finally found her version of Oscar. Amber was determined to push aside her insecurities and focus on her relief that Jade had found a kindred spirit in a world filled with desperation and greed.

A crash jolted Amber awake. In the immediate aftermath, she heard only her fast breathing and hammering heart. She gulped and grabbed her phone, checking the home security system app. Nothing had been triggered.

Jumping out of bed, Amber tiptoed to Jade's room. After a few moments of listening and hearing nothing, she began to doubt whether anything had happened. Could a remnant of a dream have put her in such a state?

She quietly turned the knob to open Jade's door and whispered, "Jade? Did you hear that?"

Amber froze when she stepped into the room. The small ceramic lamp on Jade's desk had shattered across the surface and on the floor. On the opposite side of the room, Jade was sitting up on her bed, out of breath, sweat dripping down her temples in the dim blue light from her nightstand.

"Jade?" Amber called out when her sister didn't acknowledge her presence.

Jade stared off into the distance, breathing heavily.

"Are you okay?" Amber whispered, moving toward the bed and avoiding the shards. Jade's hands trembled, but Amber knew better than to touch her sister. "Jade!" she whispered more aggressively.

Jade finally turned her head. "It was a dream," she said weakly, shivering.

"A dream broke your lamp?" Amber asked.

Jade shook her head, still struggling for calm. Amber stayed silent and granted Jade time and space to recover.

"I had a dream," Jade eventually said, looking directly at her sister. "It was"—she cleared her dry throat—"it was like before, but I couldn't stop it."

"What dream? What do you mean stop it?"

"I wake up, and it stops," Jade snapped.

"Okay." Amber held up her hands, her self-reproach compounding at having given the sleeping aid to her sister. "What's this dream? You've had it before?"

Nodding, Jade said that she had been having two types of dreams in recent months.

"Some are about Mom and Dad, like trips we had as kids—fun-memory dreams." She paused, gathering her strength. "Then one about some . . . *thing* killing a girl."

"What!" Amber breathed in horror.

"It always starts the same way," Jade explained. "There are these two girls running around by this big outdoor garden behind a massive mansion." Her hands moved apart to indicate the size. "They were playing by this pond. They were so small, Amber. Like a preschooler and kindergartener."

"Was it a memory about you and me?" Amber asked.

Jade shook her head. "I don't think so. The older one had light-brown hair, almost blond. And like I said, she gets killed."

"What happened in the dream?" Amber calmly pressed.

"They're playing, running. The little one is chasing the older one. Then this, this thing shows up, scaring them." Jade's voice rose, her fear evident. "It was floating over them. The older one pushes the younger one towards the house, but the thing, it holds out its hand, and she falls!"

"What's this thing?"

"It kinda looks human, but I can't see anything. It's covered with this ugly black robe with a hood over its face. The older girl calls out for her mother, and it picks her up, throwing her in the water."

Jade's voice broke with terror.

"He drowns her," she confessed with a quiver. "Amber, her little legs try to kick him, but he is just so big." Tears fell down her cheek as she continued, "The little girl doesn't move, like she's frozen with fear, watching until the other girl's legs stop moving."

Jade reached for her blanket, clutching it to her chest, nearly overcome with emotion. "Then, it turns to the little girl, floating, aiming for her." She cleared her throat. "I force myself to wake up. I never let it get that far. It's horrible. It feels so real, like it's coming at me."

Comforting her sister and reaffirming that she was safe, Amber realized how wrong she had been to sneak the sleeping aid. Perhaps one day she'd confess, but not now, with her sister in such disarray. Amber glanced at the desk and realized Jade's phone had broken the lamp. She must have fallen asleep with it in her hand.

Slowly, Jade composed herself. She apologized for waking her sister, insisting Amber return to bed.

Knowing there was no point in trying to sleep this close to sunrise, Amber noted the time and suggested making breakfast and watching the sun grace the world with its golden warmth, together, talking about anything other than Syndicate or their mysterious past.

Accepting her sister's hand, Jade followed Amber down the hall and downstairs. After unarming the security system and making some delicious hot chocolate, the girls walked out onto the elevated back deck, mugs and blankets in hand.

Amber led the conversation but drew out Jade's opinions to keep her mind from returning to the dream. Leaning on how she valued her friendship with Oscar, Amber asked Jade to explain how she'd met Daniel, trying to make up for lost time.

Jade lit up as she described her early college years—ones filled with hope and innocence. Amber saw a real glimpse of joy. She was happy that her sister, who had never understood the premise of friendship, had found someone who connected to her, understood her, and accepted her.

Amber held on to the blissful moment, knowing it would pass far too soon.

Chapter Twenty

THE MORNING CONVERSATION eased Jade's nerves. She admitted to her sister that although removing all stress from her life would be impossible, she needed to work on balancing the effects with awareness and action.

Their phones chimed in unison. With the employees of Syndicate still on paid leave, Jade and Amber planned on searching for any other treasures hidden in plain view.

At the office, Jade announced that she'd set another meeting with Mr. Hough, this time regarding Amy and her husband, Nathan Carlisle. She promised to join Amber afterward. Jade felt it necessary to learn all she could about Amy's husband using Mr. Hough's patented street smarts.

The not-an-investigator waved warmly to Amber as he passed her office, commenting on how delighted he was to see the girls running the company.

Jade likewise received a heartening comment about Syndicate being back to its rightful owners. Mr. Hough accepted the coffee Jade offered but declined the treats; he had other engagements. On his list of tasks that morning was retrieving some personal items for Amy to embark on her departure from her marriage. He'd accepted Jade's request the previous night, waiving any fee.

"That there girl best leave while she can, Miss Jade," Mr. Hough declared. "After I seen her husband, I know she ain't safe till she leaves."

"Mr. Hough, did he confront you?"

"Oh, I'm fine," he assured her. "No, I watched him and them friends of his. All of 'em're the dangerous type, the kind that like to show off thur power."

Releasing her necklace when she realized she'd grabbed at it, she asked Mr. Hough to take a step back and walk her through Nathan Carlisle's background.

He passed her a folder he'd brought.

"On paper, he's a fine feller. Heck, he's a hero!" he huffed with annoyance.

"Is that sarcasm I detect?"

"If folks would just use thur noggins, they'd see right past this feller's mask."

"What mask does he have on?"

"The kind that don't leave no evi-dence behind," Mr. Hough proclaimed.

Intrigued, Jade leaned in.

"Nathan here"—he indicated the folder in Jade's hand—"he's a captain on 'count'a this big 'bust' he did. He followed this shifty-lookin' feller. Not my words." He held his left hand up. "His words. He followed 'im to a shifty part of town and busted a big drug deal."

"Impressive," Jade mocked.

"If yur not usin' ur noggin'," Mr. Hough reminded her. "Now, why would this here feller be called shifty? Ain't no one I asked could tell me why other than Captain Carlisle sayin' so."

"Interesting." Jade crossed her arms over her chest, raising her hand to her lips.

Mr. Hough pulled himself to the edge of his seat. "And why's it shifty for this feller ta be in a shifty part of town at three in tha mornin' but not our brave captain? Miss Jade, I ain't no detective, but I just don't know why one man in the dark is shifty but another ain't."

Jade whispered, "What do you suspect?"

"I think that Nathan here has his hand in tha cookie jar, and by cookie jar, I mean tha drug jar," Mr. Hough declared. "I think Carlisle was at this shifty place in that shifty time meetin' this feller, and when things don' go his way, he flips out his gun."

"How do you know he had his gun?"

"Cuz that's how he was found out!" Mr. Hough exclaimed. "Thur was a gunshot, and police was called, and he was thur with that so-called shifty fella."

"Did this shifty fella say anything after being arrested?"

"Nope."

"Why?" Jade asked.

"On 'count he lunged for our Captain Carlisle and got shot!"

"How convenient," Jade said darkly.

"I looked around, Miss Jade. That big drug bust got Nathan his big break and a promotion."

"Wait," Jade interrupted, "if Nathan is so hard on crime and drugs, why is there always news of overdoses and new synthetic materials that make a person more addicted?"

"Now yur usin' yur noggin'!" Mr. Hough proudly said. "If ya ask me, his promotion runs just abou' the same time as all'a these 'surges' the news keeps reportin' on."

Jade cleared her throat. "Let me get this straight. You think Mr. Carlisle got his promotion by staging a drug deal that went wrong, then somehow made this situation worse?"

"Yur momma and dad made this company with what, Miss Jade?"

She couldn't help but smile. "With a heart."

"E'r'body always says that companies like this stay in business by keepin' people sick."

Jade nodded as she played back her mother's and father's voices explaining why they had started their company.

"If people're always using drugs, thur's always people like Nathan lookin' like heroes."

"Mr. Hough," Jade said, regarding him intently, "I respect your opinions; they're always based on logical premises. How are you so convinced Nathan is a criminal?"

He beamed as though he expected her question.

"Becaws, Miss Jade," he whispered, leaning forward, "ain't no one found that big drug bust after it was taken to tha police station, and ain't no one officially asked."

Jade took in everything as she leaned back into the sofa. Mr. Nathan Carlisle was not to be taken lightly. The cunning and strategy needed to execute such malice required her full attention if she was to protect Amy against it.

Before departing, Mr. Hough briefed Jade about Nathan's background before joining the police force. He had been a decorated soldier who chose to become an officer after completing his assignment with the military. While the majority of his family remained on active duty, he publicly announced his motivation to bring the discipline he'd acquired to civilian life.

The gift of offering one's life for one's country was priceless, and Jade had always admired that sacrifice. She also knew that soldiers underwent extreme training to survive extreme situations, and the subsequent effects of violence on the human psyche went beyond her understanding. There was no surefire way to heal both mind and spirit from such experiences.

Despite all the questions surrounding her own past and family, Jade needed to focus on getting Amy away from this man. She asked Mr. Hough to avoid Nathan until this mess was behind them. Yet again, she resolved to put someone else's needs ahead of her own.

Chapter Twenty-One

"Jade!" Daniel called out, catching her in the hall just as Mr. Hough left.

She welcomed him happily. "What's the occasion?"

"I have a meeting nearby in an hour," Daniel replied, backing a few steps down the hall and giving Amber a wave through the window. "I figured I'd pop in and see if you wanted to grab a quick snack or coffee."

"She doesn't need more coffee!" Amber announced, joining the group with a chuckle to hide her concern.

"Maybe something else," Daniel said amiably. "Would you like to join us, Amber?"

"I can't come. I have something on my calendar," Amber sighed.

"Should I bring something up for you?" Jade asked. "I think we're just going to the café downstairs, right?"

Daniel nodded, and Amber accepted the offer, saying she trusted her sister's choice before turning to jog toward the conference rooms.

Jade asked if her sister needed help, and Amber turned back, shrugging playfully.

"If you don't get my scone, who will?"

$\wp \infty$

The conference room was as ready as it could be in so little time. Amber switched on the espresso machine and double-checked the dishes before adjusting the thermostat. The room had been locked for a few days. She kept the door open, then hurried over to her sister's office to find the air purifier she was certain Jade had.

Her phone rang. The hope of Kacey returning one of the dozens of unanswered calls vanished when she beheld a number she did not recognize. She ignored it.

Placing the air purifier in the middle of the table and tapping the turbo option, Amber hung around, exasperated. How could her assistants have scheduled a formal interview without giving her notice?

She thought of Oscar and gave him a quick call after checking how much time she had before this Mr. Miles Zimmerman was expected. Pacing back and forth in her office, she begged him to help her with some sort of formal spread for the interview as the café could not accommodate her request with so little notice and Al would take too long to get there with morning traffic.

"You're the best!" she exclaimed before humming in agreement. She glimpsed herself in the large mirror beside the windows overlooking the busy city of Solas. "Yikes, Amber. You did not dress to impress this morning."

In one of the cabinets under her desk, she found emergency makeup kits and hair accessories. She glided to the disguised closet behind her desk and picked out more professional attire, then skipped to the restroom and locked the door behind her.

Within fifteen short minutes, Amber had concealed the evidence of a relatively early start to the day. She twirled in the flowy black skirt, brushed the blue-and-white floral sleeves of the blouse, and admired the light-blue hues in her makeup. Then she pinned a stunning peacock clip over her left ear, pulling back strands of black hair from a loose bun and feeling much more confident.

She took in a breath as she patted her necklace, staring off into space as an ominous feeling settled over her. Shaking it off, she headed back to the conference room.

The smell of espresso filled the air as she removed the purifier. Oscar caught her leaving her sister's office, announcing his arrival with pastries he'd brought from a nearby bakery, along with extravagant plates and silverware from his restaurant.

"Oh, you're a lifesaver, Oscar!" Amber exclaimed as she hugged him and helped with the boxes.

"Not a problem," Oscar replied.

Leading the way, she explained that she had no idea an interview was set for that morning and had been scrambling to prepare.

"Why are you alone?" he asked, placing the serving plates on the side table with smaller dishes to hold the serving spoons. "Where's Jade?"

"She's with a friend downstairs," Amber replied. "I didn't tell her about this."

"Wait, Jade has friends now? Isn't she, like, 'I don't understand how or why people stay friends' and all that?" he teased.

"I guess she needed to find her people," Amber replied, placing the last of the pastries on display. "It was bound to happen."

"What's this interview about, anyway?"

"I don't know. The calendar note just said interview."

He glanced at his watch. "I gotta run. Let me know how this goes, okay?"

"Thank you so much, Oscar!"

The elevator chimed, and a well-dressed man in his midthirties stepped out, whistling. He stopped upon noticing Amber and winked.

"Good morning, miss. Miles Zimmerman here for Amber Parker."

Taken aback by his behavior, she cleared her throat.

"Hello, Mr. Zimmerman. I'm Amber Parker. You can follow me to the conference room."

Miles picked up his pace, entering the room at her side with the confidence of a victorious warrior. She observed his body language using the few psychology nuggets she'd gleaned from Jade. He seemed self-assured as he inquired about the quiet and lack of personnel.

Chuckling, Amber said, "We gave our employees the week off as a celebration for Syndicate's new leadership."

"Oh, so that's how things are done with two women running the show."

"Excuse me?" Amber paused before offering him a drink.

"Is that really how you want to showcase female leadership, especially in today's modern times?"

She lowered her hand slowly, turning off the coffee machine.

"My apologies, Mr. Zimmerman." She plastered a forced smile. "The next time the women of this company decide to do anything pertaining to this company, I'll be sure to run over and get your seal of approval."

"Wow," Miles exclaimed with a laugh, "you're a cheeky one."

"That I am," she said, already annoyed with him in the short time that had passed as he completely ignored her effort to provide a delicious morning.

He smirked, watching her walk to her seat. "You're not at all like your sister."

Amber sneered at him, pulling her phone out.

"My goodness you're an observant man, Mr. Zimmerman. Where's your crew?"

"What?"

"Your camera and sound crew."

"I work alone, Ms. Parker."

"After meeting you, Mr. Zimmerman," Amber said, irked by his manner, "I can see why that would be the case."

Reaching to grab the nearest pastry and landing on a raspberry danish, he said, "So, are we gonna interview or what?"

Amber placed her phone on the table to record.

"You're the reporter—unless you'd like me to do both of our jobs."

With a deeper tone, he began, "I'd like to begin by congratulating you, Ms. Parker, on your new appointment. Your parents started this company, correct?"

"That is indeed correct," Amber said. Her short answer seemed to upset Miles.

"There isn't really much out there about your parents. Why is that?"

"I surely can't offer a comment on information that eludes you. Perhaps you haven't looked hard enough."

His nostrils flared, and he pressed his lips together.

"I've been looking into your family lately."

"What an honor, to be taking up so much of your time," Amber said, trying to hide her anxiety.

"Yeah, a lot of time, and not much to work with," he said with a venomous glare.

"For a seasoned reporter, Mr. Zimmerman, you aren't asking many questions."

"Here's a question for you, Amber." He leaned forward. "Why are your family's records sealed with a court order?"

"It's Miss Parker," Amber corrected. "And I can only assume that if you were privy to such information, you'd already have access."

"Amusing," he declared. "So, that's your answer to such common documents being hidden away under lock and key."

"It seems to me you're only upset because *you* aren't allowed to unlock it," Amber said matter-of-factly. "I will not be offering a comment on confidential documents."

He squinted at her, then tilted his head to the side.

"Your responses amuse me"—he paused—"Ms. Parker."

"I'm an amusing person, for a woman."

"Can you tell me why I cannot trace your family's ancestry?"

"It feels redundant at this point, but your inability to do something is not something I have an answer for."

"You and your sister are two of the wealthiest women in this country." Miles glared at her. "Yet no one truly knows where this wealth came from or how it started other than this company. Syndicate, the company with a giving heart that continues to grow and grow. But grow from what, no one knows; given to whom, other than you, no one knows." He settled back in his chair. "Tell me, Ms. Parker, why won't you disclose how you became so rich?"

Maintaining her composure, Amber calmly replied, "And what would that information do for you, Mr. Zimmerman? Why are you so desperately searching for the reason my family became rich?"

"I'm a reporter. I seek the truth. If you have nothing to hide, then you hide nothing, but everything about your family is hidden." Miles shifted in his seat, rising slightly. "What corruption are you trying to cover up? Why all the secrecy? What did your parents do that was so controversial that the highest level of political clearance has covered it up?"

Amber went from annoyed to enraged in an instant. This sneaky creature dared to tarnish her parents' reputation. With the microphone recording, Amber's emotions ran wild.

"If I were to tell you, right now, where the Parker fortune came from, would that satisfy you, Miles?" she said in a low voice riddled with anger.

The witty reporter simply leaned back in his chair again.

"So, this is the secret. I only discovered this a few days ago, and so I'm still recovering from the shock myself; but the truth must be told."

After a short and shallow breath, she continued, "Many years ago, when I was a mere infant, my parents came across the source of their ever-growing wealth. You see, Mr. Zimmerman, one day, as they were walking, they spotted a rainbow. Not just any rainbow—a *double* rainbow! They knew what they had to do, so they ran and ran until they found the end of it!"

Amber clapped her hands childishly. "They found the end of that rainbow curving into an elusive pot of gold! Oh, but it doesn't end there. Because it was a double rainbow, they were rewarded with a never-ending supply of money."

She was gratified to see him seething.

"Ms. Parker, while it's entertaining that you can be humorous at this time, the implications of these questions are far from funny."

Amber sent him a stony look. "While I can accommodate your rude comments, I will not be threatened."

"The secrets surrounding your family bear questions that no amount of evasion will remove. This isn't a fantasy; this is real. And I am only one of the many people who have asked these questions."

"With all due respect, Mr. Zimmerman, that is a ridiculous remark. My family has not hidden that we're wealthy. We contribute to copious charities and benefits, helping countless—"

"Your fake modesty doesn't work with me, Ms. Parker. Let's be real. You're a billionaire!"

"So?"

"So!" he scoffed.

"Yes, that's right: so? Did I rob a bank? No. Did I take *your* money. No! Did I commit a crime? Again, no. So why is my wealth of any concern to you?"

"I couldn't find any proof that you committed a crime, but the question is, did your parents?"

"Excuse me?"

"Ms. Parker, these hard questions must be asked, since you refuse to disclose the information."

"I don't owe you a thing. And how dare you insinuate that my parents were corrupt!"

"There are no records available to the public about James and Annalise Parker. Even the report about the fire that killed them is incomplete."

"My family records are none of your business. Having a private life doesn't mean—"

"Privacy isn't classified reports and records, Ms. Parker. There is something dubious going on here. How will anyone believe anything you say if there's no access to the proof?" He regarded her slyly with a twisted smile. "Did your parents even die in the fire, or is this a pathetic attempt to cover up proof that they faked their deaths and are quietly living off the wealth they left you?"

"You—"

"Put yourself in my place. What would you think?"

Amber slammed her hand on the table. "I think you can take your leave, Mr. Zimmerman."

With a smirk, Miles stood slowly and meandered toward the door.

"A pleasure, Amber," he said as he left, passing Oscar, who had witnessed the tail end of the interview.

She threw herself back in the chair, realizing her colossal mistake. Oscar came in with a chocolate croissant and a sheepish expression.

"I'm so sorry it took me so long to remember. I was so focused on everything I had to get done that I didn't realize why I recognized the name until after I left."

Amber thanked him for his help and his kind effort to protect her. She needed to warn her sister about the interview before Jade found out from other sources, and that talk would likely be a long and bumpy one.

Chapter Twenty-Two

THE BOARD MEMBERS' offices yielded no answers, the day ending in immense frustration.

"I don't think those documents were really hidden," Jade announced as the pair walked to the car.

"What makes you think that?"

"Well, I've worked with those men," she said, rolling her eyes at the thought of the power struggles she'd witnessed. "I don't think that's how they would have hidden something important. I think they were left there to be picked up without drawing attention."

"Jade, it still makes no sense." Amber lifted a hand in greeting as Al approached them. "Why were they all fine with making a marginal profit from Syndicate when they signed the agreement?" She grunted, shaking her head. "Never mind. The whole agreement isn't— That's not how people pass on companies or any financial entity."

On the drive home, Amber decided it was time to tell Jade about Zimmerman.

"Miles Zimmerman was in Syndicate?" Jade shouted. "How on earth did he pass security?"

After taking a breath, she waved away Amber's profuse apologies and explained how he had interviewed her when she accepted her nonexecutive position at Syndicate. Baiting and degrading her, he goaded her until she lashed out at him, causing a ripple of articles and harassment for follow-up interviews. "His articles were pure garbage—things we didn't even discuss in the interview, but he got a reaction out of me, and that's all he needed."

"You're not mad at me?" Amber asked softly.

"Why would I be mad at you?" Jade chuckled. "It's him we need to handle."

"He was just so rude, from the second he walked out of the elevator."

"That's what he does, Amber." Jade stared out the window with her hand cupped over her necklace. "Let me guess: he pretended he didn't know who you were?"

Amber nodded.

"Ugh, some things never change, but that's a good thing," Jade said with a glimmer of delight, raising her eyebrow mischievously. "It means we can use his behavior against him."

Amber's phone buzzed, and she gasped with relief when she checked the message.

"Aunt Kacey is home!" she cheered. "Oh, she made muffins. Chocolate muffins!"

At home, Jade and Amber briskly walked to the house, almost running, anxious to talk to their housekeeper. They tossed their shoes aside in the mudroom and rushed into the kitchen, where Kacey awaited with a tray of muffins. Her tea sat steeping in a mug before her as she turned a page in a book. They paused in the door like children awaiting permission.

"Hello, Jade, Amber," Kacey said with a warm smile, placing her book down. "How was your day at work?"

Jade finally stepped forward, answering, "It was nice, given Miles Zimmerman paid Amber a visit."

"Oh, that horrible man."

Amber followed her sister to the kitchen island, hoping Jade would be the one to confront Kacey.

"Aunt Kacey," Jade said hesitantly, "can we talk?"

"I would love to talk. Please join me. I made coffee."

"Decaf!" Amber told Jade sternly.

The sisters hopped onto the bar stools and leaned over the marbled countertop. Amber immediately snatched a muffin, always clear in her priorities.

There was something odd about Kacey—the way she looked, the way she sat sipping tea. It was as though a new persona had taken over. She appeared as calm as a spider in its web. Her light-brown hair was twisted in a loose braid that showed its true length. As usual, she was not wearing makeup, but Jade saw the glistening effect of her nighttime skincare routine. Her bright-green eyes twinkled as she sipped her tea.

"Aunt Kacey—"

"I'd like to start there, Jade," Kacey said, lowering her mug. "My name is not Kacey; it's Katherine."

Dumbfounded, the girls stared at her with mouths ajar.

"Kacey is what you were taught to call me, but that's not my name."

Jade and Amber shifted their eyes to one another, unsure of the implications.

"Perhaps this can help explain matters." Katherine pulled a jewelry case from her pocket, opening it to reveal a stunning diamond necklace. She placed the necklace around her neck while Jade and Amber eyed her in astonishment.

The necklace was identical to the one their mother had: a clear round diamond on a platinum pendant. Moving the stone to display the back panel, where they expected their mother's initials, they observed the letters K. E., along with Annalise's birthdate—one year off.

"Aunt Kacey, what is going on?" Jade demanded, reaching up to hold her own necklace. "Those necklaces are a family tradition."

Katherine smiled beatifically. "Precisely."

"Are you . . . our mother?" Amber asked, so thrown off her game that she could only embrace the absurdity.

"Good heavens no!" A laugh burst out. "I'm your mother's sister. I was born exactly one year after her."

"Mom and Dad were only children," Amber murmured in a daze, glancing at Jade for reassurance.

"They never actually said those words, did they, Amber?" Katherine said in a maternal tone they'd never heard from her. "I know it's hard to take in, but I *am* your aunt, your mother's sister."

Katherine gazed at the young ladies she'd cared for all these years, her nieces. Smiling genuinely, she patted her necklace the same way they often patted their own. "We are true family."

Chapter Twenty-Three

"WE NEED MORE details . . . Aunt Katherine," Jade hesitantly added.

"I'm here to answer all of your questions," Katherine said after another sip of tea, "even the ones about Syndicate and the will." She cleared her throat. "I'll even tell you about the board members."

Jade and Amber's eyes widened. Who they had thought was a kindhearted staff member who had taken pity on them, raising them after their parents had died, was now the key to everything.

"Why didn't you tell us?" Amber asked.

Katherine didn't need to ask what she meant. "Well, because your mother, father, and myself were new to this land and wanted to remain inconspicuous."

"New to this land? What does that mean?" Amber asked as Jade stared at Katherine with wide, fixed eyes.

"The place you were born is not a place one can easily visit. We came here to save you two from certain death. Our family had been targeted by someone who would kill anyone who got in the way."

Disbelief radiated from the sisters, and before she lost them to skepticism, Katherine offered the final piece she'd waited twelve years to divulge.

"My dears, you are witches born into a family of powerful witches—with a wizard for a father."

Silence fell.

Before she knew what she was doing, Amber had lurched to her feet, shoving the stool back. She wanted to be angry, wanted to rail at Katherine for making fun of them, but she was just utterly bewildered.

Then she noticed her sister sitting still and eerily calm.

"Jade, do you believe this?"

"Jade has always been able to tell if someone is lying, hasn't she?" Katherine said. "Tell me, Jade, what do you think?"

Meeting her sister's eyes, Jade whispered, "I don't think she's lying."

"Now, Syndicate," Katherine hummed, picking up her mug, "your parents' company—"

"Oh no," Amber sighed, returning to her seat. "It's bad, Jade. I knew it; it's bad."

"What's bad?" Katherine asked. It was her turn to look confused.

Jade stuttered, "Um, we found a few . . . irregularities at Syndicate this week."

"Do any of these irregularities happen to be connected to how Syndicate had a clear and traceable business line when your parents ran it but hasn't since?"

Amber nodded while Jade kept her intense gaze on their aunt.

"Do these irregularities involve your parents' will?" Katherine continued.

Jade huffed with frustration. "Aunt Katherine, tell us what is going on with Syndicate."

Acquiescing, Katherine began by explaining why their parents decided to start a pharmaceutical company.

Upon arriving with a curious toddler and a newborn Amber, James, Annalise, and Katherine needed shelter in a land that operated very differently than their own.

Mr. Porter was the first person they met, and he was instantly drawn to them and their little girls.

"I'll leave that for Mr. Porter to tell you," Katherine said.

"Mr. Porter knows about the witches and wizards thing?" Amber demanded.

"Not at first. Trust needed to be built, but yes, he knows who your parents were and who you are."

"Why wasn't the will contested?" Jade asked.

Katherine returned to her point. "Because through Syndicate, they built another form of power here. Coupled with their magic, they planned a will that was ludicrous yet unbreakable."

Jade and Amber knew the weight of money and position. They'd lived that lesson many times, and although she'd never verbally admitted it, Amber was grateful—and suspected Jade was as well—to have a name that spoke on their behalf.

Katherine went on to explain that Annalise had found it unjust that so many people suffered when there were more than enough healers with more than enough ways to treat them. In a world run by greed, so many willingly watched others suffer for profit.

Jade remembered accompanying her parents to benefits and seeing them glammed up while always reminding themselves why they did what they did. They would talk about not caring if it was a losing battle, instead focusing on fighting the good fight and doing so with honor against the companies that worked to stop them.

"A pharmaceutical company with a heart"—the phrase was in fact a secondary goal for her parents. They'd built Syndicate to provide a safe and reliable home for Jade and Amber; Amber was in awe at the good they did almost as a side effect.

"Your parents learned of a threat," Katherine said, her expression now grave. "They made a plan to confront this threat before it came after you, but before that, they changed their will in case something happened to them."

Looking down in a show of the grief still living within her soul, Katherine said, "The will was designed to steer you to Syndicate after you completed your college studies, hoping you would choose the safety net they built, but . . ." She paused to think. "But not in a direct way. They still wanted you to have a choice."

As Katherine continued, more became apparent. James and Annalise had employed Mr. Hough to find the greediest and most morally compromised men he knew—men who would agree to anything if money were guaranteed. Mr. Porter wrote contracts to please those ravenous men, making them instant millionaires and compounding their profit should they run Syndicate until the Parker sisters took it back.

"It didn't matter what the will dictated or what the business agreements between them and the board members stated," Katherine explained. "All that mattered was that they agreed. Annalise and James performed a spell that took considerable force, but it protects Syndicate from harm. *Any* harm. This is why Mr. Zimmerman's actions don't bother me. Because he can never actually do anything," she emphasized, raising her brows.

"Why?" Amber demanded.

"The spell works by persuasion. I wasn't there when they did it, but your mother told me that while some may be able to challenge it, the spell is strong enough to eventually push them away. With Zimmerman, something always distracted him, and he would simply stop."

"Until today," Jade remarked.

"I wouldn't worry too much about him. I have seen the spell deter many a Zimmerman."

"What about our birth certificates?" Jade asked. "Why are they sealed?"

"Oh, that too is the spell, dear," Katherine cheerfully replied. "'Sealed by court order' is a response that satisfies almost everyone."

"Not Zimmerman," Amber said darkly.

"Especially Zimmerman," Katherine corrected. "Mark my words, he'll find another stick to chase. I said 'almost' because it did not work on you, which to me indicated that you were ready to know who you are."

Glancing to her sister to confirm they had not gone insane, Amber asked, "Mom and Dad made a will to guide us to take over the source of power they initiated when they came here from—wait, from where?" Amber asked.

"Uporia," Katherine responded proudly. "We are from Uporia. Your parents used a great deal of magic to open a portal between the two worlds as a last resort to save you from Goliath."

Chapter Twenty-Four

"While many beings targeted our family for the power we possessed," Katherine said, "Goliath is a particularly brutal force. Your mother was the sixth daughter of the Elliot witch family and the Keeper of our family's book and power. When she married a wizard, Goliath announced that their union was an abomination and condemned them to death, along with any children they had."

"And when this guy came after us, our parents came here?" Jade asked.

"Your parents made the desperate move to a world beyond his reach, but only after he murdered your four older sisters."

"What!" Amber gasped.

Katherine paused as if to offer a silent moment in memory of those lost. When she continued, her voice was quiet, devastation creeping in.

"Goliath killed so many witches from our family, trying to get to Annalise and her girls. The whole family became a target, and losing those four previous girls showed us that we needed a new plan."

"Who are these older sisters?" Jade whispered, sick at the thought.

A fond smile crossed Katherine's face. "Oh, my little feisty Jade."

Puzzled by this motherliness, Jade also did not fight it. It was a welcome comfort.

"Are you testing me?" Katherine sounded oddly chipper now. Perhaps the happy memories outweighed the bad ones. "Maddie was the eldest; after her was Katie—yes, my namesake; then Grace; and the fourth daughter was Amelia." Her eyes gained intensity as she looked at Amber. "You're the sixth daughter, dear, and the next Keeper of the book."

"What book?" Amber immediately asked.

"The book is the Elliot family's source of power. Without it, the family's power dies. Only the sixth daughter—you, Amber—can use the book."

She smiled again at her bewildered niece.

Leaning toward her sister, Amber protested, "I don't have any book or power. I, I—"

"My dears, both of you were born with powers. You're witches!" Katherine said, spreading her arms cheerfully.

"Witches are at best folklore with some historical relevance," Jade stammered, her knee-jerk reaction being to retreat into logic.

"In this magicless world, yes. But in Uporia, witches have powers—different powers, depending on the type of witch they are. And Elliot witches are different. We have power beyond reason, but we are cursed."

"Cursed how?" Amber asked.

"The story I was told described the very first Elliot witch," Katherine said, seemingly eager to spill family secrets now. "She was banned from her coven as a child for not respecting their laws. I never knew what laws she broke; all that mattered was that she was alone for most of her life, looking and yearning for a family."

Here Katherine regarded her nieces with a loving smile.

"She built a good life for herself in a small town, keeping her power hidden. A witch without a coven or family was weakened to enemies. After welcoming her daughter, she came face-to-face with someone who wanted to take her power. It's said that her closest friend betrayed her and tried to use a spell to strip her magic, but I assume this friend did not know how to properly do it, because Elanor Elliot stopped them," Katherine declared.

"The friend then pulled out a, uh, a backup plan. A curse. He cursed Elanor, trapping her power in a scroll she carried. Upon the destruction of that scroll, her power would disappear. She was further cursed so that only the sixth daughter of her bloodline can control the family's source of power. Should the Keeper die before her sixth daughter is born, the powerful bloodline ends."

"So, Mom was the sixth daughter of a sixth daughter," Jade reasoned.

"Yes," Katherine said. "Amber is the only person who can connect to the book that holds the power of our family. If the book is destroyed, all Elliot witches would lose their power. If Amber dies before the next generation can carry the power, existing witches can still use their power, but it ends with that generation, unable to grow."

Pride filled Katherine's voice as she continued.

"We grew in strength as a family by adding to each generation. The hallmark of an Elliot witch is to grow and become stronger in the face of adversity, similar to how Elanor did."

"What do you mean?" Jade asked, sensing something beneath the surface.

"I mean after Elanor realized there was no known power great enough to break the curse, she cursed her entire bloodline to bear only daughters."

"What?" Amber squeaked. "What good did that do?"

"Well, Elanor lived a great many years ago, and child-rearing, no matter how simple it may seem to you now, is never an easy task. Much like any world, Uporia has its power struggles, and Elanor's life depended on having *her* power. She could not risk losing it if a boy were born. Having six children is already quite a difficult goal."

"That's pretty messed up, Aunt Katherine!" Amber protested. "How could anyone think that's okay?"

"I can see why this would not make sense to a young girl who has lived a considerably sheltered life, unaware of the dangers around her and with enough power in one way or another to never truly feel powerless," Katherine chastised her niece. Amber lowered her gaze.

"You mean Syndicate?" Jade interjected, slightly agreeing with Katherine's point on how protected they'd been. They had suffered, but they had never struggled to survive.

"Yes," Katherine said, taking another sip of her tea. "I can see why you disagree with the decisions of the past, Amber, but try to remember that no one ever makes an extreme decision, like traveling to another world, without an extreme need."

"I can respect that," Amber said. "But cursing her own kids still seems excessive."

"The second curse wasn't meant to remove hardship, only to lessen it. That's what Elliot witches do. We find strength in the pain. But I will admit that life itself is pretty messed up," Katherine said, nodding at Amber.

Chapter Twenty-Five

"Power?" Amber finally said after a long, thoughtful silence, shaking her head at the woman she'd realized was her aunt less than thirty minutes prior. "Witches and wizards? This, this isn't real."

"If we are these oh-so-great-and-powerful witches, where's the power?" Jade challenged, partially agreeing with her sister. She sensed Katherine believed what she was saying, but that didn't mean their alleged aunt was right.

"Oh, that will require some explanation," Katherine sighed. "But I must say I don't care for the mockery in your tone, Jade. It's quite hurtful."

"I apologize, Aunt Katherine," Jade conceded. "You need to see it from our perspective, though. Everything you've shared is the most bizarre possible answer to our questions."

"I understand how this will take some adjustment—"

"Wait," Jade interrupted as something occurred to her. "You said you're one year younger than Mom."

Katherine waited with a knowing expression for her to continue.

"If Mom was the sixth daughter, like Amber, why was there a seventh?"

"I am an anomaly," Katherine calmly professed, stacking her hands beside the now empty mug. "The rare seventh daughter born to the powerful sixth-daughter clan—a witch who is powerless."

She shifted her eyes to the mug, revealing a pain too deep to share.

"So, what are these powers, and why don't we have them?" Jade inquired to change the subject.

"Oh, do we need a wand or something?"

"Heavens no!" Katherine chuckled. "I will try my best to explain the ways of our world, but you must push aside this world's maddening view of witches or any other magical creature."

"So wands aren't real?" Amber queried.

"Well, the term is used, but it is *not* some pretty stick used to make things float," Katherine asserted. "And it is only used by wizards, full-blooded wizards. They use various inanimate objects as conduits to focus their magic for heavier tasks or powerful spells."

"And Amber and I can't do that because we're witches and only half wizards?"

"Yes, a wizard is born from two wizards or two half wizards. Your father being a wizard *added* to your powers, but you can't use his kind of power," Katherine explained. "Your father said that it was like milk and oil."

"Aunt Katherine, what is this power you keep saying we have?" Amber pushed.

Katherine sighed, passing her hand over hair streaked with gray.

"Your parents concealed them. They were gaining too much attention here."

Katherine told her nieces how their powers had unwittingly created hostility between Jade and the other children at school, and how Amber was prone to being bullied, which prompted Jade to instigate more fights.

"Your parents decided to, uh, for lack of a better phrase, put them away until you were old enough to manage them discreetly."

Narrowing her eyes, Jade studied Katherine with the undeniable sense that their aunt was still hiding something—compounded by her continued dodging of the question at hand.

"What are these powers that we were born with but don't use?" Jade enunciated slowly.

Lifting her head like a confident peacock, Katherine declared, "Your power was to know others' thoughts. You knew what a person was thinking and developed the ability to read past thoughts as well. This was the first time an Elliot witch had been born with this power."

Katherine turned her attention to Amber. "Amber, you can see events throughout time, past, present, or future. This is a power most Keepers have."

Amber reached for her necklace, then glanced over at Jade, who had been holding her stone with her arms crossed.

"Your parents restricted your powers to your necklaces," Katherine explained. "They couldn't silence them completely. After all, you were born with them. They are as much a part of you as any limb or organ, but for your own benefit, they prevented them from being, well, let's say active."

Katherine's description of their powers explained so much that Jade now believed her without hesitation. While Jade had long thought her ability to read people's behavior was one she picked up from her studies, she realized she'd carried this quality since her youth. She pondered Amber's strange knack for knowing things without witnessing them and thought back to an innocuous comment her younger sister had made the evening before.

"Amber?" Jade asked. "When we took Amy to get a new phone, you said you didn't like the look of her husband. How did you see him?"

"Well, I didn't see him like meet him," Amber laughed. "When I, uh, searched through Mr. Reynolds's stuff, I saw a picture of them in her office. A wedding photo, if I had to guess."

Jade gawked at her sister. Katherine must be right. Their innate powers had entangled with their personalities, silently guiding them.

"Amber, she doesn't have pictures in her office."

Amber denied this, stating she saw it clearly.

"I'm sure of it," Jade insisted. "The fact that nothing personal in her office showed that she's married was what made me suspect she was unhappy to begin with."

Chapter Twenty-Six

KATHERINE SIGHED with relief. "I can't tell you how long I've waited to finally share all of this with you!"

As the girls rose from the bar stools, Jade wondered how they could return to their lives after this grand reveal. While they had the comfort of knowing their company was safe, they still had an obligation to run Syndicate with integrity, and there were many obstacles.

After locking the back door and switching off the kitchen lights, Jade joined her aunt and Amber in the sunroom. She felt strangely at peace, accepting all she had learned despite having no proof. But part of her maintained a slight suspicion, if only to be prepared for any eventuality. Perhaps Katherine was telling the truth, but she'd certainly learned how to conceal it from the girls over the years. This could be another deception.

Standing in the arched doorway, she watched Amber and Katherine chatting on the couch, quietly observing the woman who had raised them. It was true that Katherine knew the girls well enough to hide certain things, but that familiarity went both ways. Jade had lived almost every day with Katherine, learning her traits and cues.

She knew that Katherine adored drinking tea and had a special section in the kitchen devoted to her blends and concoctions. She preferred loose tea leaves, tolerating the bags when necessary, with white tea being her most beloved scent. Her favorite color was violet—not pale but also not too bold. She would never describe herself as having a sweet tooth but always devoured the red velvet cupcakes Jade made using her late mother's recipe.

Trusting the instinct that had never led her astray, Jade leaned into acceptance. She might have trouble trusting others, but she trusted herself.

However, she still sensed Katherine holding something back.

"There is one more thing I must tell you before we go to bed," Katherine said, patting the chair beside the couch. "Well, two things, and the first is the reason your parents embedded control of your powers into your necklaces."

"You said they were too much for us to handle," Amber replied.

"It's twofold"—a phrase Katherine often used to describe the complexity of life. "But there was a more pressing matter that served as a greater motivator."

Katherine talked about how their powers had grown just as their older sisters' had before them. But a traumatic event gave Jade hellacious panic attacks and night terrors. The trauma she endured in their home world followed her, and nothing could alleviate the stress.

"We took you to many therapists, and none could help," Katherine said. "Annalise tried everything, but once the memory of what happened struck, all we could do was support you and hope it would pass."

The severe reaction to the memory caused Jade to scream if touched or comforted.

"It lasted for hours at a time. You would be in this fear-induced trance," Katherine told Jade. "We discovered the hold this fear had on you became stronger the more advanced your powers became, and so your parents thought it best to restrict your power."

"If Jade's power isn't gone, just, uh, muted," Amber quietly said, "how come this fear is gone? I don't think I've ever seen Jade having a panic attack."

Silent, unraveling, Jade waited for their aunt to speak.

"The trauma derived from a memory of your older sister Amelia being murdered," Katherine disclosed with a heavy sigh. "You were attacked a short time before we came here. Amelia was drowned by a horrible beast sent by Goliath."

Pure terror prickled across Jade's body as she sat motionless on the chair, staring at her aunt.

"You were so young. We never understood why that memory was so strong or how you never forgot it. Jade?" Katherine paused as the shock in Jade's face shifted and tears filled her eyes.

Whispering, trying to keep her voice from breaking, Jade said, "There's this dream; it recently became a problem. It's about two little girls playing by a pond, and they get attacked." Her lips quivered as she continued, "The older girl was drowned by this floating, black, hooded thing. That was me? I was the younger girl?"

"Jade, I'm so sorry." Katherine reached out, grasping her hand. "Based on what you said as a little girl, yes, that's the memory. I think your powers"—she turned to Amber—"both of your powers, although concealed, are growing, straining for release."

Jade was grateful when Amber changed the topic. "What about the other thing you needed to tell us before bed?"

"Oh, yes," Katherine said, returning to her usual matter-of-fact disposition. "Your powers, they can be released."

Amber's head jerked back, and Jade shook her head in astonishment.

"I'll tell you now, I don't know how," Katherine said, holding her hands up. "Your mother made it clear that the only way to release them would be of your own volition and, more importantly, desire." She dropped her hands. "They simply won't be released without that."

They sat in silence, contemplating what that meant for a few minutes. But the heavy weight of the day was catching up with all of them. Sleep beckoned, and everyone agreed that rest was desperately needed.

Politely declining Amber's company after the eventful evening, Jade declared she simply wanted to sleep and provide her mind the time and rest it needed to recover.

Soon, lying under the warm, soft covers, she rubbed her necklace, unsure of what to think. She found herself deeply pleased about her power to know people's thoughts. That the power had been seeping out into this world explained so much. But her mind couldn't help drifting to the reason for their restricted powers.

The dream that threw her into such a frozen and meek state offered a fraction of the actual memory, Jade postulated. If her power was, as Amber described, muted, then this fear, this memory, was surely much more intense than what she'd recently experienced. *Do I want this memory to be released? Or do I want it to stay repressed, and with it my powers?*

Her mother must have given her the choice for a reason.

Pushing her head back into the plush pillow, Jade pondered what it might be like to know what everyone thought. Her lips curved when she imagined the possibilities. The confidence she had when confronting Amy might have been multiplied if instead of reading expressions and body language, she knew what the woman was thinking.

In that moment, Jade realized she wanted her power. She had been born with it. It was part of her.

Everything has reason, she told herself.

But as desirable as her power was, was it worth the trouble?

She had long believed that to accept one thing meant declining another. But in this case, one could not accept power without accepting the consequences.

Jade darted out of bed. Feeling called, she drifted to the dresser, removing a small, handmade wooden box from the top drawer. Annalise had made one for both sisters, but neither had been able to open theirs. Her mother once spoke about not having the key, which seemed odd, but she'd claimed Jade would find it one day.

While the box was more a gesture of love than a demonstration of woodworking skills, Jade treasured it. She did not know why she wanted to hold this box on this particular night, but it nonetheless filled her with contentment.

Jade moved her fingers over the box's lid and the groove there—which was heart shaped. Her fingers stilled, and her heart raced at the coincidence she had somehow never noticed. Suddenly excited, Jade removed her necklace and placed the gem on the box, nestling it into the indentation. A perfect fit.

Without warning, the stone locked into place, the chain whipping out of her hand. Streaks of light shot from under the lid. Jade's jaw dropped when the box flew open.

The interior was lined with light-pink satin material cradling a single item: an envelope addressed to Jade, in Annalise's handwriting. She picked up the letter, incredulous.

Then she placed the letter back into the box, unread. Closing it, she removed her necklace from the groove, and the same light blinded her as it resealed.

She returned the box to the dresser.

While she wanted to rip the envelope open to see what other pieces of her life awaited, she knew this knowledge could not returned. She decided to be wise and wait, hoping to soon be better prepared for her mother's posthumous words.

Chapter Twenty-Seven

THE NEXT DAY came more quickly than Jade would have liked after her long struggle to fall asleep, fearing the dream would return. As she washed her face, her mind was in disarray.

In the course of one evening, she'd learned she was a telepathic witch from a different world. Her sister could peer through time and space to see events far beyond her physical scope. Amber was also the Keeper of the family's power, which manifested through a book.

Adding to this, they had four older sisters who had been ruthlessly murdered. Their parents escaped to a world she'd thought was the only world, then tied her and Amber's powers to their necklaces when Jade's trauma grew too difficult to manage.

Despite the insanity of all that, what Jade still found most unfathomable was their parents' decisions regarding the company. Having worked for two years under the corrupt men James and Annalise had purposely sought out, Jade saw firsthand how the board members, led by the despicable Mr. Reynolds, cared only about their profit. They fit into her parents' plan perfectly, it would seem, but the plan didn't make sense to her. The company with a heart had been helping no one for years.

Descending the stairs to enjoy breakfast as a family with Mr. Porter, Jade thought about how she had been drawn to the box last night. It felt as though her mind knew precisely what needed to be done, with her following its lead. She wondered if that feeling would be present in other aspects of her life now that she recognized her ability to decipher people's behavior as her witchly power reaching out.

She nearly bumped into Amber at the bottom of the staircase. Acting on instinct, she pulled her sister into the sunroom by the arm, whispering, "Quick, before Aunt Katherine knows I'm up and wants to talk."

Jade quickly asked how Amber felt about the entire revelation, in particular asking her position regarding their powers.

"Like, what do you think about you being able to see things from any given point in time? Does that sound like, uh—"

Amber hopped excitedly. "The coolest thing ever!"

"You aren't freaking out about it?"

"Not at all," Amber admitted. "Well, I'll be honest. At first, yeah, it sounded so crazy and almost like Aunt Kace—I mean, Aunt Katherine—needs help. But after sleeping on it . . ." She shrugged. "It adds up in a way that doesn't feel wrong. Wouldn't being able to see my exams before taking them have been a fun little trick to have?" She smiled ruefully.

Chuckling, Jade shared her own excitement at the notion that her instincts were so much more than that. Before she could mention the letter, Katherine called them through the house intercom, announcing Mr. Porter's impending arrival.

Holding her sister's hand after they locked arms, Jade led the way to the kitchen to bid their aunt good morning.

"Oh, Jade, I'm glad you're up," Katherine said. "I didn't call the bedrooms, thinking you might still be asleep."

"You have something you want to tell us?" Jade asked, reading her aunt's behavior—or perhaps her thoughts.

"Yes," Katherine confirmed. "It isn't a big deal, but I have the feeling it'll be hard to discuss while we're cooking."

Shooting Amber a glance, Jade noted that Katherine had prepared tea. The loose leaves had been brewing in a pot, and she seemed to have had several servings, using a special tea set decorated with tiny violet blossoms.

"I'd like to talk to you about your sisters' powers and, well, using your own, if you ever decide to release them."

Amber led the way around the table and sat, eagerly waiting for Katherine to proceed.

"First of all, I'd like to ask you, do you want to learn about your sisters?"

Jade hesitated, then glanced at Amber, who seemed equally bewildered by the question.

"I don't think it would hurt," Amber said. Jade simply nodded, though she wasn't sure she agreed.

"I told you their names were Maddie, Katie, Grace, and Amelia," Katherine began with a sorrowful sigh. "Maddie was born with the power to control fire, but it took about seven years for us to know she even had one. I think some family members took her late blooming as a sign that your parents' marriage was cursed, but eventually, Maddie's flames were the pride of the entire household. She was the first Elliot witch to manipulate fire."

After a sip of tea, Katherine continued, "Katie's power is one you're probably familiar with. It had appeared in the family before, but her control of it at such a young age was quite impressive. She could manipulate how things moved: telekinesis. Grace had an impressive power for a witch, another new one for the Elliot family: she could project an idea or feeling from one person to another. This was particularly interesting because she wasn't an empath. She could place her hand on one person and then the other hand on someone else, and both could mentally communicate without saying a word. Her power grew after a death in the family, and she was able to project a thought for people to see."

"Like a human screen?" Amber said, unsure of how such a power could be useful.

"That's a close example, but it wasn't quite like that. And Amelia's power was to heal or grow."

"What?" Jade asked.

"At first she could help plants grow faster and healthier, but after painful experiences of her own, her power grew so that she was able to speed up the healing and recovery process in living creatures, also at a very young age."

"How old were they when, uh . . ." Amber trailed off.

"Grace was killed first; she was six. Then Maddie died protecting her cousin when she was about eleven years old. Katie was ten, and Amelia . . ." Katherine paused, looking at Jade.

"Amelia was five or six?" Jade quietly asked.

"Yes," Katherine said, blinking to fight off the tears. "She was almost six. They all did their best to be the witches the family needed, but—"

"They were babies!" Amber cried out.

"Exactly," Katherine sniffled. "They did what they were told but needed to be taken care of themselves. It was devastating."

"Aunt Katherine, we don't have to do this," Jade interrupted, reaching over the round wooden table to hold Katherine's hand. "I can see it's a lot for you to talk about this."

"It hurts to live those horrible moments again, Jade," Katherine admitted, finally composing herself. "But you don't understand how wonderful it is to be able to talk about them again."

The tender moment was cut off by the house's alarm being triggered. The system was not set. They all straightened in apprehension.

"That's Al," Jade announced. "He's using the system."

Amber frowned. "That's a code gray. We're supposed to stay inside. Jade!"

Not responding, Jade darted to one of the kitchen windows with a view of the side of the property. She saw three men slinking toward the back of the house with one in the lead.

"There's three men out there," Jade whispered urgently. "Al is just one guy."

She rushed toward the door.

"And what are *you* going to do!" Amber hissed to no avail. "Oop, there she went." With a sigh, she started to follow, but Katherine grabbed her arm.

"No, Amber, stay inside. We have these protocols for a reason."

"Aunt Katherine, watch us from the window and call the police if things get out of hand. I can't just let her go."

Amber stepped outside to find Jade a few paces from the back door, with Al in front of her, stretching his arm out in protection. He announced to the intruders that they were trespassing on private property and the invitation to leave would not be extended twice.

"I'm here to talk to Jade and Amber," the leader said in a thick Boston accent.

"Sir," Al said, "your presence is not welcome. I will use force if I need to."

"Oh, I think you'll find us ready for any *force* you wanna to dish out." The man pulled his jacket up to show a holstered gun, his associates following suit. "I'm here to talk to the girls."

Al told Jade to enter the house; he would take care of this.

"Al, three guns," Jade said quietly. "Let's find out who he is."

"I'm quite confident you and your buddies aren't going to shoot anyone," Al announced. "Those service guns would need to be reported in the event of a firing, and I don't think you're here on official business."

"I'm Captain Nathan Carlisle," the man said. "And Jade has taken my wife—kidnapped, I could say. I just wanna talk."

"Kidnapping would imply that she went against her will, Mr. Carlisle," Jade loudly replied. "I can assure you she did not. She is safe."

"I need to know if she's said anything," Nathan said, stepping closer.

"That's as far as you go, Captain Carlisle," Al warned.

"My wife says things she regrets later on. It's a nasty habit," Nathan said with eyes locked on Al, yet his hands were not near his gun. "I don't wanna drag you delicate girls into our private affairs."

Nathan took another step, and before anyone had a moment to think, Al shouted Jade's name and lunged at Nathan.

Taking her cue, Jade swiftly turned, bolting for the door and shoving Amber ahead, then slamming and locking the door behind them.

Gasping for breath, the girls ran to where Katherine stood observing and recording the altercation from the window. Al had toppled onto Nathan, throwing him roughly to the ground. He kicked each of the two men hurtling toward him in the chests with a force that had them grunting in pain and falling back a few steps.

"I know that move," Jade announced. "He showed me a few things after I was followed this one time in college."

"Oh, I remember that," Katherine said.

"He said in those situations you don't strike to hurt; you strike to immobilize, then get away. That kick in the chest, it's meant to buy time so he can, yup, so he can go back to Nathan with more confidence."

"Are we seriously doing a play-by-play of Al fighting off actual police officers?!" Amber exclaimed.

Before Jade replied, Nathan brushed Al's arms off, then waved to his injured colleagues to follow him. The trio in the kitchen breathed sighs of relief when the men rushed to their car and screeched away.

Katherine expressed her deepest gratitude to Al when he came inside, nodding in satisfaction. He recommended that the girls report the trespassing to document his harassment.

Volunteering for the job, Katherine called the authorities; right or not, an older voice on the phone would likely yield a better response. She stepped out of the kitchen, describing the incident in firm, clear tones.

"Are you okay, Miss Jade?" Al asked as he caught his breath.

"She's fine, especially considering you just stopped the police from breaking in," Amber said.

"They didn't actually try to break in," Jade corrected. "But thanks, Al."

"Miss Jade," he repeated with a softer tone, "those men would not come here showing off service weapons if they were worried about the consequences."

"Oh, I see," Jade noted starkly.

"What?" Amber asked.

"Al means that Nathan came here to send a message, not to talk," Jade explained. "He wanted us to know that he knows we helped Amy, and he thinks he's powerful enough to get away with abusing his authority."

"I'd believe him. If he isn't afraid of bringing his gun here, then he knows he can get away with it," Al added.

"Great, now there's a violent lunatic making house calls," Amber said, taking a step back. "Jade, Amy was obviously right to be scared for us."

Pondering her sister's remark, Jade crossed her arms, cupping her necklace close to her heart.

"Miss Jade, may I adjust the security system, increase the volume of the alarm, and double-check the batteries for the cameras by the doors?" Al asked politely.

"Of course, Al. You don't need to ask. Mr. Porter should be here soon. You're welcome to join us for breakfast."

He politely declined his employer's invitation as it coincided with his weekly call to his mother, a fact Jade already knew.

After Al had completed his checks throughout the house, he prepared to leave for his small apartment in the back of the property.

"I sense desperation," Al told Jade, slipping on his shoes by the door. "He's probably used to getting things his way and has no qualms about making trouble."

"Thank you again, Al. It was . . ." Jade pulled back to avoid being heard by her family. "It got scary when he didn't stop coming closer, and I'm grateful I could run back home knowing you would take care of him."

"That's my job," he said, ducking his head in a slight bow and stepping out of the house.

A car pulled around, and Amber announced Mr. Porter's arrival. He walked in ready to make his famous pancakes as she relayed the events of the morning. Katherine shared that the police had not been particularly forthcoming about what they intended to do about the trespassing and assault. Their canned response was that they'd "look into it."

Mr. Porter emphatically announced that he would be staying the night. While Jade insisted they would be fine, he claimed he had already planned on doing so once Katherine told him she was going to explain the truth to them. He pointed to his packed suitcase.

Never passing up the chance to spend time with Mr. Porter, who was practically an uncle, Jade was excited to ask him how he had met her parents. In the meantime, she tried not to worry about the police officer who abused his wife and was cavalier with his gun.

Chapter Twenty-Eight

THE SISTERS HAD KNOWN that Mr. Porter lost his family before James and Annalise crossed his path. Until these recent revelations, Amber had never questioned how they'd met or what they had in common. During that significant day, she learned their mutual feelings of loss brought them together to heal.

Amber sat beside her sister on the sunroom floor and listened attentively, with Jade hugging a pillow to her chest.

Mr. Porter had stumbled across James while battling the monumental grief of losing his daughter and wife to a serial killer—a murderer he himself represented. Amber gazed at him with empathy as he described the pain that had grown overwhelming in the months after their funeral, leaving him unable to cope and unsure of what to do next.

"I was driving on this small country road. I just started driving one day, not caring where I ended up."

Beside Amber, Jade tightened her hold on the pillow.

"I pulled over," Mr. Porter recounted, his brow furrowed in sorrow. "I couldn't breathe at the thought that I would never see them again. Evelyn was the one person who saw the good in me when I didn't think there was any left."

Amber recalled that he had been a prominent defense attorney in his youth and could sense the unease lurking beneath the surface.

"And Jackie was barely old enough to know how the decisions of others could affect her." He blinked rapidly, pushing back his tears. "And your father was there, on the side of the road. He asked for directions, and I didn't know where I was."

Without a single word being exchanged, James saw the burden Mr. Porter carried. He invited him to meet his family.

"That's when I met you, little gem." He smiled at Jade. "You had the hardest time understanding that my name is James too, and you said 'Porter' so clearly . . . Somehow, I couldn't have asked for a more therapeutic moment."

Amber grinned as he shared how their parents had helped him cope with his loss, shift the blame to the right person, and then, once he had done that, accept that he would always grieve them.

Eventually, Amber stepped into the kitchen to help Katherine with the dessert plates.

"Mr. Porter and Jade are talking about Syndicate," Amber explained. "I think she's just working through her thoughts."

"Those two have had a special connection since the very first day they met," Katherine chuckled, placing the coffee mugs beside her tea cup.

Nodding, Amber slid onto a bar stool and moved the plates into place on the tray, wedging the napkins in the center. "Jade would freak if we took cheesecake out to the sunroom," Amber said. "God forbid we get any crumbs on the furniture; she'd be up all night vacuuming."

Katherine smiled fondly and tilted her head, suddenly looking thoughtful as she placed the whole cake on a platter.

"Amber, I feel like I should warn you now about an important aspect of your powers. It may sound fun to wield magic, but it comes at a cost, in pain and energy."

"Pain?" Amber asked, caught off guard "Why would using powers I was born with hurt?"

"Well, there are pros and cons to everything in life, Amber," Katherine elaborated. "To use power requires offering up your own energy. That's why Elliot witches didn't constantly use their power. Think of it like driving a car. You need fuel to make it work."

"That kinda makes sense, but why does it have to hurt?"

"Well, I don't really know," Katherine admitted. "I only know that Annalise told me her ability to see things meant her body would bear the effect of that ability."

Amber eyed her aunt attentively.

"Your power, like your sisters', grew relatively quickly. We believe it's because your father was a wizard. But you can never escape the price. I know it sounds unfair since you never asked to have it, but this is your birthright. For better or worse."

Amber grinned. "I guess I don't mind paying a price to use something amazing; it makes sense."

"If you decide you want your powers back," Katherine said, "you must be prepared to be at a disadvantage, Amber." It sounded like this part was the important truth Katherine wanted to impart.

"'Cause it would hurt?"

"Well, it's twofold," Katherine serenely replied. "The effect, that never goes away. Your tolerance to it will improve, but it will always be painful, and it will drain you." Katherine pursed her lips, bracing for an uneasy truth. "But what I mean is that, though confined, your powers continued to grow, but your ability to control even the lesser power you had as children will have to be relearned and expanded on until you master your power."

Amber contemplated the repercussions. "Would *you* want them back?"

"I don't think I can fairly answer that, Amber," Katherine sighed. "I've always wanted a power. I fear I may steer you in the wrong direction, and I will not be the one to bear the consequences."

Amber saw the haunted past glistening in her aunt's green eyes and wondered if her extended family had not been kind about Katherine's status.

The thought did not fester for long. Jade and Mr. Porter entered the kitchen. Their arms were locked into one another until Jade froze at the sullen looks on Amber and Katherine's faces.

"What happened?" Jade asked.

"Oh, nothing," Amber said lightly, jumping off the bar stool and giving her sister a mischievous smile. "We were talking about crumbs and the furniture."

⊱⊰

That night, with dinner long passed and the house armed against intrusion, the time to bid good night arrived.

Jade's thoughts lingered on Mr. Porter's story. While she had long doubted the concept of close friendship—and, even taking into account her friendship with Daniel, questioned the phrase "best friend"—hearing Mr. Porter talk about her parents made her wish she had them around now to befriend as adults.

Amber was texting Oscar about Nathan when Katherine asked Jade for a private conversation. The two sat on the top step of the staircase after Amber shuffled off to her room.

"Remember when I said that you and Amber could release your powers when you're ready and only when you truly want them?" Katherine began.

Jade nodded, eagerly grinning.

"There's something you should know about your power first," Katherine said ominously. "Your powers have continued to grow, although not with the control or skill you would have learned if they weren't restricted. Our family's initial use of power is triggered by instinct—before skill takes over, of course." She lowered her voice as laughter drifted from Amber's room. "Like weeds in a garden, unwatched and unkempt, they grow nonetheless."

"Okay," Jade whispered. "So?"

Katherine placed her hands in her lap and explained the energy required to expend and control power and the pain that accompanied it.

"So if I want to use my power, I have to, one, be prepared to replenish my energy and, two, be ready for it to affect me."

"That's for both of you," Katherine said. "The part isolated to you involves your fear as a child. Your mother was under the impression that this fear is connected to your power because the terror you felt got worse as you got older and your power grew."

"You think that just as my power will likely surpass my ability to control it, so will this fear?" Jade had already inferred a connection, but hearing Katherine voice it filled her with anxiety.

Nodding and taking Jade's hand, Katherine explained, "I know you don't remember this, but I do. I saw how you reacted to those attacks and how long it took your mother to console you; and *only* she could do it."

"You don't think I should release my powers?"

"That is not what I'm saying," Katherine murmured. "I want you to make an informed decision. I don't have to live with these consequences, so it isn't fair to steer you in any direction. The choice is yours."

Looking off to the side, Jade could only nod. Words had lost all meaning.

Katherine squeezed her hand. "I mean it. You don't need powers here."

Thankful for her aunt's concern, Jade excused herself to think deep thoughts she would never allow to be spoken.

Chapter Twenty-Nine

Lying in bed, Jade felt haunted by the decision she needed to make. Although Katherine had explained there was no pressure to release the power and the fear that would likely accompany it, something within rattled with uncertainty.

What would I tell Amber if she had this problem? she wondered, staring at the ceiling in the dark, rubbing the fuzzy coat of a stuffed shark she'd bought during a trip to the aquarium with Daniel and his mother.

Unwilling to hide from reality, she knew there were only two options ahead of her: to remain a victim of this fear and the grip it had on her, or confront it and learn how to cope with it. But it was easy to have courage when she was awake. She knew that in her sleep she would once again face the overwhelming, inescapable horror of that memory, incomplete or not.

Frustration building within her, she sat up. She loathed being perceived as weak, especially by herself. This fear had been too enormous for her to bear as a child, but she was not a child anymore. She had experienced struggle and was convinced those circumstances had toughened her, inside and out. She had also learned how the human brain and mind operated, and while she was in no way an expert, she was far better equipped than she once was.

With her determination set, her mind darted back to Katherine telling her how she had progressed in ways that impressed her mother.

The notion inspired her now. But she needed to be certain: *Do I really want to be a true and complete witch? Do I, beyond any doubt or lingering childhood fear, want to know what people think at any given moment and have the key to everyone's mind?*

Pure, indescribable joy filled her soul.

I have to have it.

She leaped from her bed, reeling for her mother's box and the letter that had awaited the bravery she felt at that moment.

She settled on the edge of her bed with the box her mother had carved for one purpose only: to help Jade decide. Taking off her necklace, she pulled her legs underneath her, then lowered it into the heart-shaped groove on the lid. Light of pristine white streaked out, and the lid swung open.

Grasping the paper, moving her fingers over the familiar handwriting, she looked to Shelby the shark for support. Then she took a breath, pressed the envelope open, and gently opened the thick pages of her mother's stationery.

My dearest Jade,

You reading this letter means that what I planned did not go the way I intended, and it probably means you are left with more questions than you can fathom.

Opening this box also means you know about your powers. Are you ready to embrace them?

I know you must feel so terrified. I can't begin to imagine the agony you're in. I never had to hide my powers or who I was until we came here, and even then, I was never forced to not use them.

If I know my sister, and I know my sister, she will teach you everything you need to know, and so I wanted to put into words a few things I don't think she will be able to tell you.

There isn't a thing in this world that I care for or love more than you and your sister. Nothing. Not myself, not your father, not even the book.

We fled to this world as a last attempt to escape annihilation. Desperation is an understatement for what we felt after the murder of your sisters. But we always knew we would go back, and so when your lives became too complex for this simple world, your father and I sought a way to return to Uporia. First we must judge if it's safe to return. If you're reading this, we have died in the attempt. But know that it was necessary.

Jade, you are the daughter of a powerful witch and a powerful wizard, and that means that you and Amber are a threat to our enemies, but you are also an incredible blessing.

I want you to release your powers. I want you to embrace them. I want you to connect with them. As with everything in life, this has a price, but the reward is well worth it. The longer you go without releasing them, the longer they will grow beyond your ability to control them.

When I tied them to your necklaces, there was a stipulation. They could only be released if you truly wanted them. There is no loophole for this condition. If you read the incantation but are still conflicted, they will not be released.

Your sister is your anchor, and you are hers. Take care of each other. Support one another. Amber will need you, as you will need her. Rise together, and you will be fine, my dear. I promise.

There are so many things to fear, both in this world and the rest, but I have also seen so much wonderment. Perhaps a little fear isn't so bad in the grand scheme of things.

You will find that knowing how and what people think comes in handy. It's a highly coveted power. Once you control it, your fears will also be better controlled. I could write a book of advice hard earned, but it wouldn't be enough. The only meaningful guidance I can give now is to embrace who you are and have faith in your sister.

Sisterhood is the backbone of our family, and our tight bonds have kept us safe for so many years. When you're ready, Jade, read the incantation. Release your powers. Be safe, sweetie, and keep me in your heart and mind.

Slowly lowering the pages, Jade let the tears flow down her cheeks. Her mother's voice rang in her mind; it was a sound she missed with all her heart. She wanted her mother there. She wanted to show Annalise how hard she had worked to make her and her father proud and do everything she thought they wanted her to do.

"A little fear isn't so bad in the grand scheme of things," she repeated, holding Shelby. Sniffling, she wiped her tears with her soft cotton sleeves.

Enthralled by what she was about to do, Jade picked up the second sheet of paper and read aloud: "Sleeping deep inside, a power within me I hide. With some help I will achieve all I deeply believe. And with the strength I hold, my new destiny will unfold. The powers that be, I call in this hour, to return my strength and free my power, to awaken what is sleeping in me so I might fulfill my destiny."

A sense of assurance she'd never felt flowed over her like a vortex of cool wind, moving her but also moving through her. Jade laughed in elation, then slipped into darkness—into sleep.

Chapter Thirty

A PALE MIST surrounded Amber as she stood in a dark room. Past the fog, she saw nothing. She could not determine where this room began or ended. She could not feel her legs or the sensation of standing but knew she was moving by the cool condensation swirling around her.

In the near distance, she spied a faint but growing light, unsure whether she was moving toward it or it was drawing closer to her. The light soon overtook the darkened room, illuminating the ominous environs into an undefined and seemingly endless bright canvas.

An unfamiliar sound reached her ears as a figure emerged. She trod closer to the abstract image, the view sharpening with every step. An involuntary smile spread across her face, and her heart raced when she discerned her mother's features.

The gray silhouette shifted, and color saturated the scene, filling her with warmth and calming her thudding heart. She now saw her mother sitting on a child's bed, gently brushing a little girl's hair. The girl's black hair swirled between her mother's fingers, and she wore the citrine necklace. Reaching for her throat, Amber found her own missing.

Wonder engulfed her. She gazed at her mother with watery eyes, observing her in a way she couldn't before. The depth of this experience went beyond that of memories and photos. Her mother stood in front of her with a younger Amber, swaddling her in a tenderness she desperately missed.

All at once, Amber floated up like a helium balloon. In her newly elevated state, she now saw and heard them moving and talking. Cheerful giggles echoed.

"We're almost done, Amber."

With the delicate French braid almost complete, Annalise continued speaking, though the little girl did not seem to be paying attention. "One day, Amber, you'll find yourself all grown up and thinking your life is going according to plan. Then you may discover new information you don't know how to break down.

"You're lucky, my little flame. Being the Keeper of the book, it's a feeling like no other. Connecting to it, feeling it push your power, and, when you're ready, using its power. It's one of the greatest feelings. From one Keeper to another, you're gonna love it."

A small sigh escaped Annalise's lips. "And now, Amber, young and warm but capable of starting a raging fire, I must warn you. You cannot abuse the book. When you feel its power, you'll be able to do things many cannot, but you must use it wisely. There is no one who can stop you but yourself, and Keepers have fallen into the trap of abusing this fact."

Then something happened that Amber could never have predicted. Annalise shifted her gaze to the Amber floating above. "The book is yours to use, and like all things, you have the responsibility to treat it and your family with respect." Little Amber betrayed no reaction, and the older one finally understood that her mother had been talking to her the entire time, not soothing the daughter in front of her.

"My not-so-little Amber. This projected memory is proof of how powerful you can be, and so, I urge you: take the book, connect to it, and be the Keeper I know you can be. Control the book and know that its power is a double-edged sword. Use it to keep your sister safe. You are each other's net."

Annalise smiled, a tear glistening in her eye. Amazed that her mother had been able to see her future self when that conversation took place, Amber realized how much she wanted to take this grand power left for her to claim.

"You were born the Keeper, Amber." Annalise's voice echoed as she turned to finish the braid, little Amber giggling. Amber descended back into a mist, and the image faded.

As the silhouettes narrowed to a dark speck, she heard the final words of her mother's message: "All you need to do is claim it."

Chapter Thirty-One

AN EXPLOSIVE, SHRILL SCREAM awoke Jade from her unexpected peaceful sleep. Recognizing Amber's voice, Jade threw herself from her bed and ran.

"What on earth?" Katherine gasped, stumbling out of her room as Jade reached Amber's door.

Mr. Porter rushed up the stairs, and Jade, fearing the worst, flung the door open, ignoring the knocking rule for once. Amber lay curled in the fetal position on her bed, sobbing with her hands over her head and screaming, "Make it stop!"

Jade yelled her sister's name but did not get a reaction. Before she could think of what to do, a sharp, hot pain seemed to split her head in two. She collapsed, holding her ears and gritting her teeth through the agony. Finally, she cried out, unable to move yet desperately wanting to flee. She felt as though her brain were boiling.

Frantically calling to Amber, Katherine urged Mr. Porter to help Jade. They tried but were unsuccessful in shaking the Parker sisters out of whatever state had overcome them.

The pain consuming Jade's consciousness slowly dissipated, and her surroundings sharpened back into view. She blinked several times, staring out at Mr. Porter and Katherine's stunned expressions, then shot her gaze back to Amber, the pull of the pain lingering in her head.

Amber whimpered, taking in long, deep breaths and releasing them slowly.

"Amber?" Jade managed to rise to her knees, shivering at the residual heat between her ears. She pulled at her left ear. "Are you okay?"

Amber shook her head nervously.

"What was that?" Jade asked, moving to her right ear as she tried to subdue the sensation of a metal rod heating inside her brain.

Amber quivered. "I have no idea. I had this dream about Mom. She was telling me about the book, and then I woke up and remembered Aunt Katherine was going to make blueberry waffles." She paused, placing her hands over the crown of her head. "This crushing headache hit me! It feels like something is slowly being placed over my head, like—"

"Like an elephant stepping on your head," Katherine thundered.

Wincing, Jade turned. "Please, talk softly."

"My goodness, Jade—"

"Aunt Katherine!" Jade cried, shaking her head and pulling her ears. "Please, speak quietly. This really hurts!"

"Jade," Amber whispered, "she hasn't said a word."

Dumbfounded, Jade squinted back to find Mr. Porter eyeing the girls in a most confused manner, as if doubting the sanity of everyone in the room. Katherine, however, was smiling, rocking on her heels and beaming from one Parker sister to the other.

"When your mother tied your powers to your necklaces, she knew that your best chance of survival lay in both of you accepting your powers, or neither," she explained. "So the spell was designed so that only Jade could release them, but both of you must want it." Katherine took a step closer. "You released them." It wasn't a question. "These are the effects of your powers."

"No one used anything," Amber croaked. "I didn't even know—"

"I haven't made waffles yet," Katherine interrupted. She pointed at her nightgown and robe. "I planned to but haven't quite gotten there."

"Wait." Amber popped up, rubbing her temples. "I saw you, in the future?"

Slowly lowering beside her sister on the bed, her head now ringing, Jade realized that this was why her mother had left a letter only for her.

"You didn't *say* that the pain Amber had was like an elephant stepping on her head?" Jade asked quietly, still considerate of Amber's headache. "I, I . . . I knew your thoughts."

Nodding with jubilation, Katherine joined her nieces on the edge of the bed. Mr. Porter drew nearer, radiating concern.

"The book is all that's left," Katherine declared. "And that happens to be tucked away in my room."

"Oh, right," Amber exclaimed, dropping her hands away from her head. "I get the book!"

Above Amber, from thin air, appeared a book, which landed gracefully in her hands.

All four froze in astonishment. After a glance at her family members to confirm with wide eyes that what she had witnessed had in fact happened, Amber moved her finger over the edges of the book.

It was covered in smooth, aged leather embossed with an intricate black floral design. She moved her fingers over the creases and cracks in the spine. It was not a large nor a heavy book. She flipped it open and found only blank pages; it seemed like nothing more than a journal meant for daily writing, excluding its exaggerated exterior. She'd anticipated a large, heavy book when Katherine explained that the book had been passed down through generations of Elliot witches, spanning hundreds of years. She'd also assumed something would be written in it.

A jolt of electricity zipped through her body, and she instantly knew that the book transformed into whatever the witches of each generation needed. Excitement suffused every inch of her as she held the magical object, already connecting to the energy on an instinctive level.

She looked up at Jade and knew they'd made the right choice; in that moment, both felt the missing pieces of their identities click into place.

"So, we did it?" Amber asked her sister, holding the book as proof. She felt a tidal wave of energy flowing around her yet saw nothing move. She held on to that feeling, hoping it would last forever.

"I think we did." Jade's smile accompanied a look of wonder. "We are whole!"

Chapter Thirty-Two

Jade and Amber were a bit dazed as they prepared to return to work days later. The rest of the employees would be returning as well, and the sisters' time spent getting used to their powers had taken their focus away from the task they'd hoped to accomplish at Syndicate while everyone was out.

Considerably late, they grabbed their bags and rushed out the back.

"Girls," Katherine called after them, "remember, using your powers will take up energy." She handed each of them a temperature-controlled lunch box through the doorway.

Jade couldn't help a sarcastic comment, but she heard her aunt's thoughts and immediately apologized, succumbing to the heat building in her skull.

"I wish I knew how to stop it," she cried. "It's not as hard as before, but it hurts so badly." She was also not a fan of the weakness that followed.

"I know you may not want to hear this, but the only way to gain skill with your powers is to use them, actively," Katherine said,

"But we have!" Amber whined, applying slight pressure to her temples.

"No, you haven't. Your powers have been triggered by instinct, not because you have chosen to use them. It may feel impossible, but you'll get the hang of it."

"I don't even know what that means," Jade exclaimed. She tugged her bag's strap back on her shoulder.

"Well, think of exercising a muscle," Katherine explained, glancing at Al waiting patiently by the car. "The first time you contract that muscle, you need guidance, like putting your hand on the area to focus your attention on it."

"But this isn't an exercise," Amber grunted.

"I know it doesn't feel that way, but I've been told the principle is the same," Katherine insisted. "Try to make your powers work for you today, deliberately, and we can recap when you get back. Your powers have grown since you were children, so it may take time to gain control."

The car ride proved excruciating for both. Amber curled over in her seat, holding her head and muttering complaints about sensory overload from the strangers they passed. Jade explained this behavior to Al by saying Amber was nauseous, hiding her own agony at Al's innocuous thoughts screaming in her mind.

The girls entered the Syndicate building gingerly, knowing the lobby would bring incredible suffering. Jade suggested they try Katherine's advice and use their powers on purpose. Maybe that would stop them from buckling under every little thought or glimpse they caught.

Unsure of how to do this, Jade told Amber to head upstairs to reduce the stimulus and then attempt to stay focused and aim her power as a first step. Perhaps she could take it further after knowing what that initial step felt like, with the magic itself guiding her.

Amber gratefully hurried to the elevator.

Jade sought no such protection for herself. She peered around the busy reception area, watching the people march in all directions. As she leaned against a wall out of the way of the swarming crowd, she discerned a pattern to the hectic room. No one misstepped or ran into another. So many thoughts bounced around her mind, but rather than struggle against the pain, she tried to find a similar order, focusing on the meaning of the thoughts.

They were all there for work, and their busy lives were foremost on their minds. A man rushed past, and she connected him to a thought about needing to get to a meeting. She glanced at a woman wearing a peeved expression and realized that this stranger's coworker was taking credit for her work.

No one seemed to notice she was there. No one except for one man whose thoughts now rang clearest in her mind.

JJ the security clerk noted her stepping aside and was worried something might have happened after the email he'd received the previous week regarding Miles Zimmerman sneaking into the building. Smiling in response to his friendly care and concern, she was astounded to make two distinct discoveries in that fleeting moment.

The first was that she had a friend in JJ without even knowing it. He may not have sought out her time or attention for recreational pastime, but he also did not view her merely as a source of benefit. He was genuinely concerned for her, and he meant to approach her when possible to see if she needed help.

The second and more intriguing realization was that she had stumbled into actively using her power. In the bustling room, she did not try to push people's thoughts away but rather leaned into the discomfort and pain, looking past it to utilize the gift she was born with.

Pulling her ear to alleviate the ringing, she headed to the elevators with an ache but also the awareness of what she was capable of if she leveraged her innate passion for the human mind.

Rushing into her office, Amber closed her door and threw her bags and lunch box on one of her couches. She immediately went to the desk and grabbed the remote for the blinds to dim the ridiculously bright room. As the blinds began their descent, Amber heard a light tap on the door.

One of her assistants stood by the sparkling glass door. Squinting to find something on her that indicated her name, Amber sighed, "Yeah, Purple, what is it?"

Her assistant flinched, hesitating, then timidly excused herself.

"No, no," Amber blurted, asking her to come in but to kindly close the door as the hall behind was far too loud. "I just have this incredibly painful headache, and I really need to not, uh—trigger is a good word. I need to not trigger it."

Lunging forward to catch herself on the desk and then crouching low to get her bearings, Amber grunted from the pain of a vision, ignoring Purple's terrified expression.

"Oh, sweet buttered buns," Amber gasped, taking a beat before pulling herself to stand. "Okay, Purple, I'm going to venture a guess, and let me know if I'm right."

The assistant nodded nervously.

"You don't want to be my assistant, but you don't want to get fired," Amber said, falling into her desk chair and dropping her head back to stare at the ceiling. "You took this job because your mother is ill and she had to move here for treatment. The pay is why you're here, but it's a pharmaceutical company, so you're hoping for a better fit." Amber exhaled, finally lifting her head to look at Purple. "Am I right?"

A confused Purple muttered, "Miss, I'm—"

"No, please," Amber interrupted, trying to head off anything that would prompt another vision. "It's fine. You're not fired. I'll talk it over with Jade and look at your résumé to find you another position, okay?"

Purple thanked her, practically leaping out the door, but not before another crippling vision overcame Amber.

"Oh no!" Amber cried out. "Purple!" Holding the top of her head, Amber groaned, wishing she could give everyone another week off work.

"Yes, miss," Purple replied, poking her head back in, followed by Blue and Green.

"You guys aren't planning on going to that new restaurant across the street for lunch today, are you?" Amber asked, grinding her teeth.

They all nodded, with Blue replying, "We often go out to lunch on the first—"

"Perfectly fine!" Amber interrupted forcefully. "How about instead of the new place here, you go to, uh, Maroon?"

"Miss, that's a ten-minute walk from here and one of the most exclusive restaurants downtown?" Green said in astonishment.

"Only the best for my people." Amber sighed as her pain began to lessen. "I know the owner and can get you on the list. Just don't go to the new restaurant today. We wouldn't want anyone getting sick or anything." She nervously chuckled, grabbing her phone to text Oscar.

Minutes later, the hum of the blinds closing on the other side of her office granted her the privacy she desperately needed.

"That book better be worth it," she whined, slouching across the office to the couch to retrieve her treats.

Midbite, Amber felt a twinge in the back of her neck—the unmistakable pull before an image appeared in her mind. She saw her sister walking down a crowded hospital hall, looking for one room in particular.

Jade stopped by the nurses' station and received directions to room 2319. The nurse pointed behind Jade, and she turned and strode to the last room down the hall. She knocked on the door, but before she could enter, someone grabbed her shoulders, pulling her into the stairwell. Jade wailed as she hit the railing with considerable force, and when she turned, her cheek was swollen red and bleeding.

The man towering over her breathed heavily, furiously; it was none other than Nathan Carlisle. Seizing her arm, he pushed her toward the stairs—and the image faded away, leaving the pressure of the world filling Amber's head.

"Oh no. Jade!" she gasped, grabbing her phone and calling Al. She barked at him to be ready for her, running over to her desk and grabbing her purse. She took two full-sized candy bars from the lunch box Katherine had prepared and rushed from the office.

With Al set to meet her by the building's front entrance, Amber hurried to the elevators.

"Okay, Amber, think," she instructed herself, alone in the small chamber. "She was in a hospital. Which one?"

Playing back the scene of the nurses' station gave her the clue she needed.

"Solas General! Good, that's right around the corner." Armed with the details of the hospital emergency department and the room number, Amber leaped to save her sister from Nathan as the doors opened.

She realized she was still on the twenty-fourth floor and cried out in frustration when she saw Mr. Porter and Mr. Hough talking. In her hurry, she'd failed to push the button for the lobby.

"Mr. Porter, I can't talk," Amber gasped, moving to the side.

"I came by to check on your, uh, headaches," Mr. Porter said.

"Yeah, I had a really big headache, Mr. Porter," Amber said urgently. "Nathan's going to attack Jade!"

"What?" both men demanded in unison.

"Al is downstairs. Let's go. I think he's gonna throw her down the stairs!"

When the doors finally opened on the first floor, all three rushed to the car, with Amber hollering for Al to take them to Solas General's emergency department immediately. She shouted that Jade was going to be attacked by Nathan.

"Al, I know Jade hired you for your extra skills. Use them all! Just get us there, fast!"

Al wasted no time darting down the road. "Miss, do I have your permission to incur tickets?"

"Yes! Whatever you need to do."

Chapter Thirty-Three

"Excuse me?" Jade quietly prompted a busy hospital employee, not wanting to disrupt her day. The overworked employee did not immediately respond as she juggled the circus spiraling around her.

Such moments were when Jade typically felt small and unimportant compared to the people helping, improving, saving lives. However, she did not succumb to the feeling this time. Searching desperately for someone else to assist her, Jade felt ignored. She had not stumbled into the ER by accident, nor was she here to spread good cheer. She was Amy's emergency contact.

Amy had been attacked on her way to an exam. A passing student found her badly beaten after following her groans to an empty room. Once the ambulance had brought her in, the hospital called Jade, who summoned a private car service, unaware that Al had decided to stick close following Nathan's visit to the house.

"Excuse me." Jade raised her voice to catch the nurse's attention and became agitated when the women acknowledged her presence with a glance only to immediately overlook it. She knew what she had to do, and she hated having to do it.

Position and stature were rare privileges. Not using them did not offset the power spread; it only exaggerated it. She'd also learned that while sometimes it was best to make one's way through life gently and respectfully, in other areas, one must simply get things done.

"Miss," Jade said firmly, leaning slightly over the counter, "I'm looking for a patient. I'm not comfortable saying her name, but she came in not too long ago." The nurse looked down at her papers, not responding. "I was told that she requested I come. My name's Jade Parker."

The nurse finally looked around, then focused on a tablet, grabbing it and hanging up the phone.

"The young lady who was beaten at the community college?" the nurse asked, barely loud enough to be heard over the ruckus. "You're the emergency contact? Ms. Parker?" She pointed to the plaque hanging beside her, which recognized the Parker family's contributions to the hospital.

"Yes," Jade sighed. "I haven't been told anything. Where is she?"

The nurse called someone to take over her post, then walked around the circular counter and asked Jade to follow her. The clamor died away as they headed down the hall, allowing the young nurse to speak freely.

"She came in slipping in and out of consciousness, badly hurt," the nurse said, peering at the tablet in her hand. "They cleaned her up, but she still needs to see the on-call OB before they move forward with, um, the other treatments."

"OB?" Jade asked, halting. The nurse swerved to the side of the hall to get out of the way and stopped alongside her. Jade winced in pain, then tugged her ear. "She was pregnant?"

"She didn't know," the nurse whispered. "I don't think she planned on being pregnant. I saw this before with a rape victim, but I'm not the nurse on her case."

"Why do they need an OB right away?"

"The pregnancy . . ." The nurse paused, recalculating. "The attack was too much. The OB needs to let her know that the miscarriage, it wasn't, uh, complete."

"Oh no," Jade quietly gasped, realizing the difficult situation ahead of Amy.

"Her room is the last one on the left," the nurse said after being called back to her station. "Room 2319."

Jade's mind was a storm of emotion. She had inadvertently barged into a precarious situation, considering Nathan's profession, and the repercussions were building. Furthermore, Amy clearly trusted Jade, since she was listed as Amy's emergency contact. All of which pressured her to help Amy out of this mess.

Jade was veering toward the room when she heard her sister calling her from behind. Stunned, she stared as Amber halted in front of her, collapsing over her knees and gasping for air.

"I've been looking for you!" Amber announced, then held up a finger while she caught her breath.

"What's going on? How did you know I was here?"

Lifting her head, Amber exhaled and patted her forehead. "I, uh, had a headache."

She froze when the door to the staircase behind Jade opened. Nathan lunged through the opening, forcefully wrapping his arms around both girls and slamming them against the door to Amy's room, then shoving them inside.

The girls crashed into each other and hit the floor, momentarily immobilized. Nathan barricaded the door with a portable table, throwing the food it held to the ground. He grabbed Amber's hair and yanked her to her feet as she screamed. Backing into the corner, he gripped her hair at the base of her skull.

Jade jumped to her feet, meeting her sister's terrorized expression as Amber trembled, her face red.

"Nathan," Jade said, "let her go."

"No," Nathan barked, pulling her hair tighter.

"I understand that you don't like people interfering with your private affairs," Jade said, "but trust me when I say you are crossing a dangerous line. Let her go!"

"Why do you think I'm here? For that little wench!" he yelled, flinging an arm at Amy, who was now sobbing on the bed behind them. "She has more on me—"

"Let her go!" Jade shouted, hearing the door shake behind her and the alarmed voices of Al and Mr. Porter.

"Or what?" Nathan growled with a sinister glare. "What're you going to do about it?" He smirked, bringing Amber closer to his face. She strained away from him.

Jade deliberately relaxed her shoulders and tilted her head, regarding Nathan through narrowed eyes. This shift rattled him; Jade sensed it as she entered his thoughts.

"Does my sudden calm scare you, Nathan?" Jade murmured.

Before he could speak, Jade said the words echoing in his mind.

"There's only one woman who reacted to your— You think it's strength. Okay, fine, let's call this 'bravado' strength. Only one woman has ever made you feel scared."

"What?"

"Your commanding officer in the military, Eliza Gardener."

"How do you know about her?" Nathan demanded, his grip on Amber's hair loosening as he glared at Amy. "How does she know!"

Looking into Amber's teary eyes, Jade said, "You're getting clumsy, Nathan. Making a big mistake by, oh, you wanted to kill Amy, not beat her up."

Flustered, Nathan darted his gaze between Jade and Amy.

"Hey!" Jade shouted at him. "Look at me. I'm the one messing with you." His eyes refocused on her with a tinge of madness in them. "Let my sister go, now."

Pressing his lips tightly together, Nathan thrust Amber forward. Jade managed to catch her but could do nothing to stop their attacker from diving for the open window and crawling down the fire escape, disappearing with a clang.

Jade kicked the table away from the door, still holding Amber, who hunched into her sister's embrace, crying.

Al jerked the door open.

"He left through the window!" Jade shouted.

Mr. Porter rushed to the girls, asking Amber if she was hurt as Al and Mr. Hough raced from the room. Finally calmer, Amber lifted her head and wiped away her tears, announcing she was fine.

A nurse attended to Amy, who was in a hysterical state, and shouted for a doctor and a sedative. Stepping out of the room to give Amy privacy with her medical team, Jade checked Amber for injuries. Amber insisted she was unharmed. Al returned, informing Mr. Porter that Nathan had not been found and that Amy should not be left alone.

"Nathan wants to kill her," Jade said, holding Amber's hand. "She knows too many of his secrets."

"I'll talk to Mr. Hough," Al announced. "He said it may be better for Amy to transfer to another hospital."

Understanding the mountain of paperwork ahead of them, Jade asked Mr. Porter to take Amber to the cafeteria for a snack; she felt obligated to be present with Amy.

As the two headed downstairs, Jade sighed with relief, knowing how badly things could have gone for her sister—or for her, had her sister not shown up. Their mother was right. They needed each other.

Chapter Thirty-Four

Before returning to the room, Jade encountered a familiar face in the hallway.

"Jade, are you okay?" Daniel asked, lifting his hand toward her cheek, which was pulsing bright red.

"Yes," Jade responded distractedly as she tapped on her phone.

"I heard the nurses saying there was an attack. Is that what happened to your face? Who did this?"

"Oh, my goodness," Jade gasped in sudden realization, putting her phone away. "I completely forgot about today—"

"Jade, what happened?"

"Nathan is what happened," Jade said. "He attacked us and used Amber as hostage."

"What? Who is Nathan?" Daniel gasped.

Jade hesitated. "Okay, so, between us, okay, Daniel?" She pulled him to the side, waiting for his agreement before continuing, "We have an employee at Syndicate who has been living in a violent home situation."

She looked down at her phone, tapping a few replies, then returned her attention to Daniel.

"Amber and I helped her leave him. Like, a new place to stay and people to help her find a new job, counselors and therapists, new phone, everything. And I think it worked because he came to our house to send us a message."

"Wait." Daniel held up a hand. "A physically violent man came to your house?"

Jade nodded. "Al showed him a thing or two, and he left, but I got a call from the hospital as soon as I got in today, saying this employee was brutally—and, Daniel, I mean brutally—beaten."

She paused as someone passed them. "I was coming to see her when Amber showed up. Then he threw us into the door." She gestured to her red, swollen cheek.

"Where was Al?" Daniel demanded.

"Nathan blocked the door," she said. "And after he let Amber go, he bolted out the window."

"Wait, where's Amber?"

"She's with Mr. Porter, to distract her from all of this. Oh, great, he's here!" She waved at a rapidly approaching Oscar.

Oscar quickly asked about his friend, and Jade reiterated her whereabouts, then introduced the two men.

"Oscar, I need you to take Amber home. Can you do that?" Jade begged. "I know she won't want to leave without Al, so I need someone to ride home with her."

"Why won't she be with Al?" Daniel asked as Oscar nodded.

"I'm staying here until Amy can be transferred to another location."

"Why are you taking care of this? Why is this guy targeting you and Amber?" Oscar inquired.

"Her husband attacked her, left her for dead, and Amber and I were the ones who got her away from him. I can't just walk away."

"Why can't the police watch her?" Daniel asked.

"Her husband is police. He's a captain, and from what I heard, he's influential. The police will watch her, alright, but they won't protect her." Given her brief foray into Nathan's mind, she had no doubt that he would come back to finish the job.

The two men who had just met exchanged looks of concern.

"Oh, there's Mr. Hough," Jade announced. "I need to ask him to handle a few things. Please, Oscar, will you take her home?"

"Yeah, of course. Where is she?"

"Third-floor cafeteria," Jade responded, waving to get Mr. Hough and Al's attention. "Don't tell her why you're here, though. Let me do that. You'll never convince her."

Oscar promptly sought the quickest path to Amber. Jade asked Daniel to give her and Mr. Hough privacy, and taking a step back, Daniel insisted he would wait until she finished.

Over the following hours, Jade saw Amber safely off with Oscar and Mr. Porter for company. Standing at the entrance of the hospital as they departed, Jade realized a new fear had been unlocked. Seeing her sister handled in such a way filled her with rage and a terrible sense of helplessness. She vowed to never be that weak again.

Al contacted several private security companies, who offered their services free of charge. While payment was nothing to worry about, Jade was pleased to see this honor among men working in the protection service.

As the clock drew closer to midnight, Jade finally found a moment to sit, catching her breath with a deep sigh.

"Bet you're wondering, *How did I get myself into this?*" Daniel chuckled, approaching her from around the bend with two cups of coffee.

"Never a dull moment, right?"

"Is Amber okay?" he asked.

Peering down the hall, Jade spotted Al by Amy's room, talking to the hospital workers preparing her for transport.

"I think she will be," she sighed. "I haven't had a chance to talk to her. But the look on her face, the way she shook when he had her—I can't unsee that."

"I'm sorry you went through that, Jade."

Jade snapped her drink away from her mouth. "You came to see me at Syndicate—"

"Well, I was pretty booked this morning, so I thought I could hop in for a quick discussion."

Jade's eyes darted to the large clock behind him. "Daniel, I'm so sorry!"

"Don't worry about it. A lunatic attacked you."

Al approached with the medical team as they wheeled Amy to the ambulance. Jade joined them, comforting Amy and insisting she was not to blame. Reflexively, Jade tugged her ear as she informed Amy that Mr. Hough would be riding with her to the new hospital.

"I'll come by tomorrow, okay?" Jade told her, still tilting her head in an attempt to hide the pain. Upon the ambulance's departure, those left behind meandered toward the parking exit, and Al asked Daniel if he needed a ride.

"You've been here all day," Jade said apologetically.

"I run a foundation, Jade," Daniel chuckled. "I can take my meetings in a hospital." He thanked Al for the offer. "I have my car."

"Let's give that discussion another go tomorrow, okay?" Jade said as Al took her bags and the stack of paperwork. "Text me. I can come to you, or we meet at Syndicate. I'll clear my schedule."

By the time Daniel drove off, Al had arrived with the car.

Amber sat alone on her bed, trying to calm her racing heart. Nathan was out there, Jade was still at the hospital, and Amber felt helpless. She curled up and struggled to process the emotions overwhelming her. Helping Amy was probably more important now than ever, but Amber feared something awful happening.

As Amber lay in the dark, hugging a small pillow, she gradually felt a soft tug. A delicate, invisible pull toward her dresser. She knew what was summoning her. She did not know how she knew; she simply did.

The book was calling her, yet it didn't feel like a call. The hum was more intrinsic than external. Sliding her feet over the edge of the bed, Amber padded over to the dresser, both excited and confused.

The gravity of the pull grew until she stood in front of the open drawer, the magical book below her, urging her to pick it up.

With a desire she could never describe, Amber picked up the book, and a tingling rush swept through her body. She felt complete holding the book, as she had the first time. While the book's external characteristics suggested it was an inanimate object, to Amber, this was the one friend that was perfectly in sync with her unique self.

Smiling, she took the book back to bed. The most unusual phenomena occurred; somehow, it was like the book was transcribing in her mind. No words were needed between the two kindred spirits, and Amber giggled.

"It's nice to meet you, too. Even though I feel you know me better than I know myself."

The soft rush of gentle static overcame her as the book explained their bond. In essence, the book confirmed, it was whatever Amber needed it to be. While the book did not elaborate on what that entailed, Amber was satisfied with the progress she'd made.

"Oh, interesting," Amber whispered. "Anything—like, anything?" Sensing a gentle warning, she smiled. "Okay, okay. Something small."

Amber had prepared for Jade's return by setting out a cup of warm milk and three chocolate chunk cookies in the sunroom. Katherine and Mr. Porter went to bed once Jade texted everyone that Amy had left the hospital.

Jade fell onto the soft couch. The sisters chatted about the alarming events and using their powers as Nathan crashed into their lives yet again.

Amber explained her vision to Jade, relaying something the book had since told her regarding future events not being set and easily changed. Thankful for her powers, albeit dreading the almost constant effect they had on her, Amber shivered at the thought of what would have happened had she not arrived at the hospital in time.

"Jade," Amber whispered, "I've been waiting to show you something. Actually, to try something. The book told me that as the Keeper, I have two important connections with it. One, it expands my power, whatever that means, and two, I can connect to it to use its power, when I'm ready."

"And what does *that* mean?" Jade asked.

Amber shrugged. "It depends on the Keeper's connection to the book, like how strong it is or something."

"But what *is* the book's power?"

"It's very subjective or dependent on the Keeper. I have to build a good connection with the book. After that, and I quote, I can do 'so much more.'"

"How are you not frustrated not knowing what the book can do?" Jade huffed.

"Because," Amber giddily said, holding the book up, "I connected to it for the first time!" Vibrating with excitement, she handed Jade the book, explaining what had happened.

"When I picked it up, it was the coolest thing. I knew what it was telling me without hearing a single word."

Jade was captivated as Amber continued.

"You know how you get this feeling like something is just right? Like you *know* the answer even if you don't know the answer? Like a really good guess?"

Jade nodded.

"It's like that," Amber said with a proud grin.

"So, you talk to the book?"

"Communicate is how I'd describe it."

"What did it communicate?" Jade questioned.

"It told me about expanding my power!" Amber almost squealed. "It said that my power to see events can be pushed a bit further by using the book. It can show me the scene with more clarity and depth."

"No way!" Jade exclaimed.

"But it doesn't show perspective or intentions or stuff like that, just a scene like a rolling film of time. It emphasized that."

"Wow." Jade fell back in the cushions. "This day definitely did not go according to plan."

"Well, it's about to get even crazier because I'm gonna use the book!" Amber announced. She knew that using the book in any capacity would drain her energy more than her power did, yet she needed to start somewhere.

Glancing down at her phone, Jade asked Amber what she wanted to see.

"The book said something small, so . . ." Amber hummed, plucking the book from Jade's lap. Holding the book tightly, she searched for the sensation that had overcome her when she first connected with it. Once she felt the book, she pulled in more focus. She requested to see a memory she barely remembered. She squeezed her eyes shut as a force wrapped around her.

The book rose from her hands and flew open, to a page about halfway through the book.

Both pages glowed brightly with a translucent halo. The golden hue appeared almost silky, a ripple gliding across the pages. As the sisters gazed down on the silken canvas, an image unfolded.

The perfectly clear scene animated through splashes of color. Amber saw her father walking down the staircase of a house she recognized as their childhood home. James was carrying ten-year-old Amber to the car, his daughter limp with sorrow.

"Dad, please," Amber begged. "I don't want to move to a new school. Ariel's birthday party is next week, and I know I won't go if we change schools." Amber's tiny hands held her father's cheeks, trying to get him to agree before they reached the waiting car.

"Sweetie," James said, placing her gently on the ground and crouching down to her level, "the school isn't a safe place, not anymore." He gently pinched her chin. "Do you know how terrible

I'd feel if anything happened to you? You're my baby girl. I don't want you getting hurt."

"I promise, I won't talk to any strangers. I won't talk to anyone!" Amber pleaded.

James chuckled. "I know you'd do anything to stay with your friends." He hugged her, nudging her to the open car door. "I'll talk to Ariel's dad, okay, sweetie? Your mom and I will try to keep up all of your friendships, especially with Ariel and Keyana, but your safety, and Jade's safety . . ." He nudged Jade, who was sitting in the back seat with her arms crossed, pretending she didn't hear. "That comes first."

"But—" Amber squeaked.

"Just because something isn't first on my priority list doesn't mean I don't care about it or that I'll forget."

The younger Amber relented, then jumped into the car and slid her seatbelt on. James acknowledged Katherine with a wink, mouthing, "Thank you" before he shut the door.

The glowing pages fading, Amber studied his face as he watched the moving car, his words echoing in her mind. The color disappeared, and the book shut gently, sinking to her lap.

Amber and Jade stared at each other with teary eyes, knowing they felt the same way. Their father and mother had sacrificed everything for them. From coming to a new world to building a company that guaranteed their wealth and stature, James and Annalise showed with everything they did just how much they loved their family and how far they'd go to protect it.

Feeling immensely weak, Amber decided to sleep in the sunroom, pulling a throw pillow and blanket from the storage ottoman in front of her. Jade rose and unfolded the blanket, then grabbed the larger cushions from the couch and joined her sister in a makeshift slumber party.

Too exhausted to comment, Amber snuggled in, in awe of her own power.

Jade used her phone to arm the security system. Looking back at Amber, she reveled in the amazing reality of who they were. She did not regret for a minute releasing their powers.

After a few more taps, Jade succumbed to the heaviness dragging her eyelids shut and soon fell asleep, afraid of so many things in their past and future but secretly enjoying the excitement of it all.

Chapter Thirty-Five

AMBER BLINKED, glancing at her watch and discovering she had slept in. She pulled back the blanket carefully wrapped around her. Knowing what an active sleeper she was, she luxuriated in the comfort of knowing Jade must have covered her.

She shoved her disheveled hair into a messy bun and stumped into the kitchen, following the random sounds in hopes of finding Jade.

"Good morning, Aunt Katherine," Amber trilled, stretching her arms high.

"Good morning, Amber. I see you slept well."

"I got really tired last night."

"Oh yes." Katherine nodded. "Jade told me you used the book and made it clear that I was to let you sleep for as long as you needed."

"I don't think it's that bad—using the book, I mean," Amber said, pulling out a stool and sitting. "I don't think I have ever felt that tired before, but I'm fine now."

"Amber, it's almost noon," Katherine chuckled, cutting a sandwich she had assembled. She had several volunteer projects before summer festivities began and was about to head out now that Amber had woken up. "But your tolerance for this fatigue will get better. It won't ever leave completely, much like the effect of using your powers, but it gets easier." Katherine pulled crackers out of a sleeve and sighed. "Or that's what I was told."

Amber bounced off the stool to change into professional attire.

She was applying a thin layer of foundation when the pressure of a headache emanated from the crown of her head, signaling an imminent vision.

Through the throbbing pain, Amber saw Jade in a restaurant, sitting alone but with two glasses in front of her.

The waiter was replacing the other glass while Jade politely asked for more time to finish her own. Nodding, the waiter mentioned that the first course would be out shortly, and Jade grinned as he walked away. Tugging at her sleeves, she surveyed the intimate restaurant and sighed.

Jade was dressed in a way not seen by most. Her dark-brown hair was loose and flowing. Black pins tucked strands back from her face. Her makeup was not the professional style she often wore; instead, her eyelids boasted hues of light violet, and her brown eyes danced with the subtle cat-eye liner and mascara. She wore a black, knee-length dress and a sheer navy cardigan.

Her eyes shifted to a hall in the back where a wooden sign displayed WC. Her jaw tightened when a man emerged, affixing his cufflinks before confidently striding in her direction.

Jade produced her polite business smile as he sat, nodding when she commented about his drink being replaced.

"So, where were we?" he asked, looking at her intently.

Jade spoke with distinct tension in her voice. "Oh, you were describing your work."

"Yeah," the man chuckled. "It's really great getting this promotion. I was up against three other employees who worked at the company before I joined. It's really humbling."

"What is it you do again?"

"I'm an executive director at First Lights, the electrical company."

Jade was only marginally bothered that he did not return her question.

"How long have you been working there?" she asked.

"A couple of years."

"That's quite an impressive leap you've made."

He smiled, basking a moment before continuing, "The people who lost out may not like me after this. Nothing they can do about it, though."

"I can't imagine anyone being upset with you for being the best person for the job," Jade said with a hint of incredulity, tugging her cardigan snuggly over her chest.

"Oh, Jay, these three women have been working there for ten years, each thinking she has what it takes to make it on the executive level."

"And they don't?" she asked, shifting her weight.

"Well," he hummed, "they all have families, and those commitments get in the way."

"Oh, commitment to the job is a serious point," Jade responded. "How did they balance that in the ten years they were working there?"

"I'm gonna be honest, Jay," he snickered, "I don't really know. But I've seen it a million times. Women get caught up with this idea of wanting a career and bust their butts, climbing the corporate ladder, but then a few missed games or family time, and they bail on work."

"My name is Jade," she grumbled, picking up her phone and sending Amber a text asking if she was available. She received an immediate reply that her sister was studying with friends. "You've been calling me Jay all evening. I prefer my name."

"Oh, come on," he protested. "This is a date; let's take it easy." He snapped his fingers to call the waiter over.

Forcing a smile, Jade quickly sent another text, to Daniel, asking him to call so she might leave politely without a fuss. "It's a first date, Jarred."

The man made an inelegant comment to the waiter regarding the pace of the food before he moved his attention back to Jade still on her phone. "How about I'm the only guy who can call you Jay?" he said with a twisted quarter smile.

The corner of Jade's mouth twitched as she placed the phone down.

"How did you know about me? You know, to ask for this appointment?"

"I was telling my old mentor, Reynolds, about my promotion, and he suggested I take you out." He leaned back in his chair. "He taught me everything I know, so why not take him up on taking the infamous Jade Parker out for dinner?"

Jade's right eyebrow arched. "I thought this was arranged by his assistant, Amy. Don't you know her?"

Shaking his head, he replied, "Does it matter?"

Jade excused herself to answer her vibrating phone. After a few practiced responses, Jade told the caller she would be there immediately and hung up. She stood quickly, flooded with relief as she caught the waiter and asked for her coat—and to kindly put the gentleman's dinner on her tab.

The man's stunned expression as Jade rushed out of the restaurant was the best part of the night.

She peacefully walked up the side streets, mindlessly staring up at the twinkling lights of the busy yet quaint shops. Then she stopped with a genuine smile and waited for Daniel to join her near the crosswalk. He'd agreed to accompany her until Al arrived.

"So, how was the date?" Daniel laughed.

"Insufferable," Jade cried out with a gasp. "Oh, he really thinks he's the bee's knees."

"Never quite understood how that phrase came to be," he said, leading them away from traffic.

"I'm sure *he'd* have a story for it." Jade smirked. "I don't think this 'try new things and step out of my comfort zone' racket is for me. Ugh, he called me the infamous Jade Parker."

"Ouch!" Daniel said, opening the door to a nearby restaurant and holding it for her, then asking about her beverage of choice.

The scene began to fade out on Jade waiting for a table with Daniel, who graciously took her coat.

Guilt struck Amber at knowing Jade had reached out to her first. She recalled the many responses she'd glibly dashed off to Jade during those first years at college, annoyed at the constant messages and viewing them as a nuisance when in fact it was comforting to know Jade was always there.

Amber quickly completed her makeup, then glanced at the book as she stood to leave. Filled with the urge to pick it up, she answered the silent call. Intoxicating energy coursed through her body. The book seemed to be hinting at its need to stay hidden.

"Oh, you're right," Amber exclaimed. She walked to her dresser, then tucked the book away in the middle drawer. The book conveyed something like a purr, and she giggled, then gently closed the drawer—but not before the book shared one more thing with her.

Chapter Thirty-Six

"Excuse me, Daniel," Jade said politely as her sister streaked toward her office door and quickly retreated after seeing Jade with someone. "I'll be right back. I just want to check on Amber."

A soft knock drew Amber's attention, and the sisters convened briefly about Amber's exhaustion, with Amber sharing what Katherine had told her about building a tolerance.

"I'll come back after my meeting with Daniel. I need your opinion on a couple things," Jade confessed, stepping back to leave.

"Why do you need my opinion?" Amber asked.

"Well, the first is a Syndicate thing, and the other is an Amy thing."

"Oh, okay." Amber nodded, but instead of leaving, her sister came closer.

"I'll tell you now," Jade said, unable to hide her anxious tone. "I 'heard' something Amy thought of last night and confirmed it this morning when I saw her."

"What?" Amber whispered.

Leaning in, Jade revealed that Amy had been thinking that she "should have never saved the files" on a drive dating back years. Amy felt guilty for the Parker sisters being caught in the middle of Nathan's revenge scheme but initially said nothing, fearing Jade would be angry with her.

Nathan Carlisle had been emotionally abusive from the day he moved Amy away from her family, progressing to physical abuse a year later. Throughout their four-year marriage, Amy had secretly saved files and data about the many meetings he conducted at their house, making a digital record that could put him away for a very long time.

"What did he do?" Amber asked, intrigued.

"I have no idea!" Jade said. "I wish I could scan her mind. All of her thoughts were very general—at least, to me they seemed general."

Amber gave a mischievous grin. "That's a nifty little power ya got there, Jade."

"Yeah," Jade reluctantly replied. "I like being able to know what's on people's minds, but I sometimes feel bad for infiltrating their privacy like that."

"Infiltrating? That's a pretty specific word."

"That's what it feels like," Jade admitted. "I'm so grateful to know what she's thinking because of how crazy Nathan is, but she didn't tell me that information. She didn't want to."

"You're not going to do anything with it to hurt her," Amber replied. "You're not snooping."

"Yeah, but still. Privacy is a big deal. The hypocrisy of it all is kinda unsettling."

"What are we gonna do?"

"We're going to develop our powers and be able to control them so we're not infiltrating people's lives unnecessarily."

"Unless we want to." Amber nudged her sister.

"Unless we *need* to," Jade emphasized before turning to leave.

"I've, uh"—Amber paused before continuing—"I named the book."

"You named the book?" Jade chuckled. "Like a pet?"

"Its name is Avania," Amber declared.

"I like that." Jade grinned before leaving the office, winking as she passed the transparent wall.

Jade apologized to Daniel for interrupting their meeting, but he insisted there was nothing to apologize for. He was simply pleased that they could discuss the matter he'd initially come to talk about the previous day.

Daniel wanted to collaborate with Jade again but not like they had as students. The goal was to provide more options for the patients the foundation served. He never called the foundation his, even though she hadn't actively contributed since her junior year in college. He always referred to it as a product of both their efforts.

Jade reminded him that she would need to formally discuss the concept with Amber as she was the business-minded sister and fellow owner of Syndicate. He expressed eagerness to show Amber the progress the foundation had made.

"How's Amber after yesterday?"

"We still haven't talked about it," Jade sighed. "But I think we have, um, an idea of how to proceed with Nathan Carlisle."

"Jade, what happened was intense."

"You bet it was."

"No," Daniel said, taking a step closer. "For you." He held her gaze. "I know it was Amber he grabbed, but he attacked you both, and you saw this maniac hurt your only remaining family member and couldn't stop him." He studied her face for a moment. "That isn't easy to experience. Are *you* okay?"

He gave her space for her emotions, and she accepted it gladly.

"He hurt my little sister, Daniel," she whispered. His brow furrowed in consternation; Jade usually referred to Amber as her younger sister, but she was unusually emotional about the situation.

"Jade, if you need help, I'll do anything."

"It'll be fine," Jade responded with a subtle smile. "With Al and Mr. Hough's street smarts, I'll make sure he doesn't cross that line again."

"I know you're capable," Daniel warmly added. "I know you can take care of it. But if you need anything, after Al and Mr. Hough's street smarts, ask me. Okay?"

"Okay," Jade chuckled, "I'll ask."

His smile indicated he was about to speak, but Amber bounded in.

"I'm sorry to barge in like this. Hi, Daniel. Nice to see you again." She acknowledged him with a wave. "Jade, we gotta go. Something went off at the house, and Aunt Katherine isn't answering. Al's downstairs. Grab your bag. I'll get the elevator." With that, she was gone.

Jade kicked her corporate heels off, ran to her desk to retrieve her small purse, and slipped into the running shoes stored in the closet. She asked Daniel if he was okay to walk himself out. Understanding of her abrupt departure, he said he would call later to check on things.

Jade arrived at the elevator to see her sister anxiously waiting for the doors to open, bolting inside when they finally did.

"It's Avania," Amber whispered. "It—I don't know; it's calling me or trying to connect. It said someone other than us was close to it and about to get it."

Confirming on her phone, Jade relayed that the security system was offline. They desperately watched the lights illuminate the descending floor numbers as time moved impossibly slowly, then ran to their car in the garage, Al at the ready, to head home and find out who was searching for Avania.

Chapter Thirty-Seven

Conveying to Amber that Katherine was out of the house and safe, Jade returned her phone to her pocket as the sisters waited for Al to finish sweeping the house. Amber connected to the book but could not sense the danger she had felt.

When Al emerged from the back door, Jade sprang from her seat, followed by Amber.

Al verified his employers' suspicions. "There was a break-in."

He suggested packing an overnight bag; he did not think anyone should stay in the house until a new security system was installed.

Amber ran ahead to find Avania, leaving Jade and Al to discuss the concerns about the current security measures and how they would likely increase now that Nathan had entered their lives.

She entered her ransacked room to find the book discarded on her bed. "Really?" Amber said, staring at the book with intrigue as she pulled her overnight bag from the closet to pack. A rush of energy overtook her when she grabbed it, grateful that Avania looked like nothing more than an empty journal.

"Is Avania okay?" Jade asked, leaning into Amber's room, awaiting her sister's permission to enter. Nodding, Amber indicated the general state of her room—her clothes thrown about haphazardly and the contents of her dresser tossed on the ground.

"I think this was Nathan's doing," Jade somberly said, moving some clothes from the corner of the bed to sit. "I think he's trying to scare us."

"It worked," Amber replied, placing the book inside her bag. "I think we're in serious danger."

Then Jade caught her sister by surprise. "I want to retrieve the drive."

"You want to antagonize him even more?"

"I want leverage!" Jade emphasized. "Whatever Amy has on that file, she was sure it could be used against him."

"How can we be certain? Her thinking something doesn't mean it's true or that it would actually work," Amber said.

"He's willing to kill her for it, so I know that's his biggest weakness."

Amber whimpered under the effects of a sudden vision. She crouched and tucked her forehead into her knees until the scene had played out in full, then revealed to Jade that the men who'd broken in were police officers. "We need to be careful, okay?"

Agreeing with her sister, Jade informed Amber that she knew where the drive was hidden. It was in a small portable safe, the key hidden in another location. Their first step would be to obtain the key, which had been placed in a small yellow envelope taped behind lockers near a gym by the train station. Amy had been thorough since she suspected Nathan was following her.

"So, how are we gonna get it if she couldn't?" Amber asked, zipping her bag and accompanying Jade to her room.

"I think that with Amy," Jade said, gasping at the chaos in her room, "Nathan knew what he was up against. She's his wife." She pulled her travel case from the closet. "But with us, he needs to show his dominance and strength because he doesn't really know ours."

"Oh, I see what you mean. He's trying to scare us into giving up," Amber said, watching her sister pick up scattered articles of clothing.

"Exactly." Jade blew a tuft of hair from her eyes. "Unlike him, we have *real* power. We may not be captain in a prominent police task force, but we have our reputations, our money, our connections—and . . ." She gestured between herself and Amber.

"And we have our real powers," Amber finished with a sly smile.

"I'd say we need to work on those."

"We must exercise them!" Amber crowed.

"While I can appreciate Aunt Katherine's analogies," Jade said with a half smile, placing folded clothes in the case, "athletes don't practice in a vacuum. They have teams of people watching them and providing constant feedback." She held for a dramatic flair. "Then they adjust their performance for optimal results. We need to strategize with our powers, to push them and ourselves to new limits and gain control."

"You almost always have a plan," Amber commented. "Do you have a plan for getting the key?"

Jade nodded triumphantly. She told Amber about her plan to go to the gym in disguise so they would not be obvious on nearby footage. Once they had the key, they would find the safe that held the drive. They would need to go at night to remain undetected.

Squinting, Amber felt the lingering headache grow. She stared off into the distance, and when her attention returned, worry spread across her face.

"That plan won't work," Amber proclaimed. Jade stopped packing her toiletries and furrowed her brow. "Nathan has people following us! After they came here, he assigned three teams to follow me, you, and Al."

"My goodness, he's paranoid."

Amber shook her head. The vision had so much more to tell. She grabbed a candy bar from Jade's purse and took a bite, still overwhelmed.

"I saw us going to the gym, and we were in disguises," Amber explained. "You had a blond wig, and I looked pregnant." She shivered. "We got the key."

Jade's frown deepened.

Amber tugged on her sister's arm and explained, "Our disguises worked on the teams following us, but not Al!"

"Amber, I'm lost."

"When we go to get the key, I'm assuming we didn't tell anyone, but Al follows us, and he's followed by Nathan's people."

Jade had clearly not accounted for Al's commitment.

Amber continued to describe the scene. When Jade and Amber returned to an empty parking lot to retrieve the car they'd rented for the occasion, they were met by Al, who was shocked by their appearances. Jade's attempt to explain was interrupted by two men coming from behind Al, demanding the drive they presumed Jade had.

One man pulled a gun out and aimed it at Jade, shouting for the device. Al placed himself in front of Jade, who in turn stood in front of her sister. Their driver calmly told the men to stand down, urging them to consider the consequences of shooting.

"He kept telling them that shooting anyone there would bring more attention to Nathan, and I think it worked, 'cause the guy lowered his gun," Amber said. "But then he jerked it back up, taking a step to the side to talk to you."

The officer showing his badge informed Jade that if she didn't give him the drive, he would shoot her sister.

"You told him we didn't have it, that the gym only had a key." Fear took over as Amber spoke with quivering lips and tears in her eyes. The image was fresh in her mind, and she uselessly closed her eyes in reaction. "Jade, he shot Al!"

Jade knelt next to her sister.

"Jade, they shot him, then looked at us and said they wanted the drive," Amber tearfully said. "We can't do that plan. They'll kill Al."

"We won't, Amber," Jade assured her, flapping her hands to calm her sister. In a very un-Jade-like move, she wrapped Amber in a hug, pulling back after ten full seconds. "We aren't risking anyone's safety. We'll think of another way to get the key and drive."

Katherine's calls from down the hall drew their attention, and Amber quickly wiped her face. "We're not telling her or Mr. Porter, right?"

"Not yet," Jade confirmed, returning to her case and closing it before Katherine entered the room.

Chapter Thirty-Eight

JADE NEEDED TO KEEP Nathan away from her family. While she felt the advantage of having her power, Katherine and Mr. Porter could easily become collateral damage in Nathan's game, and she was not prepared to lose anyone else.

The night in the hotel was pleasant, yet Jade could not hide her discomfort at sleeping in a new bed. Katherine left ahead of the girls since the kindergarten center she volunteered at was a considerable distance from the private hotel. Al purchased and implemented a new security system, then searched the house for anything Nathan's men might have left behind.

Jade left Amber to her personal day; Amber had spent time with Avania late into the night and needed to rest and reflect on matters. After dressing for work in her own room, Jade left a note near the tray of treats she'd ordered for Amber with the proper heating instructions. Then she popped her head into Amber's room to check on her sister before leaving for Syndicate.

The ride was filled with remote working. The Parker sisters were planning a big change for Syndicate. After discussing a collaboration with Daniel's foundation the previous night, Jade and Amber agreed on an idea that would allow them to restructure Syndicate away from prying eyes. Syndicate would be relocating to a smaller, more economical building outside the luxurious spotlight where the company currently resided.

Jade had surveyed several locations and given Amber her top three choices while granting Amber the time to search with her own real estate agent for business properties. Wanting to avoid additional complications, Amber limited herself to the options Jade found acceptable and agreed on the infrastructure of one particular building but questioned the location and the layout.

Jade believed that settling a pharmaceutical company among logistics-based businesses would likely be viewed as an odd choice, but it was one that would allow her and Amber to rebuild Syndicate in the way that best suited them. It might also keep outsiders from prying into Syndicate's past. Jade wasn't sure of the limitations of her parents' protective spell, so better safe than sorry.

Noting that the buildings would require immediate construction, Jade arranged for interior designers to visit each location to provide an estimate and timeline. Amber requested time to think about the designs, which comforted Jade as she worried her sister would quickly comply to appease her.

Thanking Al, Jade slid out of the car with a plain box of baked goods from the hotel's bakery and the breakfast bag Katherine had ordered that morning stacked on top. She passed by her usual acquaintances, wishing them a pleasant day.

A rogue thought intruded as she waited in the lobby for the elevator. She stood with dozens of other people making their way to work. Out of all the thoughts surrounding her, one reflected malice and the desire to harm Jade.

Not recognizing anyone around her and not sensing Nathan's presence in the thought, she stepped into the elevator and tried to accept that some individuals in the world simply did not like her.

Jade returned to her own busy thoughts about the tasks ahead, mentally prioritizing them. She glanced toward her sister's dark, locked office, then greeted both her and Amber's assistants and handed them the box of desserts. Swiping her badge to unlock her office, Jade entered and switched out her comfortable shoes for the heels she kept in her closet, quickly examining her face. She'd been feeling nostalgic for the braids her mother used to make, so this morning she flaunted a stylish French braid.

Jade picked up her ringing phone and then left for Mr. Porter's office; he had a document regarding Amy that he wanted to discuss in person, promising that it would only take a moment.

Leaving the room cheerfully, Jade paused as the same thought she'd sensed before rang painfully in her mind. She stopped by her assistant's desk but saw no one. Unsure of how to perceive what her power was doing, she left to meet with Mr. Porter.

Jade felt uneasy upon her return to her office. The thoughts were louder and unmistakably near as she stepped inside, yet no one was around. Her heart pounding with every step, she froze when she heard, quite distinctly, *Ah, there she is.*

Jade decided to be smart rather than succumb to the anxiety. She immediately texted Mr. Porter, who called the building's security team and the police. She was certain someone was in her office. While at first she feared a connection to Nathan, a cursory dive into the lurking mind eased her worries on that front.

Jade was on the edge of the couch closest to the door, pretending to be idle on her phone, when Mr. Porter briskly entered her office, accompanied by three security guards. By this point, she knew exactly who the intruder was and what he was after. She gestured to her closet door, which was closed; she had not fully closed it when she switched her shoes.

The security guards thrust the door open, then leaned in to grab someone, accompanied by loud expletives.

Miles Zimmerman was yanked out with a disgruntled sneer and dragged from the room. Jade explained that he was after Mr. Porter, seeking evidence for yet another smear article founded in falsehoods and misinterpretations.

When two police officers entered the lobby to collect him, Jade and Mr. Porter met with them to explain Zimmerman's history of harassment and that they would be formally pressing charges against him for trespassing and theft.

When Zimmerman vehemently denied such an allegation, she simply gestured to the carrier he had across his chest with several papers inside.

"Mr. Zimmerman, Mr. Porter and I will see that these charges stick because what you took was in fact stolen from Syndicate." She crossed her arms and shifted her weight to one side. "But you'll find nothing of what you came for in that folder."

She smirked, loving the power that hearing his thoughts and intentions gave her over the lowly man.

"Do you really think you won?" Miles snickered. "These bogus charges will be dropped. I have my own connections."

Jade stepped closer as an officer moved aside to make a call. Mr. Porter watched Jade curiously, and she realized she felt like a completely different person.

"How's Molly?" Jade taunted with a wicked smile.

Miles gaped in stunned silence, regarding Jade as though she were the Grim Reaper.

"Come after me or my family, Mr. Porter included, and I'll make sure Molly's case is reopened," she said flatly.

With enough information to warrant a very public conversation at the police station, Jade saw in his eyes and read in his thoughts that his view of her had shifted—from little girl to dangerous enemy.

Later on, Jade informed Mr. Porter that Molly was Zimmerman's former coworker, before he shot to fame writing about the scandals of the rich and powerful. Miles convinced Molly to bait a serial rapist who murdered his victims after holding them captive. His unrealistic goal was to catch the criminal in the act and become a legendary and legitimate reporter.

Instead, Molly was abducted, held for a month, and raped throughout her captivity. Eventually the police tracked her phone to a cabin in the woods. Miles faced severe criminal charges for obstructing an ongoing investigation. The case was handled quietly as a favor to his well-connected family, but should he cross Jade's path again, Molly's case would get the attention it deserved.

Mr. Porter complimented Jade's composure. She blushed and apologized only to be told that her strength and determination were admirable qualities, and from Mr. Porter's point of view, everyone in Syndicate welcomed it. While working under the board members might have her believing that confident women were considered overbearing, Mr. Porter encouraged her to lean into becoming the leader he knew she was.

It was then that Jade stumbled upon the realization that she hadn't merely heard Miles's thoughts; surely he hadn't been thinking of Molly in that very moment. Somehow, she had searched his mind.

With a childlike grin despite the lingering pain in her head, Jade basked in the notion of expanding her power and felt hopeful about gaining control and preventing thoughts from bombarding her mind.

Amber greeted an exhausted Jade with dinner at the hotel. Knowing her sister would never eat on a bed lest crumbs scatter through the bedding, Amber pulled Jade down to sit with her on the floor, to chat before Katherine returned.

Jade laid a cloth napkin over her lap and settled the metal tray on top, lifting the lid to reveal a true classic, chicken parmesan. Eyeing the marinara sauce, Jade was cautious with her food as Amber presented Avania in front of her like a prize on display.

"So, I asked Avania something last night, and it said it could show me but that it would also knock me out since I haven't worked up my tolerance yet. This is why I needed to stay behind today. I knew I was going to be tired afterwards."

"What did you see?" Jade asked, swirling the pasta around her fork.

Exhaling, Amber closed her eyes, connecting with the book. After a few seconds, the book levitated into the air and flew open along the middle seam, the two pages melding into one golden, glowing canvas. Jade edged closer to see what Avania was about to show.

An image came into focus. Jade recognized the room from their childhood home before the fire.

Holding hands, Annalise and James entered, sliding the doors shut behind them. James crossed to close the door leading to the adjacent room, then set his eyes on his wife, clearly worried.

"Annie," he cried, going to her, "you're the strongest person I know. We're going to do this. Then Jade and Amber will be safe here."

"What if I can't, Jamie?" Annalise asked weakly. "This place barely has any magic. It took everything I had to tie the girls' powers."

"You're not alone," James gently replied, cupping her cheek. "A seventh-son wizard is here, and you're the Keeper of the Elliot witches. *We're* going to take care of this."

Annalise smiled, holding his hand against her face. After a gentle squeeze, she nodded. "Don't think we have much of a choice anyway," she said, moving her hands in a circular gesture, overlapping one another. The book appeared above her, floating like a faithful angelic lieutenant.

James grinned. "That's my girl." Kissing her forehead, he placed his hand in his pocket, whispering a few phrases. When his hand emerged, it held a stick, which expanded into a grand staff. James twirled it around, leaving a glowing trail that reflected in his gaze.

Annalise closed her eyes and called for the creature that had followed them back from Uporia. In a matter of seconds, the ground rumbled, shaking the room.

A black, pulsating cloud appeared, accompanied by a growl and two blood-red eyes.

"How dare you call me here?" it roared through no discernable mouth.

"We dare and we did," Annalise responded. "I take it you followed us back."

"An easy enough task, witch!" he snarled at her. "Especially when there was no one guarding the portal."

"You can't go back," James announced, calling the cloud's attention. "Goliath will not hurt our girls."

The dark cloud jerked as it yelled, "Watch your mouth, you foul beast."

"He would send a shapeshifter only to gain some advantage." James stated the obvious, giving Annalise time to harness the book's power to attack. "That advantage ends here."

"You fools are—"

"You know what," Annalise interrupted, "I'm sick and tired of having my life torn apart because of him. He killed my daughters, my family, you little parasite." The book above Annalise shook as it glimmered along its edges, the glow intensifying until the book was a blinding ball of light. "He will not get my girls."

The cloud began to scream in agony, steam emanating from within, though no flames were seen. James whipped his staff to create a vortex that immobilized the beast. Holding his staff tighter, he looked toward Annalise, who had her eyes shut, focused on her power as the Keeper channeled her family's magic.

The dark void lowered to the ground, screaming to Goliath, "Oh, master! I vowed never to use this weapon, but now I must, for they are too powerful."

James darted to Annalise as she grunted forcefully. The black cloud shrieked, followed by a roaring explosion that blew the walls apart and engulfed the room in flames.

Jade's heart broke watching the fading image of the house burning. The pages dimmed and the book closed, returning to its former position in Amber's hands.

She had no words.

"Yeah, that was me this morning," Amber said, placing Avania to the side. "I guess we were right. They were killed, but not for their money." She rose and fell back on the bed. "Apparently, by a shapeshifter that works for Goliath."

"This changes nothing about the fact that they're gone." Jade stared down at her food without the slightest desire to consume it. "It changes nothing, but it changes everything."

Chapter Thirty-Nine

"Aunt Katherine, what do you know about shapeshifters?" Amber asked, stretching as Katherine plated breakfast. The previous night had ended in a consensus to prioritize obtaining the drive, but Amber was still curious about the creature.

Katherine hummed. "Well, if you mean similar to animal shifters, let me tell you werewolves and vampires are beings of this world, so I truly wouldn't have an answer for that."

"Animal shifters?!" Amber demanded.

"Yes, but again, they are not like the images depicted in stories here."

"And shapeshifters?"

Katherine sighed. "They're rare and very few, but I've heard they can change to any form they please."

"Are they dangerous?" Amber asked.

"Their power is their ability to shift," Katherine remarked. "What they do with that power is subjective and personal, much like you and Jade, I would assume."

Katherine and Amber wandered onto the balcony, and the older woman glanced over with an arched brow. "Is there—"

A shrill scream erupted from Jade's room. Amber hurtled toward her sister with Katherine only steps behind her, throwing the door open to reveal Jade sitting up in bed with tearful eyes, staring straight in front of her.

Amber called to her sister but received no response. She slowly approached, noting Jade's extreme focus and heaving breaths.

Jade pulled her arm away when Amber reached out, tugging the covers over her. Wanting to comfort her, Katherine approached the other side of the bed, whispering Jade's name.

"Jade, what's wrong?" Amber begged.

"I've seen her react like this before," Katherine murmured, "but I have never been able to help her."

"What?"

"I think this is another episode from the memory of Amelia's death," Katherine somberly said, studying Jade's terrified expression. "This is why your mother tied your powers to the stones, because these episodes were becoming too much to handle."

"Jade," Amber called louder than before, "you're safe. Whatever you saw isn't here. Jade!"

The lack of reaction alarmed Amber, who turned to Katherine.

"How did Mom stop these episodes before?"

Katherine helplessly shrugged. "I wasn't around. I think she sang a song or a lullaby."

"Fine," Amber huffed, jumping to her feet and rushing out to return seconds later with Avania. "I have Avania, Jade. I'm gonna see what Mom did and try to do it too, okay?"

"Amber, keep speaking to her!" Katherine encouraged. "Her eyes shifted when you spoke."

"I'm right here, Jade, and I'm gonna help you."

Amber had already connected to the book but shifted focus when Jade broke her sightless stare to look at her. Her breathing was erratic, and sweat dripped from her forehead as she looked deeply into Amber's eyes, folding her lips over each other, fighting the mental strain.

"Let's breathe together," Amber said tremulously. "In, one, two, three. Out, one, two, three. Long abdominal breaths, just like you showed me."

Encouraging her sister by breathing along, Amber was relieved when Jade joined her after a few inhales. Roughly five minutes passed. Then Jade looked around the room, her breath still shallow.

"Jade, what happened?" Amber asked again.

"The dream . . ."

"The one with that black thing and the little girls?"

"It was so much worse, Amber. It felt real, like I wasn't dreaming. I had nowhere to go."

Jade spoke weakly, plucking at the covers. Finally catching her breath, she told her sister and aunt about the event that had completely taken over her senses, paralyzing her with terror.

Jade was playing with Amelia, chasing her, when the rustling of the trees behind them interrupted their merriment. Amelia thought it was an animal and hushed her sister, calling her to the side of the pond.

A towering, cloaked figure appeared, hooded and hovering in the air with no discernable feet under him. He cackled maniacally as he drifted closer to the girls.

That was when Amelia pushed Jade to run.

Jade, two and a half years old, stood and ran a few paces before the creature hurled a rock at her, tripping her and leaving her frozen in fear at the sight of him descending upon her sister. She stood back up with a scream. "Amelia!"

Amelia, terrified, yelled again, telling Jade to get their mother. The older girl threw her arm out toward the grand house behind them, and vines thrust up from the grass beneath Jade, pushing her to run. But the giant figure's evil shriek petrified her, and she tumbled to the ground once again as a swarm of rocks ripped the vines apart.

When Jade looked up again, the dark figure was looming over the pond. She dimly heard water splashing. She called out to her sister but was immediately confronted by bright, glowing green eyes from the black abyss of the hooded face, staring right at her.

Then the splashing stopped.

The beast crept toward Jade, leaving Amelia draped over the little stone wall, her head still submerged in the water. As the flowers and vines around her body withered, a loud, furious scream erupted behind Jade. She did not move, and the black being retreated toward the greenery from which it had emerged.

James desperately pulled Amelia from the water, sobbing while her mother screamed again. Annalise moved her hands in a circle over her protruding abdomen. Avania appeared, floating alongside her, and Annalise glared at the beast that had murdered her child with the full force of her Keeper power. The hovering figure screamed in agony, exploding in the air and leaving no evidence of its existence.

Jade's parents carried Amelia's body away as Jade stood alone, still unable to move. Beside her, the cloaked figure reappeared, sending Jade scrambling away and calling for help.

"No one can hear you, little girl." The dark void of a face turned toward her, the bright-green eyes regarding Jade with eerie fondness. "I hope you don't mind. I'm admiring my work."

"It's only a dream," Jade whispered, attempting to convince herself. She had an odd, overlapping sensation of being both woman and girl.

A laugh echoed through the vacant forest.

"A dream? Oh, little girl, this is more than a dream. So much more!"

Jade, still silent, peered around her, trying to gain a grip over her mind.

"Oh, this is a sight." The figure drifted lower. "It's nice to see that my plan worked."

Jade stared into the faceless hood, unable to look away, her eyes filling with tears and her forehead dripping.

Finally, her defense mechanisms triggered. She recalled a tactic she'd learned as a child, from her father: when she felt overwhelmed by fear, she could seek comfort in facts.

"Little girl?" Jade said, showing all the courage she had, as infinitesimal as it was. "I think you're mistaken."

"There is not a mistake," he chuckled. "Why are you not crumbling in fear?"

"Because I'm *not* a little girl. Who are you?" Jade demanded.

"I'm the one who killed your sister," he bellowed with joy.

Reminded of Amelia, Jade briefly succumbed to her anguish and trembled.

"Are you Goliath?"

The thing seemed startled. "You know of Goliath. You aren't a child."

"I told you I wasn't. Are you Goliath?" she repeated, bolstered by the creature's uncertainty.

"You are not worthy to be in the presence of Goliath."

"So that would be a no."

"Goliath's focus lies in great matters far beyond your paltry clan of conjurers."

"Nothing is worth killing children," she snapped at him.

"Children?" the faceless figure shrieked. "Those are the spawn of the undeserving! Call them children if you like. It softens the hard reality of what you are."

"And what am I?" she demanded.

"The unholy product of a union of two species."

"Goliath has been targeting the Elliot family since before I was born," she pointed out.

"That's not my concern. I have no issues with the sixth-daughter clan," he announced.

"Then *why* did you kill my sister?!" Jade shouted.

"She is the product of something that cannot be. My job is to illuminate them."

"That's a ridiculous justification for murder," she exhaled. "You would only fear someone with more power than you."

"You imbecile," he cackled. "I have been tasked by the Goliath for one job and one job only: to destroy the offspring of the witch and wizard."

With her voice breaking, Jade stammered, "You and your not-so-great Goliath—"

"Mind your tongue, witch. Your power is not what you think it is," he hollered,

"It's enough to scare you into trying to kill me when I was a defenseless child."

He unleashed a victorious laugh. "Was? So, you have grown and escaped Goliath."

Jade, slowly folding beneath the weight of her anxiety, said nothing.

"Oh, you're such a witch, thinking you know everything."

"I won't deny my fear, but I won't let it consume me either," Jade stated more to herself than to him.

"But it already has, hasn't it?" he taunted.

Jade grew weak in the knees.

He bellowed again, "Ah, this gives me great joy. You will *never* escape the fear of me."

"Wha—"

"Why do you think Goliath sent me to kill you and your sister?"

Jade shook her head.

"I have *never* failed," he bragged. "I have a reputation for finishing my job without fault or fail, and he hired me to rid the world of the last of the Keeper's daughters." He laughed again. "When your family came, I knew I couldn't kill you. But I had one last task to complete."

Jade fell to the ground again, throwing her arms over her head as he rose.

"You fool! I seared into your mind the fear you felt the moment I attacked." His glare intensified. "Remember my parting gift. You can never outgrow or escape your mind, and thus, you will never outgrow or escape your fear of me!"

The figure had grown in size and now towered over Jade. All she could do was curl up and hide her head in her chest, paralyzed once again with anxiety, anguish, torment, and fear.

Katherine sighed when Jade revealed the true extent of the horror inflicted on her.

"Jade," she whispered to gently draw her attention, "the memory you're describing may not be accurate, considering how young you were."

"What do you mean?" Amber asked.

"What I mean is that this figure—this hovering, faceless, dark, hooded figure—may not be what actually attacked your sister but is rather a visualization based on what your younger self felt when he attacked."

"Aunt Katherine, dumb it down for me. What does this dream signify?" Jade demanded.

"I would say there's some good news and bad news," Katherine replied, rocking slightly on the bed. "The bad news is that this creature probably was not as terrifying as you're seeing in your dreams. It's your mind extrapolating."

"How is that bad?" Amber inquired as she leaned closer to Jade, still keeping some distance.

"Because this means that this . . . Let's call him a man to make it less intimidating. This man most likely knew he would not survive. Since he couldn't kill you, he made it impossible for you to be as powerful as he assumed you could become."

Jade shook her head, fidgeting with a tassel of the blanket wrapping her. "How? I'm beyond confused and still frazzled."

"Okay, okay. Now, remember I'm only guessing," Katherine warned, "but I think he 'seared' into you the fear you felt back then to hold you back. He must have known that your powers are connected to how you feel—on an instinctual level, of course. By keeping you in a constant state of fear, he ensured you wouldn't develop your powers."

"That sounds far-fetched," Amber interjected, though she was immediately struck by the fact that their entire lives had become far-fetched.

"I would agree, except for the tiny little fact that he said as much in Jade's dream, and it worked!" their maternal aunt announced.

Jade and Amber stared at Katherine.

"Even when we came here, those dreams would send you into a frenzy for the entire day. You weren't even actively using your power. It's terrible, awful, but it *worked*."

"Until Mom removed it?" Jade said, slowly lowering the blanket.

"Yes. Your powers—for both of you, that is—were not helpful at the time, and muting the memory was an added bonus. It just goes to show you, there is always a way."

"Even if that way means postponing the inevitable and letting the fear grow beyond my control, without me knowing about it so I have no way to cope or handle it?" Jade spat.

"Was it a perfect solution? No. Was it the only viable one at the time? Yes," Katherine stated.

"That's harsh. Whatever this guy did, it's seriously affecting Jade," Amber said.

"I don't mean to take away from how you feel," the older woman replied, patting the blanket in front of Jade, still careful not to touch her. "I'm simply saying that we needed to solve that problem, and this was the only way to do it at the time, and it wasn't easy. There is little magic in this world, so it took a lot for your parents to push down the memory with your powers."

"Forgive me for not feeling so grateful right now. I can still see that thing hovering over me," Jade grumbled.

"Which brings me to the good news," Katherine announced with a smile.

"We definitely need it," Amber replied.

"Jade, you're able to know what that 'man' intended!"

"Please don't take this the wrong way, but you're *way* too happy," Jade snapped. "It doesn't matter if we are these crazy strong witches in Uporia. We don't live there, so it doesn't matter."

Katherine cleared her throat. "Apologies. I'll try to tone it down. But, Jade, I don't think you understand what this actually means!"

"Like Jade said, dumb it down for us, Aunt Katherine. We missed a few days at witch school," Amber teased, trying to lighten the mood.

"Alright." Katherine rubbed her hands together. "This man was somehow able to imprint fear in your mind, right? Now *I* know that this 'man' did not survive; your mother killed him. I saw the body. But, Jade, you were always so sure he talked to you after Annalise threw him back into the forest. Your parents knew this couldn't be true, but we didn't feel it was the right time to break this down, with you being so scared."

Jade and Amber nodded.

"Whether it was his own power or not, he used mind control on a witch who has mind power as well."

The sisters nodded again, gesturing for her to continue.

"I think this dream or memory means that while he was 'imprinting,' Jade went into his mind and learned what his plans were." The cheerfulness seeped back through. "You did to him what he did to you, to some extent, when you were a mere toddler! This means you're stronger than anyone ever expected."

"Jade? Are you okay?" Amber asked, easing closer to her sister.

"*I* imprinted on him," Jade whispered. "I imprinted on him when he was imprinting on me?" She stared off into the distance.

"My goodness, I regret using that word," Katherine chuckled.

Amber sighed. "Yeah, we got that, Jade. She's a little too eager about that part too, if you ask me."

"I beg your pardon, young ladies!" Katherine scoffed.

Jade exclaimed, "If you're right, that means I knew his thoughts, but the trauma twisted events in my memory to make me think we had a conversation."

Amber stared at Jade with amazement.

"Does that make sense or am I losing it?" Jade asked, desperately seeking confirmation. "That means I *can* control it, right? If it's my power that took in this information, and this conversation I'm remembering is just my brain piecing together the information, then I think I may be able to control the memory."

Jade let out a breath.

"If I can separate the fear of what happened to Amelia from what I learned from that thing's mind, I think I can."

A smile spread uncontrolled across Katherine's face. "And this is why I am excited about your powers," she exclaimed. "Jade, this is an excellent deduction, and above all, you're actively choosing to not be victimized by this event that happened so many years ago. I can't help feeling proud."

"I'll feel proud when I can do it."

Chapter Forty

Jade and Amber covertly made their way to Syndicate, discussing the drive and the messy business of retrieving it before Nathan. Jade wanted to ask Mr. Hough to get it; he had helped Amy get settled under an alias and would be able to wheedle out the safe's location after safely retrieving the key. Amber had no objection, provided Mr. Hough was told of the risks and was given the option to decline, citing her vision of Al. Jade agreed.

Before leaving Amber's office, Jade reminded her of an appointment with the contractors that afternoon. The decision to move Syndicate commenced with Amber in the loop but Jade taking point. Jade set to work completing her short list of tasks before her appointment as Amber took over restructuring Syndicate's employees and departments, promising no layoffs and a simple adjustment.

Walking back from HR, Amber held a copy of the announcement that Syndicate would be implementing various changes in the very near future. She glanced down the hall before entering her office and saw her sister on the phone, pointing to her computer.

Amber felt the pounding headache of a vision begin, an image playing out in her mind, and barely made it into her office, shutting the door for privacy.

An anxious Jade paced beside a small stage covered with brightly colored banners that announced an award to Syndicate for its dedication to charitable funds made in James and Annalise's name. As she nibbled on her fingers, Daniel approached from behind a curtain. He asked where she had been. She snapped that she was waiting, hoping that Amber would make a last-minute appearance since she'd agreed months in advance to take over the acceptance speech.

Jade frantically explained that she had been focused on her assignments. She pulled out her phone, tapping it aggressively and ignoring Daniel's attempts to calm her nerves.

"I can't go up there, Daniel!" she shouted, throwing her phone on a nearby table. "I can't go up there and take this award in my parents' name without formally addressing, well, everyone involved! I already have the board waiting for me to mess up, especially with graduation right around the corner—"

"I'll do it," Daniel offered.

"What?" Jade said, peeking at the door behind him.

"I've given tons of speeches like this. I won't be as formal, but I'll get by and say that although you're here to wave and smile, you, oh, you have laryngitis and can't speak."

Shifting her attention to Daniel from the closed door, Jade blinked, stupefied.

"No, I can't ask you to do that."

"You didn't," Daniel said with a charming smile. "I offered, but I won't go over there and try to scramble something together without your blessing."

Jade released a breath of relief, her shoulders relaxing. The gaze she directed his way was filled with warmth and gratitude.

"I would really appreciate that, Daniel."

"And I would be honored," he said, grabbing a pen from his inner jacket pocket, then making a joke about his navy tie before scribbling down some words on several napkins. Jade jotted down some ideas of her own, then returned her focus to the door.

Guilt overcame Amber as she reached for the snack-sized bars on the coffee table. Her regrets for abandoning Jade were now compounded by the revelation of moments Jade herself would probably never share.

Amber could see what Jade meant about invading people's privacy. She was left riddled with remorse at Jade being on the receiving end of such an intrusion.

Then she felt another vision headache spreading. Upon spotting her sister's face alongside the podium where Daniel stood, she stopped the image, forcing her power to respect Jade's private pain.

When she opened her eyes, she grinned, proud of herself for actively stopping a vision. If only she could actively start them.

She returned to her desk as she recalled her sister's words about using their powers strategically to gain control over them, as well as Katherine's description of their powers being triggered by instinct. Accepting that her power could be tamed and controlled, Amber felt her confidence grow.

After placing a much-deserved order from the café below, Amber got to work poring through the documents delineating the restructured departments and the best employees for each one.

∽∾

The buzz of her phone's alarm caught Jade's attention as she looked away from her screen. The concept of time had escaped her as she went over the renovations the new offices would need. Since the building had remained vacant for over a year, it needed repairs in addition to any aesthetic changes before Syndicate moved in.

She locked her computer screen, packing away a folder with her notes on each of the contractors she'd hired. Humming, she switched out her heels for comfortable shoes.

She texted Al to confirm her appointment and locked her office door. Amber's blinds were drawn down, a clear sign of desired seclusion. Jade paused by the corner of her office to place her keys in her purse.

The ear-piercing pain of her power led to the thoughts of a very familiar somebody.

Aunt Katherine said shapeshifters were rare, but the one that killed Mom and Dad worked for Goliath. She said they could change into anyone or anything. Was that how he was able to gain so much power? By tricking people?

Jade tried to cut off Amber's thoughts, but the heat between her ears would not dissipate.

Oh, Oscar. I forgot about dinner. Dang it, okay, okay. "Of course I didn't forget. Meet you tonight."

Jade dropped her bag, holding her head and pouring her energy into blocking out Amber's voice. She had no intention of ferreting out what those close to her did not wish to share themselves. After a stifled grunt, all that remained was the painful ringing in her ears.

She exhaled in relief, feeling one step closer to controlling her power and apologizing to Amber's assistants, who had run to her, radiating concern. Brushing it off as a migraine, Jade knocked on Amber's door to tell her she was leaving and coming back later to pick Amber up.

As Jade pressed the elevator button, she resolved to continue actively practicing her new skill. She replied to Mr. Hough after she stepped onto the elevator, and he agreed to retrieve the key—taking every precaution to protect himself and his family from Nathan. He also agreed to confront Amy about the safe and attempt to collect the drive everyone was so determined to acquire.

Jade smiled at Al when he took her bags, then opened the door for her to enter and embark on the next step in Syndicate's journey.

Chapter Forty-One

DINNER HAD ALWAYS BEEN the time of day the girls most enjoyed because they could decompress with Katherine and get her perspective on matters of the day. After Al had cleared their return to the house, they entered the kitchen to find Katherine drinking tea and reading a book and dinner awaiting their arrival.

As they ate, Jade discussed her meeting with the contractors, sharing how grateful she was that her power had been helpful in selecting the one that did not seek to cause more damage than necessary for a bigger paycheck. Katherine, as expected, was thrilled to see Jade advance in her skill. She also rejoiced in Amber's using the book to build her tolerance.

A turn in the conversation allowed Katherine to explain another aspect of being the Keeper. When any Elliot witch died, her power, whether it was one she was born with or one she had gained, reverted to the book. When the Keeper gained enough skill with the book, she could connect to her deceased relatives' power through the book.

This came at considerable cost, but Jade was in awe at the potential Amber had at her disposal, eager to know when Amber would be ready for such a thing.

"Oh, girls," Katherine chuckled, sipping her tea. "Remember, it takes power to use power, so there's work ahead of you, Amber. Also, our family must always be mindful that our power comes from a place of pain. The very first Elliot witch was alone in the world; she was ambushed and cursed. It was painful to have her ability to protect her family tethered to a piece of paper, but she saw beyond that," she said.

"In an ironic twist of events, her pain made the book powerful. Our family's power comes *from* pain, but it also grows *with* pain." Katherine placed her fork down as she finished her roasted vegetables. "Your mother losing her daughters in the way she did gave her the power to use the book in ways our mother never did."

"What is the book's actual power, Aunt Katherine?" Jade asked, leaning over her plate. "You said Amber controls it, but what does it do?"

"Amber doesn't really control it," Katherine corrected. "The book holds the culmination of the power of all Elliot witches past. Amber has the ability to access and wield that." She dropped her gaze. "I've never heard a true explanation of the book's power other than that it does what the Keeper wants at a magnitude she never could have imagined," Katherine sighed, looking back to her nieces, "paying the price of that power soon after with extreme fatigue and pain."

"That is awesome!" Jade gasped, glancing at Amber, who was silent.

Amber nodded slowly. "I only connect to it to show me things, and that's incredibly intoxicating. If I didn't get tired, I wouldn't stop. But that's all I can manage for now."

The trio cleared the table before Katherine left them to themselves.

Amber primarily discussed the new office space, along with how she'd divided the departments to make the space functional for various research collaborations, allowing for further infrastructure to be rebuilt.

Then she mentioned her assistant Purple. "She was walking around like I'm some predator about to pounce," Amber vented. "I know I need to establish a sense of authority and all that, but my goodness, she shook like a leaf on a windy day!"

Amber placed the last of the dishes in the dishwasher. "Maybe Mr. Reynolds got to her, but Green and Blue aren't that way, so guess what?" she asked rhetorically as her sister wiped the counter.

"After a series of headaches, I found out that she never wanted to be my assistant! In fact, her background is in social work, but she was pressured to take the position. Spoiler alert, it was Reynolds."

Placing the cloth she'd used in the appropriate bin, she continued to speak, then circled the island to approach her unusually silent sister.

"Turns out, her mom's sick, and she needs help with the medical expenses, so she couldn't leave even though she hates it. Don't worry," Amber chuckled. "I assigned her to a new department after the move. She's going to work with Daniel's foundation."

Amber abruptly paused, having come full circle to find her sister frozen, staring off into space. As she called out to Jade to no avail, the pressure built for her to act. She recalled her mother summoning Avania, but Amber could only connect to the book where it lay safely ensconced in her room. She had no clue how her mother had called it.

She resorted to shouting for her aunt. Katherine rushed in at her niece's frightened cries, then hurried off again to find Avania.

"Jade, it's okay. Ugh, if I could just make a vision appear that—"

Suddenly, the pain around her crown peaked, and an image developed in her mind.

Amber saw a garden; she recognized it from before her parents' death. Annalise was holding a young Jade, approximately six years old. Jade had been crying, wiping her wet cheeks and red, puffy eyes.

"Why does that dream keep coming back?" Jade begged while Annalise rocked her limp child in her arms. The image began to fade before further details unraveled, leaving Amber dazed and shocked at calling a vision but frustrated at its uselessness.

With no idea of what else to do, Amber reached out to her petrified sister and touched her arm.

A crippling torment overcame her in an instant. She screamed and only regained awareness when Katherine pulled her away from Jade.

"What was that?!" Amber shouted, tears flooding her eyes.

A forced breath escaped Jade's lips, and she curled over the counter, then crawled to the floor, crouching in agony, her head buried.

"Amber," Katherine called out, drawing her attention.

"I think I saw what she sees," Amber exclaimed. "I think I felt what she feels!" She turned to her aunt with wide, fear-stricken eyes. "How can she feel that and be so calm?"

Shushing Amber, Katherine stroked her hair as she offered her a hug, explaining that everyone reacted to fear differently.

"No." Amber pulled back. "You don't understand. That wasn't fear; that wasn't fight or flight. That was—"

"Like you're stuck in a vortex of terrifying emotions, fear, terror, and horror, all worse than the next, but you have nowhere to go, no tricks to snap you out of it, no safety net, nothing," Jade mumbled from the floor.

Katherine gradually helped her up, then walked the sisters to the sunroom.

"Jade, that thing . . . it was awful." Amber gulped. "How it held Amelia underwater while she fought to live, you hitting him to break her free."

"I didn't hit him."

"Um, yeah, you did. After she told you to run home and nudged you with those vines—were they vines? He grabbed her hair and held her underwater, and you ran to her and hit him, screaming to let her go."

"That's not what happened," Jade quietly said, looking away.

"Yes it did," Amber insisted. "I can't believe you were only two and trying to save her from that thing. Then you held your ears like—"

"Like you were using your power," Katherine interrupted, looking thoughtful. "Jade, when you were that little, whenever you used your power, the pain was always too much, so you held your ears."

"You used your power to try to save Amelia," Amber somberly concluded.

Katherine nodded. "In Uporia, every Elliot witch was always on guard. Even powerless me had to be strong. The girls took on that trait early in life."

"Well, that's just messed up," Amber complained.

"Can you two stop?" Jade shouted. "Just stop!"

Amber and Katherine said nothing, waiting for Jade to continue.

Still out of breath, she hissed, "I don't know what you're talking about, but that's *not* what I see. I didn't fight or hit him after Amelia told me to run for help." She glared at Katherine. "I didn't grab my ears or use my power." With her attention not fixed on either one, she continued, "I just sat there, I watched him kill her, then Mom came and killed him."

"How can we see two different things?" Amber pondered.

"As we discussed, I believe what Jade sees is her perspective of the event, seared into her with the fear," Katherine said.

"That wasn't fear," Amber retorted. "Fear is seeing a snake in the garden when you thought it was a hose." She shivered at the memory. "That, what I saw and felt, that's cruel."

Jade looked away from her family in deep thought.

"Wait, that's it!" she suddenly exclaimed.

"Um, care to share with the rest of the class?" Amber teased, glad to see liveliness return to her sister.

"I think I know how to stop this fear from taking over."

"How?" Katherine asked.

"Avania!" Jade rejoiced, all signs of her fear erased. "Amber, you can use Avania to show me exactly what happened, so I know what is real and what that thing put into my mind."

"How will that stop the fear?" Katherine inquired.

"I'm not sure," Jade responded, checking her phone to see if Mr. Porter had arrived for their first night with the new security system. "Amber, would you be willing to do that?"

"Of course," Amber agreed, hoping neither of them would ever again feel as she did when she held Jade.

Katherine excused herself to let the last member of their broken family in, handing Avania back to Amber. Jade leaned on her sister as Amber connected to the book, eager to find the missing piece to her curse.

☙❧

"Are you sure you aren't too tired?" Jade asked.

"Not yet. I will be after, but you *need* to know this, Jade."

"It doesn't feel worth it to have you zonked out just because I need to see this. I don't even know what will happen."

"Hey," Amber said, squeezing her sister's hand, "*you* are worth it, okay? I don't know who has you thinking you're a burden. You're not."

Jade smiled at Amber, wiping a tear away before it fell.

"So, we are looking for what happened to Amelia. Not what you think you saw, or what crazy villains imprinted in your mind. The objective, whole truth."

Jade nodded, curling her lower lip inward as anxiety filled her.

Avania flew from Amber's hands and hovered in the space in front of Jade. Amber's eyes were shut, but the tension around them began to ease. Avania whipped open to the middle of the book, lowering and creating the luminous blank canvas once again.

The splotches of dark colors quickly formed into an expansive stone mansion surrounded by forest.

As the scene of the pond behind the house came into focus, Jade pulled closer to see her younger self running joyfully after Amelia. The girls looked truly happy, far more beautiful and happy than in her dreams.

"Remember, Jade," Amelia warned, "Mama said not to go by the water. I can't pull you out if you fall in."

Jade's eyes swelled with tears at seeing herself as a little sister. Amelia held young Jade's hand and hugged her, taking a blue rose she'd grown from the ground and placing it behind Jade's ear. Jade giggled, and they went back to chasing each other.

Jade did not want this scene to end. She did not want that little girl, the girl she once was, to grow up. She did not want to see what would come from the trees behind them. She wanted to stay young, happy, innocent—a younger sister with an older sister who grew flowers in unusual colors. But Jade was an Elliot witch, and despite all the wonder that came with that name, pain was stitched into every atom.

The dark cloak appeared gradually from the forest as it always did in her dreams. It towered over the children, who stood frozen in fear, fluorescent-green eyes glowing at them. Amelia moved first. She pushed Jade forward, telling her to run and not stop.

As tiny Jade stumbled away, the cloaked figure shrieked, shooting a black orb in her direction. Jade smacked face-first into the ground, rolling quickly to see the creature grab Amelia's throat.

"Leah, no!" Jade's high-pitched yelp drew his gaze back to her.

Amelia raised her hand and touched the stone wall of the pond behind her. She dug her hands into the stone, cupping a few pieces of grass. Thin, long, dark-green vines grew from the ground beneath Jade, helping her to her feet.

"Run, Jade! Get Mama!"

Jade turned to run, pulling free from the helpful vines. Again a shriek echoed all around, and another dark orb flew in Jade's direction, ripping the vines to shreds.

Jade rolled to the ground, her body covered in dirt, and scrambled to all fours in time to see the cloaked creature plunge Amelia under the water. Like a soldier trained for battle, Jade sprang to her feet and ran to the figure without hesitation, yelling at him to leave her sister alone.

She struck with her tiny hands, swinging them at the rippling cloak. Her determined expression disappeared when she encountered nothing tangible.

As the monster stared down at her with fiery eyes, Jade collapsed at his nonexistent feet, holding her ears and whimpering.

No water splashed from where Amelia hung; she was still. Still holding her ears, Jade opened her eyes to see the vines wither around her sister's body. The vibrant blue rose, which had fallen beside her, wilted away to rotten brown mush.

The low cackle came closer to Jade but suddenly twisted into a yelp. With Jade still on the ground, holding her ears, the black cloaked figure was hurled through the air and landed splayed across the trunk of a wide tree. James ran to Jade, laying his wooden staff on the ground. Taking a second to make sure she was not hurt, he then shifted and pulled Amelia out of the pond.

The figure returned, and Annalise stood defiantly in its path, her fury at the sight of her murdered daughter translating to instant action. She moved her hands in a circular motion. The book appeared above her, floating in the air with a bright glow.

"You barbarian!" Annalise yelled, the glow intensifying.

"Elliot Keeper, you know I hold no ill will against your clan," the figure said flatly, floating closer. "I am acting on contract."

"Children are spared from contracts," James sneered, hauling Jade into his arms.

"Hear this, you abomina—"

"No," Annalise roared. "No more listening, no more reasoning, no more. She was barely . . ." She wiped the tears and briefly settled a hand on her round, protruding stomach. "You tell Goliath—no. Better yet, I'll tell him when I deal with him myself." Annalise squeezed her eyes shut, the book shining like a raging flame above her.

The cloaked figure screamed in agony as light streamed through rapidly appearing cracks in its form. Annalise sank to her knees under the effort. The assassin's agonized cry grew until nothing but silence remained. Amid that utter quiet, Katherine caught up to the group, out of breath.

"So, it has a body," Annalise said with an empty voice, observing the pile of bones and char before her. Katherine ran to her limp sister and helped her up. In somber misery, everyone drifted back to the mansion, Jade hanging over James's shoulder, whimpering at the sight of Amelia's lifeless body cradled in his other arm.

The color and focus of the vivid scene slowly disappeared, and the glowing pages dimmed, closing as the book floated down to Amber.

"Jade, I . . . I'm so sorry," Amber said softly.

"Was that what you saw?" Jade asked, allowing her tears to fall at last.

"Some of it. Avania only shows objective things. I think I originally saw it from your side. I don't think I'm supposed to be able to, but when you were in that state . . ." Amber shrugged.

"Aunt Katherine was right," Jade said, feeling strangely calm. "It tried to use some sort of mind power on me, but I used it back. What I see in the dream is my own interpretation of the whole thing, from that young age."

"Jade, how does this help?" Amber asked, getting closer. "I'll be honest, I thought we were going to see something that wasn't as bad. Something that would help you. That was so much worse."

"It does help," Jade replied. "Maybe not much, but now I know what's real and what isn't."

Amber seemed to break out of a daze, shaking her head. "I can't believe that was Mom!"

Jade gave a half smile.

"Like, she killed that thing with the book. That's not the Mom we knew."

"If Elliot witches grow with pain, Mom must have been in agony."

Jade didn't know what else to say at that moment, and the sisters spent the night in her room.

Chapter Forty-Two

"How was Jade after last night?" Jade overheard Katherine ask Mr. Porter.

"I can tell you she seems like her normal self this morning," he replied.

"You're such a lawyer," Katherine laughed.

Jade sang good morning as she entered the kitchen, then told Katherine that Amber was recovering after their evening with Avania.

Jade headed off to work, with Mr. Porter following. Al, ever the gentleman, was prepared with an umbrella, keeping pace with her until she reached the car door; peaceful spring showers were expected throughout the day. She waved to Mr. Porter as they drove off with him close behind.

Jade tugged at her ear and realized two cars were tailing them as they left the neighborhood. Eavesdropping on their thoughts, she learned that the first car was the team Nathan had tasked to follow Al. She assumed the others had been assigned to her.

While alarmed by how closely these men were following her, she delighted in her ability to know what they were thinking, even while in a moving vehicle beside her. She scoffed at their demeaning thoughts toward her and her sister but expected nothing less from men who willingly followed Nathan's command. She learned that these men had no information about the whole operation but that Nathan had a pull over them, making them loyal minions.

Al used the garage entrance, informing Jade that he too noticed the cars following along. He urged Jade to be wary. As she marched the few steps from the car to the building and then to the elevator that would take her to the lobby, she tried to ignore the stares from the men parked nearby. Knowing the drive was her only advantage against Nathan, she discreetly texted Mr. Hough, eager for an update as she had much to attend to that morning.

Passing her sister's dark office, Jade continued down the small hall and greeted one of her own assistants. She was shocked when the assistant announced that a gentleman was waiting to talk to her; he had not given his name.

This man had apparently stepped into the restroom down the hall to freshen up. Her assistant referred to him as charismatic and confident. Alarmed, Jade entered her office promptly to prepare for any scenario.

She switched out her shoes and closed the blinds but left the door open as she checked her makeup for smudges and let down her hair, which had flattened where she leaned against the car seat. Before Jade could pull her hair back with a clip from the basket under her desk, she heard the bathroom occupier's thoughts. Unlike with her friends and family, she did not fend them off.

She turned as the man exited the restroom and beelined for her office, his mind occupied with self-admiration. Peeking through the blinds, she studied his stride. She observed how he flashed a side smile at everyone he passed. She marveled at how people were seemingly unaware that it was all a facade.

She took in his exaggerated confidence and exercised her budding powers to dive beneath the surface. Although Nathan emanated arrogance, he was in fact terrified.

Jade felt at ease but kept it hidden. She had the upper hand mentally if not physically. She remained still, her eyes focused on him, deliberately holding back a reaction as he entered her office.

If Nathan was audacious enough to drop by her place of business after everything that had been disclosed, then perhaps Jade needed to respond in kind.

Closing the door behind him, Nathan turned to Jade and simply stood with a smirk, attempting to rattle her. She maintained eye contact and thought back to the previous night with Amber and Avania, homing in on who she was: a witch—an Elliot witch and half-wizard hybrid from another world. She belonged to a family so powerful that they had been hunted down as defenseless children.

An Elliot witch, as Katherine had said, was not to be taken lightly. She fixated on her mind-blowing power—a power she had used instinctively as a toddler. A power that gave her the ability to know everything she ever wanted to know about anyone in any given moment. A power that Nathan was *powerless* against.

He stood a few feet from her desk, resting his hands in his pockets.

"Surprised to see me?"

Keeping her emotions in check, Jade sat behind her desk and signed in to her desktop computer, closing her laptop. She did not offer him a seat.

"Surprised isn't the word I would use, Mr. Carlisle." She smiled pleasantly. "Nauseated would probably be a better fit."

"I have that effect on people," he snickered. "The anxiety they feel when dealing with me causes all sorts of tummy aches."

"I wouldn't go about calling myself intimidating, then using the words 'tummy ache,' Mr. Carlisle," Jade said, her tone wry.

"Whatever you say, little Miss Jade. I'm not the one who's sick to my stomach."

"How's your wife?" she sassed.

"Enjoyin' her time, while she still can."

"Oh, I bet she is. Never wanting to be around you is something we share."

"I thought a girl like you would appreciate a direct approach." He dropped into a chair uninvited. "So, I came here to, well, be direct."

"If direct is what you want, then directly leave."

"Where is the drive?" he demanded.

"Not with you."

"Don't make this harder than it needs to be. Amy made a mistake copying those files. She has no idea what she's done, and I *want* it back."

Internally, Jade rejoiced. Nathan was panicking, and she read every thought attached to that feeling.

"Considering the fact that you are in my office begging, I think the only person having a hard time is you."

"This is a polite gesture, a peace offering for your ignorance. Give me the drive."

"This is a rude gesture. No."

"Jade, I have the power to hurt you, your family, your friends," he said as he leaned forward from the edge of his seat, his dark-brown eyes filled with irritation. "Don't lose face by pissing me off and begging me to stop."

"Oh, I think I struck a nerve," Jade taunted as she pulled on her ear. Nathan was not explicitly thinking about what was on the drive, but Jade filtered through the surface, searching his mind slowly and expanding the skill of her power. "Mr. Carlisle, the drive is *not* going to be given to you. This is what us little girls call leverage, and little girls like to play with their leverage."

"I wouldn't do that if I were you," Nathan growled.

"You can't fathom the idea of being me," Jade continued, poking the bear.

"I said I would be direct, so I will." He smacked his lips in an attempt at masculinity. She grimaced. "Your sister didn't come to work today because she's at home. Asleep, from what my friends can gather. And if I am not mistaken, she'll be alone at some point."

Jade tilted her head to the side, staring intently.

"Your biggest weakness is lying down, defenseless on a bed, with nothing but a high-pitched sound for protection and a police call that takes eight minutes to respond to. Eight minutes is more than any one man needs to teach a *little girl* a lesson." He pushed back in the chair, presuming victory. "Your biggest weakness is your sister, and I will give the order to hurt her if I don't get that drive."

Jade slowly stood while maintaining eye contact. She was no longer squirming nor tugging her ears.

"You imbecile," Jade said almost indulgently. "You've done nothing but state the obvious."

She slowly circled the desk as she spoke.

"Amber is the only living member of my family. She is my business partner, my best friend, my life." She grinned, enjoying the uncertainty in his gaze. "Running around threatening her is not the best use of your time."

She crossed her arms as she stood in front of him, well within reach, and leaned back on her desk. "The best use of your time, Mr. Carlisle, would be realizing that my sister is *also* my greatest strength."

Jade then lowered her tone. "She's the reason I am who I am. She is my greatest *power*. And by threatening her, you fumbling fool, you've triggered my anger. Did you think I would cower away?"

Confident in her power, Jade leaned into it, sifting through his mind with more ease.

"You just pushed the big red button marked with big red letters warning you not to push the big red button." Armed with the knowledge of why the behavior she exhibited was intimidating to him, she whispered, "You come near my sister or anyone I know, and I assure you, that drive will be the least of your problems."

Nathan's face creased into a confused frown as he looked at her.

Jade stood tall, knowing her advantage had paid off. In Nathan's memories she detected the similarities between her condescending, forceful tone and the tone his commanding officer in the military had used. Replicating the behavior created in Nathan an unconscious submissiveness.

"The drive contains every piece of incriminating information about the web of crime you're involved in—from the drug activity to personal attacks on other police officers who found out. But the worst piece of information on the drive is your military record. I suspect that's what worries you most. Because you were not honorably discharged."

Nathan was on his feet and had retreated a few feet before Jade could blink. She allowed a smile of satisfaction to cross her face.

"You used your family's connections behind their backs to get into the police force and lied to them about how you became a captain. That's why you parade around with that Boston accent: you're a walking facade."

Empowered in a way she had never felt before and would never again lack, Jade continued, "Your fear isn't of being caught for the plethora of crimes you committed. You're worried about what your powerful benefactors will do to you. And you don't want your family discovering that you were kicked out of the military."

Nathan's face went red, and his breathing grew labored.

"Mr. Carlisle," Jade softly said as she built up tension with a stare, "you dare mention my sister's name again, and I will personally go talk to your father, who lives at 8004 Cherry Hill—"

"Stop!" he shouted. "How do you know about him?"

"Know what? That he isn't the senile old man you keep telling everyone he is? That he's enjoying the peace and quiet of retirement, but if he heard that Nate is being his mischievous old self again, he would come down here and fix things right away?"

"You can't."

"You watch your step, because I can, and *I will*," Jade snapped back. "You will back off and stay away from my family, or so help me, everything you hold near and dear to you will come crumbling down. Everyone will know about what a fraud you are; everyone will know that you planned that drug exchange so you could take credit for the bust, only to slowly return the drugs in small increments."

She leaned back against her desk again. "A genius plan. Go to a drug lord and promise them guaranteed sales if they allow their bulk products to be confiscated and then replaced and sold for double the cost."

Nathan glared at her in disbelief. "You can't know that. The drive hasn't been opened."

"Because by threatening my biggest weakness, you awaken my biggest strength," Jade calmly stated. "Get out of my office, and stay away from my home and my family."

Pulling on the sleeves of his jacket, Nathan swept out of Jade's office without the charisma he'd flaunted upon entry. She went to the door and watched him walk straight to the elevator as the coward she knew him to be.

Jade felt accomplished. His threat against Amber had pushed her to use her power in a way she hadn't before. She had searched his mind for specific details she needed.

She gazed into the distance, lost in her thoughts as she finally returned to the task of pulling her hair into the clip. When Daniel knocked on the door to her office, she jolted, then cheerfully gestured for him to enter.

After a polite greeting, a few chuckles, and grabbing some drinks from her fridge, Jade asked, "What brings you in?"

"Maybe I just swung by to talk."

"That would be delightful, but . . ." Jade said as she passed him some chocolates.

"But both of us run busy lives, yeah." He sighed. "I came because of Lucy."

She remembered texting Daniel about Lucy the previous night. His sister had invited Jade to several lunches that were all politely declined. Hoping Daniel could explain her position, she asked him to be an ambassador to Lucy.

Jade released a deep breath. "I'm so sorry to involve you, Daniel. I usually can handle my social life, but—"

"Oh no. I get it. Lucy, uh, Lucy is—how can I put it?"

"An acquired taste?"

"Exactly! She won't stop, too, kinda like a pigeon in the park. Once you feed it, it follows you around."

"I don't want to hurt her feelings," Jade said.

"I can't guarantee they won't be hurt," he cautioned, "but I can guarantee she sees the difference between friends and acquaintances."

Daniel stood to exit, a bit rigid in his movement. He held the door's handle, then turned back. "Jade, who was that guy?"

"Who? The gentleman before you?"

He nodded

She rolled her eyes. "That was Nathan."

"The guy that beat his wife?"

"Yup."

"And put her in the hospital?"

"Yup," she casually responded, placing her hands at her sides, arms akimbo.

"The police officer that came to your house and freaked Al out?"

"The very one."

"Call me crazy, but why is he visiting you in your office?!"

"I wouldn't say visiting is the right word," Jade huffed. "He tried to intimidate me into giving him something."

"Tried?" Daniel asked, concern in his voice.

"Did you see his face when he left?" Jade grinned. "The table has definitely turned."

"Jade, that guy is a nutjob," he protested.

"Most guys are, no offense," she quipped, attempting to diffuse the tension.

"Allow me to rephrase," Daniel said. "He's desperate."

"How do you know that?"

"Because people who aren't desperate don't go around attacking their wives and attacking people they don't know in a public space, and they don't parade into other people's houses, showing off their weapons."

"Or breaking into houses," Jade added. "I agree; 'desperate' is a good word."

"He broke into your house?" Daniel demanded.

"Um, yeah. Just a little."

"He broke into your house, just a little," he reiterated, looking bewildered at her calmness.

"Yeah, Al got a new alarm system. Only took a few days in a hotel—no biggie."

"Jade, that's the very definition of a biggie," Daniel said and stepped closer to her. "What's going on?" In a softer manner, he asked, "Why aren't you being careful?"

"I am being careful," Jade emphatically replied. "I'm just not allowing him to walk all over my life."

"He was in your office, and he was shouting."

"Daniel, I really appreciate your concern, but I put him in his place today," she declared. "And I don't want to tell you any more, for *your* protection. This man, he likes to prey on people's weaknesses, which means he's conscious of his own. I discovered exactly what that is, and now he knows to back off."

Jade moved away from Daniel and added, "But if he finds out who you are, he'll try to hurt you to regain authority, and I simply can't have you and your family become pawns in his game." She shook her head. "You said it yourself: he's desperate."

"Do you hear yourself? Hurting my family, regaining authority, 'pawns in his game'? Jade, this is ludicrous. Please, turn him in for attacking your friend and let it go. This is going too far."

"First of all," Jade snapped, "I can't turn him in, not now. His reputation is still in good standing. Turning him in now won't help anything, but it could hurt his wife a hell of a lot."

"Jade, we aren't living in a perfect world where good wins over evil," Daniel pleaded. "Don't hurt yourself trying to win a battle in a war that can't be won."

Jade elected to ignore him. "Secondly, he threatened Amber. Just now, he said he knew she was home, and he threatened my little sister, Daniel." She inhaled deeply, aware of the distress she'd exposed with her choice of words.

Daniel finally fell silent, shaking his head. After a moment he said, "Promise me you'll ask for help when you need it. I know you won't stop, not after he crossed the line with Amber. But promise me that."

Chapter Forty-Three

After Nathan's appearance, Jade reached out to Mr. Hough to give the go-ahead to retrieve the drive and strategize the next step.

Arriving home, she ran to Amber's room. She'd snacked all day rather than eating a full meal and was famished, yet duty called. She halted in the arching doorway of Amber's open room to behold her sister terrified on her bed. Panicked that Nathan may have done something after all, Jade rushed to her side, asking if she was hurt.

"I, I just had two visions," Amber squeaked. "First time I got a double like that, and I know they aren't necessarily in order."

"Amber, what's wrong?" Jade pleaded.

"Nathan has this weird-looking computer," Amber said. "I think that's where he keeps all of his important information."

"Okay."

"In the vision, he was walking around this barely lit room, and he was on the phone. He said the drive hasn't been accessed." Amber released a breath, reaching for the water bottle on her bedside table. "He said the thumb drive Amy used was one of his. The instant it's put into any device, he'll get a GPS signal and can track it."

"Wait," Jade asked, bewildered, "that's a real thing?"

"He was serious, Jade. It's like he's waiting for it to be plugged in."

Realizing that explained some of Nathan's comments, Jade grabbed her phone to text Mr. Hough and warn him, muttering, "Amy told Mr. Hough where it was, but he didn't say when he was going."

Amber was almost in tears as she continued, "Jade, the other vision was him finding Amy." She paused as her sister locked eyes on her. "It doesn't end well. We need to do something, and fast."

"Get dressed," Jade said darkly. "Mr. Porter is on his way, and we're gonna need to get him and Aunt Katherine up to speed."

"Up to speed about what?" Amber asked, pulling herself to the edge of her bed and gingerly swinging her legs to the floor.

"I have a plan," Jade confessed. "I've been thinking about it for a while, and we need a family discussion to work through the bugs."

Amber wobbled toward her closet, settling on her robe.

"Also, I think we should give Syndicate the rest of the week and next week off," Jade announced. "That will give every department time to come in and pack for the move in increments."

"Are we move-in ready?" Amber marveled, momentarily distracted from the current drama.

Jade nodded. "In a week and a half, yes. I saw the new space today. The major issues are set to be resolved by that point, and then it's mostly cosmetic stuff, which can be completed after the move."

Amber yawned as Jade headed out to the hall. "I have a few calls to make. I'll meet you downstairs, okay?"

Amber flew through her emails as she waited for Jade in the sunroom, coming across the thread regarding the construction site and the latest reports. She had just finished drafting an email to be sent to HR for the time-off announcement when she heard the back door open and the merry sound of laughter from Katherine and Mr. Porter.

Wasting no time, Jade gathered everyone to share what was happening and her plan to solve the problem. She finished up with a list of some people involved. While Jade was unable to break down the entire list of affiliations, she mentioned one couple she'd encountered at benefits.

Nathan had lied about his background and built an impeccable reputation, making alliances with people on both sides of the law—all documented on one military-grade laptop, as Amber confirmed in her vision. Amber believed her vision was accurate and that accessing the computer would be equivalent to walking into the lion's den.

With worry evident in his tone, Mr. Porter warned the girls that desperation pushed people to make mistakes, but it also made them violent, as had been made clear already.

After everyone agreed that the drive needed to be obtained, Jade revealed that Mr. Hough was retrieving it. Then she shocked them by adding that she no longer believed holding the drive as leverage would keep them safe indefinitely. She shared that despite what she'd told Nathan, she also had no illusions that tattling on him to his father would put a stop to the whole mess, especially if Nathan's bosses got involved. If anything, he would become more dangerous with nothing left to lose.

"The drive would only buy us time until he and his powerful friends find a way around us."

She then proposed an additional piece of insurance: stealing the laptop from Nathan.

Katherine was appalled by the thought of Jade stealing anything.

"Fine, call it long-term borrowing," Jade said. "But the drive only has a fraction of the information."

"The drive won't stop Nathan, but the laptop will?" Amber asked.

Jade looked over to Mr. Porter, who nodded.

She explained, "The laptop gets his friends involved, and trust me, he doesn't want them in his business."

Slowly shaking her head, Katherine again mentioned the risk involved.

"My next step is to talk about how we break into his house and steal"—Jade rolled her eyes at her aunt's frown—"or 'indefinitely borrow' his laptop. Anyone not willing to be an accomplice can leave now. I promise I won't be upset. I just can't spend time convincing you. Either you're in or out, please."

"After seeing what he'll do to Amy, I'm all in," Amber said grimly.

"Of course we're helping, Jade," Katherine retorted with a smile to take the edge off as Mr. Porter nodded.

Jade then informed the group of the teams following Jade, Amber, and Al, describing their loyalty to Nathan and their attention to detail.

Mr. Porter and Katherine would take a day trip with Al, making it appear as though Jade and Amber were also in the car. All three cars would need to follow them to provide the sisters the freedom to execute the next step.

Next, they needed to figure out Nathan's base of operations. A police officer of his caliber would have an unlisted number and enhanced security. Amy's address of record was a PO box, so that was no help. Jade had recently been in contact with Mr. Hough, but safely communicating with Amy to learn her former address would be a complicated and slow process. Jade felt too much urgency to wait, and she didn't want to drag Amy back into things.

She emphasized that Nathan would be hard to follow.

"Instead of one car following him, I suggest we use four cars!" Jade announced.

She had lined up four cars of similar makes and models to be driven by four different people, all following Nathan and taking turns passing him and then falling back.

"Four drivers?" Amber asked, pointing at herself and Jade.

"Me, you, Oscar, and Daniel," Jade replied. "I know you aren't a fan of driving. Daniel will get the cars, then pick us up before we go to the police station. You can practice a little until Oscar joins us."

"I *can* drive," Amber nervously chuckled. "I just don't like it."

"We'll all be on a group call to communicate who is passing and who is making him think he's being followed. The key is getting him to second-guess himself."

"Why would we want him to even think he's being followed?" her sister asked, mystified.

Jade's expression was sheepish. "Honestly, I just assume he'll be on the lookout for that sort of thing, and no one here is an expert. So I'm making it part of the plan. If he never spots any of us, well, better safe than sorry."

"Then what?" Mr. Porter asked. "What happens after you follow him to his house, or wherever he's holed up?"

"The boys will take care of the cars. Then Amber and I will get our disguises on with the padding under our clothes; in case a neighbor sees us, they won't be able to provide an accurate description. Amber can use visions to see door codes and where we need to go once we're inside. I'll use my power as needed, too."

"Then you get the laptop?" Katherine inquired.

"Yes, that's the hope," Jade said. "Daniel and Oscar will come back for us at a pickup point near his house, and they'll bring us home."

"We can be each other's alibis," Amber announced.

"We only need an alibi if we get caught," Jade said, winking at Mr. Porter, who appeared on board but still worried.

The family agreed to the plan and worked through the minor details before dispersing to prepare for the following morning.

Jade privately asked Amber if she was truly fine with breaking the law, giving her sister the chance to walk away. Recalling her vision of how Nathan reacted to finding Amy, Amber was confident that the only way to stop his madness was for a higher authority to order him to back off.

Chapter Forty-Four

Working throughout the night and calling different contacts, Jade finalized the necessary details. The next morning, Al followed Katherine's instructions in assisting Jade and Amber as they packed up the car. They aimed to be subtle but conspicuous to their stalking teams, and from what Jade gleaned from their thoughts, the act was working.

When the time for the first deception came, Katherine entered the car as Jade waited beside her. Al then walked behind the car, ostensibly to assist Jade. Lowering her head as if to take her seat in the rented car, she instead ducked down and crawled along the bottom of the vehicle, toward the open back door of the house. The car was perfectly positioned to hide her clumsy dash.

With their usual town car parked in front of the garage, Amber was able to perform the same fake-out when she and Mr. Porter "entered" the car.

The girls sat in the dark house, watching from the front entrance's camera to ensure that all three cars followed Al. Then Jade called Daniel to pick them up.

Jade was adamant about Amber having sufficient time to practice her driving skills. Amber drove Daniel and Jade to several stops using her phone's navigation system, deliberately taking various routes across smaller side roads and merging with heavy highway traffic to test herself.

At each stop, Daniel helped Jade carry the items she'd purchased back to the vehicle.

"When was the last time you used cash?" Amber teased, backing up the car. She had regained some of her confidence with driving.

Daniel eventually asked why Jade had purchased items from different convenience stores.

"I got a few things Amber and I will need in order to follow Nathan. He obviously knows what we look like, so I got us some . . . facial distractions." She held the false beards and mustaches aloft as Amber turned onto a small dirt road leading to the parking lot where they were to meet Oscar and receive their respective cars.

"So, I figure you paid in cash and went to different stores to be sure that, in the unlikely event anyone looks into this, there isn't one store with a record of you buying everything. Makes sense," Amber said, turning the car off. She faced her sister in the passenger seat and glanced at Daniel in the back. "But how did you find four similar cars on such short notice that wouldn't be traced to us?"

Jade grinned. "Daniel got the cars. I needed some extra help," she said, shooting him a meaningful look.

"My stepdad helped," Daniel added.

Oscar approached the car, and Amber opened the driver's door, giving him a fist bump.

Pointing at a vending machine beside the parking lot's pay station, Jade quickly excused herself with the explanation that she and Amber had skipped breakfast.

Amber introduced Daniel to Oscar and leaned back as the two men discussed the situation. Jade was making her way back to the car when a vision came to Amber.

She welcomed her visions that day, despite the pain, as an added measure to keep everyone safe.

With flushed cheeks, she looked at Daniel. "You know, speaking about family, recently Jade and I have been learning more about our mom and dad."

"Oh really?" Daniel asked with polite interest. "What'd you find out?"

"Oh, not much. One cool thing was that Mom had six sisters. How crazy is that?"

"Aunts are the best," Oscar said. "My aunt is that one person I can talk to about my mom and not feel bad."

Amber continued, "Jade and I were talking about what it would be like to have that many kids." She glanced over to Daniel, who was peering at his watch. "What do you think, Oscar?"

He pondered. "Haven't really thought about kids, to be honest. But I think having a son would be nice. I never knew my father."

"What about you, Daniel?" she asked casually as Jade opened the car door. "Do you ever think about it?"

Jade froze with her eyes locked on her sister.

"I kinda see myself with a daughter," he replied. "Don't know why, though."

Jade apologized for the selections she'd brought. Oscar burst out laughing when she said she was not familiar with the different foods offered. After distributing the goods, Jade informed them that Daniel would be the one to drive to the police station and wait for Nathan to leave. The other three would be nearby to follow suit.

"Amber and I will have these to help hide our features." She held up a bag, repeating her assumption that Nathan would likely notice being followed. "In all likelihood, he'll spot at least one of us. That's why it helps that the cars are similar."

"So, he'll avoid one car, like that three-right-turns trick, but will still have three other cars that can follow," Oscar said, walking ahead with Amber to the cars Daniel pointed out.

"Yep. I asked you gentlemen to bring caps to hide your faces, but he may try to get a look if he lets you pass him, which is why I brought extra disguises."

Amber searched through her bag and found a plethora of items for her and Jade, noting the additional padding Jade had packed in the overnight bag for when they finally approached the house.

Upon reaching the cars, Daniel finally asked, "Why are we following him? Why do this if the goal is to make him think he's being followed but pull back?"

Amber didn't know how much to share, but Jade was prepared for such a question. "We need to know where he lives and keep an eye on him if we're going to turn the tables. As for making him paranoid, Nathan's people taunt us by standing by the street and staring at us all day. I want him to have a taste of his own medicine. Then maybe he'll make a mistake," Jade admitted. Amber tilted her head at the response, knowing that a partial truth was far easier to remember than a lie, even if Jade's explanation wasn't the real reason they were following him.

With a group fist bump instigated by Amber, the four friends entered their respective cars and headed toward the police precinct, all but Daniel pulling to the side of the road before they were close enough to see the entrance.

Soon enough, Nathan exited the building and entered his car.

Like a swarm of ants working in unison for the colony, the foursome took turns following Nate. Jade guided them all on the group call, shuffling the drivers behind the police captain. When Oscar suspected he'd been spotted, Jade instructed him to fall back and allow Amber to follow for a time.

Jade stayed close by, occasionally invading Nathan's thoughts to determine the next best move and adapting accordingly. The plan moved along smoothly as he took an exit to the left with Amber behind him in a cap and a false mustache. Daniel soon took over, removing his own cap as he did. Before long, Jade was the chosen car, following Nathan through an affluent neighborhood with her beard secured over her face and a zipped hoodie to hide her feminine neck.

When Nathan emerged from his car and stumped into a house, the group convened a few blocks distant to discuss the next part of Jade's plan. Daniel and Oscar would return their cars and use another conveyance to come back for the sisters.

The boys then drove off, giving Amber and Jade the privacy they needed to complete their plan, albeit not with an exorbitant amount of time.

Padded and hooded, the Parker sisters marched with wide steps to the property line, armed with the knowledge gathered from Amber's visions about Nathan's security measures. He primarily had cameras around the entrances but none in the house, not wanting footage of covert meetings.

After another vision, Amber announced that Nathan was on his way out, speaking to someone on the phone about Amy. He mentioned meeting someone downtown.

They hid behind a shrub, the branches prodding and poking their flesh as they waited for him to drive away. When he was gone, the two had a whispered discussion about the best point of ingress.

"I don't think the cameras are operational," Jade professed, hunched over beside her sister. "Can you call a vision to see if I'm right?"

"They don't work that way, yet," Amber giggled nervously. "But I'll see if I can figure it out."

Nodding to her sister once she'd regained focus, Amber confirmed that, true to Jade's suspicion, the cameras were not in use. He'd either installed them to keep up appearances or simply hadn't gotten around to connecting them in his haste to set up a new base after Amy's escape.

"How did you know that?" Amber asked.

"Try spending some time in that guy's head," Jade announced. "You get a feel for how he thinks." Studying the door, she continued,

"Okay, this lock doesn't have a key, only a number pad. I think we need that code."

"Another vision?" Amber whined.

"Yes, but wait. No doubt he'll get an alert if the code is used. He'll probably turn around when that happens. So we want to wait as long as possible."

"What if we wait too long? Or what if he forgot something and comes back?"

"Then this is our protection," Jade replied, pointing at her head and nodding toward Amber's. "But if it comes down to it, you run. I mean it. Get out of the house, run, hide, and don't come out until the coast is clear."

"It's scary that you've thought of everything," Amber said, creeping with Jade to the front of the house. "Beneficial but scary."

They waited a good fifteen minutes, endeavoring to look like they belonged in the shrubs of the enormous house. Finally, doing as her sister instructed, Amber pulled on nitrile gloves, then punched in the code. As the lock cleared and the door popped open, she muttered, "Ugh, I hope we have some painkillers, 'cause this is going to be one rough night."

"Prescription *and* over-the-counter analgesics," Jade announced as she shook the medium-sized backpack containing the items she'd brought. "I also have some electrolyte drinks in case we need a boost, and the snacks from before, of course."

"Scary," Amber repeated. "Oh so good, but still scary."

"When Nathan walked up to the house before, he stood in front of the door for a few seconds, but then he stood in the doorway," Jade whispered, leaning slightly into the opening. "I think you just disabled the lock, not the security system."

Pulling in her lips and hiding the pain of her headache, Amber called another vision. "Sweet buttered buns!" she gasped, turning to Jade and pointing at the corner staircase visible from the doorway.

"There's a motion sensor there that will trigger an alarm if the code isn't used within a minute."

"Do you know the code?"

"Yes," Amber declared, "I have it. How many measures does this guy need?"

"You'll have to tell us where to go."

"Yeah, I figured," Amber mumbled. "This is it. Ready?"

Jade nodded, biting her lower lip. They walked into the expansive hall, and Amber quickly punched in the code by the entrance with Jade by her side.

Jade followed her sister through the house and up a staircase to the second floor, noting the sophisticated layout of the home. Wondering aloud how he could afford such a place, they concluded that either a criminal benefactor installed him here or he must have legitimate wealth outside of his extracurricular activities, because he certainly wasn't shy about drawing attention.

With Amber's guidance, they found a closet filled with dusty clothes. Amber pushed some aside to reveal an antique doorknob. She then pressed the circular cold metal rather than turning it, and the door swung open with a click. Amber glanced at her sister before stepping into the room, which was essentially an extension of the closet lit by a small lamp on a desk. Also on the desk was a gray laptop.

"That's it." Amber pointed at the device and the cord beside it. "That's the laptop I saw him using, and that's the charger."

Jade grabbed the machine and cord, placing them in her bag quickly so they could leave before being discovered. The two traced their steps back to the stairs.

Amber glanced through the wide window at the end of the hall and froze, grabbing Jade's arm. "Jade!" She pointed urgently at Nathan's car pulling in. "He's here."

Alarmed, Jade stepped back from the window, pulling Amber with her. She whipped her gaze around, assessing their options.

"Amber, once he gets inside, we won't be able to talk. Keep your hood on and stay close to me, okay?"

Amber nodded. "You have a plan, right? A 'scary that you have such an oddly specific plan but still good that you have it' plan?"

"I have a working plan," Jade said quietly. "Just stay close and follow my lead."

They scampered down the stairs and toward the front door. "Okay, he'll likely walk in and turn on the lights, so we can't hide here, but we don't want to go further into the house." Jade opened a small door, verifying that it was a coat closet. "Let's get in here."

"What if he puts his coat away?" Amber anxiously whispered.

"He wasn't wearing a coat," Jade stated. "He'll likely go check on the room upstairs."

Amber trembled.

"I won't let him hurt you."

As the door clicked open, the girls entered the closet, softly closing it behind them. Jade tried to map Nathan's position by the footsteps clunking across the hardwood floors as she stood in the dark, struggling to stay ahead of the plan she'd insisted on pursuing.

But she doubted herself. Listening to her sister breathe, Jade regretted involving Amber. She held her hand, then tapped her sister's nose to indicate the need to control her breathing.

The moment Jade dreaded had come; she heard Nathan shuffling outside the door. The pain she felt as she reached out with her mind was minuscule compared to the consequences of being caught, so she opened to Nathan's thoughts.

Nathan suspected he had been followed but called the teams he'd put on Amber and Jade to make sure. The response confirmed his fears, followed by the alert about his code being used at the house. Knowing there would be no video evidence of the intruders, his only hope to gain leverage on them was to catch them in the act of breaking in.

That last thought reassured Jade. If Nathan went upstairs to check on his belongings, she and Amber might have an opportunity to escape undetected.

This optimism did not last. Nathan had no reason to suspect they'd found his laptop; his arrogance convinced him that it remained safely hidden. Jade began to panic when he contemplated searching the lower level's nooks and crannies. The floor cracked slightly with his steps, and she knew he was approaching the coat closet.

Her mind flooded with anguish over what would happen to her and her sister. She squeezed her eyes shut, wishing with all her might that he would just go upstairs so they could make their escape. Amber squeezed her hand, and Jade opened her eyes, both staring down at the light seeping under the door and the moving shadow on the other side.

Then, Nathan took step back. A phone call. Jade mentally sighed with relief as he pulled out his phone to answer.

"Hey, yeah, I'm gonna be late. I had to go back home. Somethin' was off with my security system. I don't care if you're tired." Nathan paused for a few seconds. "Are you kiddin'? They're smart, but they ain't that smart. There's no way they'd do that. Look, I gotta go. I heard something upstairs. I'll call you back in the car."

And suddenly he was gone. The coast was clear.

Jade tugged on Amber to follow her outside. "There's no time to explain. We're safe, but we gotta move fast. We'll text the boys there."

Without hesitation, Amber followed her sister's lead, stopping whenever she did until they arrived at the car. Jade pulled out the medication and gave two pills to Amber with a bottle of water as they huddled in the back of the car.

"Jade, that was so close," Amber exclaimed after gulping down water. "It's crazy how close we were to getting caught. I mean, he was right there."

Jade did not speak, feeling a bit dazed.

"Jade? Are you okay?"
"I think I did something," Jade quietly said.
"What did you do?"

Chapter Forty-Five

Safely in the back seat of the car, Amber held her curiosity like a dam about to burst.

"Jade!" she finally exclaimed when Jade reached for her backpack, startling her sister. "What did you do? Did you forget something?"

Pulling candy from her backpack, Jade shook her head and exhaled in disbelief.

"I think when Nathan was about to open the door—I *think* I made him think something was upstairs."

"I'm confused. What do you mean?" Amber said.

"I mean, I think I somehow added a thought to his mind," Jade stated, shifting her attention and body toward her sister. "I think I changed his perception of what was happening so he wouldn't open the door."

"You controlled his mind?!"

"Well, that's an exaggeration."

"Pishposh," Amber scoffed. "Are you serious? You really made him think something was upstairs so he wouldn't open the door?"

"I *think* I did," Jade replied. "I knew he was coming to open the door 'cause I knew what he was thinking. And I was thinking that if something made him go upstairs, we could leave."

"Oh, sweet grilled corn!" Amber squealed. "You controlled his thoughts!"

"Amber—"

"No, that's not an exaggeration," Amber interrupted. "How cool is that! Your power is so awesome!"

"It was your power that got us inside. Heck, it was your power that showed us the laptop to begin with."

"Geez, Jade. Take a compliment."

Jade chuckled, then admitted, "I'm grateful that my power was able to get us out. Seeing his shadow get closer and closer was . . . Let's just say I was scared."

ൕ

When Oscar and Daniel arrived together, Jade switched places with Oscar and reminded him to stop briefly at a couple of bars or restaurants before taking Amber home with photographs of their fun night out, ready for a worst-case scenario where they'd need to provide an alibi.

Al was returning home after the mission, so the Parker sisters went their separate ways, agreeing to meet at the house within two hours.

Oscar dropped Amber off after buying her a milkshake at their second stop. She waved to him from the door as he passed through the gate, then pressed the button to shut it remotely.

Listening to a message from Katherine informing Amber of her estimated arrival times, Amber's headache grew, and she prayed for relief from a day of using her powers.

She gasped under the sudden onslaught of yet another vision, rushing to the back door. Breathing heavily, she searched in the box of keys hanging near the back door. Then she ripped open the back door to find Daniel standing there.

"Daniel, what in the—"

"Amber, I tried calling!" Daniel cried. "You didn't answer, but Jade had the gate key."

Patting her jacket pockets, Amber realized she'd left her phone on the kitchen counter.

"What's wrong? Where's Jade?" she demanded, not spotting her. "Daniel, where is my sister?"

"She's in the car. I can't get her to move, and she screams if I come near her."

"What happened?!" Amber barked, dashing toward the car.

Following, Daniel recounted, "We were driving down a street not too long after leaving you. We saw him on the other side. I'm positive he didn't see her or me, but that's when—"

"When what?"

"Amber, she just froze." He stopped by the car, staring down at Jade, who was in the passenger seat, blank faced and trembling. "She was shaking but didn't say a word."

"Did you touch her while she was shaking or when she froze—like, physically touch her, even a tap?"

"Yeah!" Daniel burst out. "And I asked what happened, then she screamed, so I backed off."

Amber studied Jade and took a deep breath. She knew what must have happened but was unsure how to fix it.

"Amber, what's going on?" Daniel demanded, stepping beside her. "Did something happen at Nathan's?"

"No," she quickly replied, "I don't think this has anything to do with that."

"Then what? I've never seen Jade like this."

"Daniel, I can't tell you. She wouldn't want me sharing anything without her permission," she said, looking at Jade. "Thank you for bringing her home. I can take over."

"And what do I look like?" he snapped. "A hired chauffeur?"

"Daniel—"

"No, Amber!" he interrupted, not raising his voice any more than it already was. "She's my friend. I know she's your sister, and that wins, but it doesn't mean I lose!" He then lowered his volume. "I have never seen her react like this, so please, tell me what Nathan did."

The tricky game of not telling the truth but not lying had begun.

"Daniel, I wish I could talk about this, but look at Jade. Is this really the best time?"

"Just tell me why she freaked out like that. Why is she *still* trembling?" Daniel persisted. "Just tell me what he did."

"I honestly don't know. She seemed okay, but maybe it's all too much."

"Did he approach when we left you at his house?"

"No," Amber replied, exasperated. "The goal was not to get close to him at all; it was just to, I don't know, mess with him like he's been messing with us, but—"

"But?"

"I think Jade underestimated how much this whole thing would affect her," Amber said. "Nathan has been playing this mental game with so many people for so long, he makes it look easy. I think it got to her."

"I'm not going to open the door," he whispered, taking a step back. "Maybe she'll react better when she hears you."

"Please don't take this personally. Jade hides her anxiety really well and hasn't shown this kind of, uh, behavior since we were little."

Daniel said nothing. He simply watched as she opened the door and Jade flinched. Careful not to touch her sister, Amber whispered, "Jade, it's me, Amber." Jade's breathing remained shallow and fast. "You're home. Can you come inside? I promise I won't touch you."

Jade's eyes shot to her sister, locking on. She moved her legs to the side and slid out of the car, then tottered into the house with her back hunched over, her hands still in the hoodie's pockets, the backpack still in the car, not looking back or speaking.

"Daniel, I'm sorry," Amber said, grabbing the bag and walking backward toward the house. "I'll ask her to call you tomorrow, okay?"

He closed the passenger door without a word, his mind clearly busy.

Inside, Amber found Jade sitting in the kitchen with her legs pulled up on a dining chair, her whole body slumped over. Her hair was out of place, and her lips quivered.

"Jade," she said calmly as she closed the door and locked it, "are you feeling better?"

Not a word escaped her terrified sister's lips, and Amber grew concerned. She left in a rush to get Avania. Upon returning, she saw Katherine and Mr. Porter surrounding Jade with Katherine holding him back from touching her.

"I got Avania!" Amber exclaimed. "I can see how Mom calmed her down."

She connected to the book, grunting, then exhaled in frustration. "Avania says I can't. I don't have enough energy to see the whole thing—not now."

"Amber? Are you okay? Your lips are pale," Katherine asked.

"I had to use my power a lot today," she groaned, rubbing her temples, "and the pain medication still hasn't kicked in."

"Rest. Jade will be fine, but you can't push yourself like this. That's not how this works."

A cough from Jade drew their focus back to her. When they asked how she was feeling, she explained that the fear had struck again, but even though she knew the events were exaggerated in her mind, the fear seemed stronger.

"Is it because your power got stronger?" Amber asked.

"Your power got stronger?" Katherine demanded.

Jade simply accepted the drink Mr. Porter handed her while Amber explained how Jade had been able to drive Nathan away with a thought. As expected, Katherine practically jumped with joy at the news.

"Did you get the laptop?" Mr. Porter asked.

Nodding and pointing to her backpack, which Amber had laid on the kitchen island, Jade had another confession to make. "I have something to show all of you."

She slowly moved her hand to the inner pocket of her hoodie, unzipping it and pulling out a black thumb drive with bright flames along the side.

"Is that what I think it is?" Katherine exclaimed.

Jade nodded. "Mr. Hough brought it when we met up with Oscar in the parking lot."

"You had it the entire time!" Amber demanded, livid at her sister for hiding such vital information.

As Mr. Porter looked on in disappointment, Jade expressed that they had every right to be angry with her.

"Why didn't you tell us?" Katherine demanded.

"Nathan is *not* going to stop!" Jade explained. "Even with this drive, we need that laptop so we can see what's on it without him barging in here."

"You thought I wouldn't agree if I knew you had the drive?" Amber yelled in disbelief.

Jade shook her head, looking over at Katherine.

"Well, you are absolutely right, young lady," Katherine insisted. "I know this man has crossed the line, but breaking into his house when you didn't need to—"

"Aunt Katherine, *we* broke in," Jade firmly replied. "You aren't responsible if he comes after us."

"I am your aunt, Jade Elliot Parker," Katherine emphasized. "And whether I am legally responsible or not, my concern and duty towards you does not waver."

"Aw, Aunt Katherine," Amber said.

"No, Amber—"

"Katherine, let's leave this conversation for another time," Mr. Porter interrupted, "when emotions, fears, and headaches aren't running high."

Katherine marched out of the room, saying she needed to freshen up after being in a car all day—a code for wanting to be alone.

"Oh, and Daniel . . ." Amber hesitated.

"What about Daniel?" Jade quickly asked.

"I think you should call him," Amber added, "and maybe before Aunt Katherine is done."

Jade excused herself, leaving the kitchen as Amber shared how exhausting the day had been to a kind and compassionate Mr. Porter.

Chapter Forty-Six

Jade returned to see Amber pacing around the table. "Oh, Jade, this is bad. It's so, so bad," Amber lamented.

"What happened?" Jade asked. "I was away for like a minute."

"Sometimes, a minute is all you need," Mr. Porter sighed, shaking his head.

"Nathan knows about Oscar!" Amber whimpered. "He knows how long we've known him and that I invested in his restaurant. I think he knows about Daniel, but he definitely knows about Lucy."

"What? How?" Jade asked.

"I only got a small vision, but I think he's planning on going after them," Amber cried. "Oscar's restaurant took everything he has. If Nathan goes after him—"

"He's not going after Oscar, Amber." Jade halted her sister's train of thought, holding her arms gently. "We won't let him. We're taking the next step, tonight."

"What's the next step, kiddo?" Mr. Porter asked, joining the girls.

Pulling the drive out of her pocket, she declared, "We're opening this."

"Aunt Katherine is taking a shower. I don't—"

"I'll go ahead." Jade took the lead, sliding the backpack on. "You have your key to the new offices, right, Amber?"

Amber nodded, looking at Mr. Porter.

"Let's meet up there. I'll go ahead and see what's on this. Come when Aunt Katherine is ready."

"Why can't I come with you?" Amber pleaded.

"Because Aunt Katherine and Mr. Porter need your power to get past the men outside. And if Nathan finds me quickly, you can be my backup. I'd rather he didn't catch us both again," she said, thinking of what had happened at the hospital. She didn't want any of them in danger.

"Why can't all of us go together?" Mr. Porter asked.

"Wait," Amber hushed them. "Avania."

She ran over to the book, taking it in her hands. A moment later, she jerked in startlement, her eyes going wide.

"No way!" she exclaimed, looking exhausted but nonetheless joyful. "She says I mastered the power I was born with. Using it today, that was the final push."

With her eye twitching, Amber shot a glance at Jade, her breath growing ragged. "Jade, he found out the laptop is gone." She paused, clearing her throat. "He's going after Amy—with a gun. He knows where she is. He tracked her phone using an email."

Jade growled in frustration. "This man."

"Jade, he can't kill her for something we did."

"I know."

"How are you going to protect yourself from him?" Mr. Porter demanded.

"I may not have used my new skill enough," Jade admitted, "but I can still hear his thoughts and navigate around them. I'll sneak out back and order a ride from the neighbor's house. As soon as Aunt Katherine is ready, come to Syndicate."

Creeping around the house, avoiding the motion sensor lights, Jade left Mr. Hough a voicemail warning him that Amy was compromised and to explain why they were going to Syndicate. She paused briefly at the sound of a rustling tree, which revealed a roaming cat.

Jade swiftly moved through their neighbor's backyard, calling a ride on her phone. Soon she would find out who was above Nathan on the food chain of corruption.

Chapter Forty-Seven

WITH TREMBLING HANDS not attributable to the cool spring night, Jade unlocked the door, stepping in to inhale the scent of newly painted walls and cardboard. She passed through the lobby with a glance up at the clean, shiny slate spelling out the company name above A PHARMACEUTICAL COMPANY WITH A HEART.

With pressure mounting to put Nathan in his place, she hurried on, leaving the area lit. Gliding the backpack's strap off her shoulders, she continued to where her office would be, dodging various discarded items before entering a room that was not as spacious or luxurious as the office she currently had. It was empty other than a table saw and stacks of cardboard boxes.

She had just placed her belongings on the table saw when she heard a loud bang from the entrance, coupled with her name being called. Immensely grateful she'd locked the door, Jade slowly crept back out to see who was there, texting her sister to apprise her of the situation and urge her to hurry, fearing Nathan might have arrived.

Her horror mixed with confusion and sweet relief when she spotted Daniel by the door, tapping the glass window.

"What on earth is he doing here?" Jade thought out loud as she unlocked the door.

Daniel pushed it open, out of breath and most definitely out of sorts, asking if she was okay.

"Yes, I'm okay," Jade replied. "Almost had a heart attack, but other than that, I'm fine."

"You're the one pushing the buttons of one of this city's most notorious officers," Daniel shouted.

"Daniel, what are you doing here?"

"You thought, what, that coming out to this part of town at this unholy hour with that ridiculous drive would be just fine?"

"How do you know about the drive?" she gasped.

"Lucy told me!" he announced.

"Lucy? How does she know anything?" Her headache was of a different kind now.

Daniel yelled, "Lucy is plain old dumb Lucy! She's the same as she ever was. She heard you while hiding out somewhere." Daniel stepped closer to Jade. "She's not the reason I'm here."

"I know, but it's okay, really," Jade attempted to reassure him. "I have my phone on. I promised Amber I'd check in and everything." She patted her jacket pocket and realized it was empty. "Where's my phone?"

"Jade, seriously?" Daniel snorted in anger. "You're just holding that drive in your hand. You have the one thing Nathan has been gunning for this entire time." He broke off as Jade ran toward her office, indicating for him to follow. "Jade, if this were anyone else . . ."

"There it is," Jade exclaimed, grabbing her phone. "Let me just text Amber so she knows."

"You're not really listening, are you?"

"Yes, I am, Daniel. But we're almost out of the woods with Nathan, I promise," she said after she unlocked her phone.

"When did this plan come about?" Daniel questioned. "We spoke last night. You were—" He stopped abruptly at Jade's shocked face as she put her fingers over her lips, slowly raising her gaze from the text message.

"Nathan," she whispered. Amber had received a vision of Nathan approaching Syndicate, noting the lit lights, and walking in. Her sister was on her way with Katherine and Mr. Porter since Al was not on duty that night.

"Jade, what is it?"

"He's coming here." She looked through her office door and pulled on her left ear, pushing the limit of her ability to detect whether Nathan was close. As she strained, Daniel saw her discomfort and worried, allowing her to unintentionally hear some of his thoughts. She stepped closer to the office door.

"How do you know he's coming?" Daniel quietly asked, following her.

Jade froze in the hall outside her office, holding out her arm to stop him from going further. "I didn't lock the door when you came in," she muttered, turning her head to him, all her confidence stripped away in a moment.

"No, I don't think you did," Nathan announced, rounding the corner.

With nothing but the short distance of a hall separating Nathan from his targets, the severity of the situation began to sink in.

"We've got to stop meeting like this, Jade," Nathan chuckled, drawing nearer.

Daniel pulled Jade behind him as they both paced back into the middle of her office.

"You don't seem so well, Nathan," Jade retorted, desperately trying to gain an advantage. Nathan's thoughts were racing; he had improvised his drive to Syndicate based on information he'd received from his men. He had brought his gun, and in his hopeless state, he was committed to using it.

"Nathan, I'd like this to be officially stated." She flicked her phone and began to record. "You're on private property, and you are *not* welcome."

"You think that little video is going to stop me?" Nathan snarled. He then looked at the table saw and spotted his laptop. "What the hell is that doing here?"

As he darted to the machine, Daniel grabbed Jade and walked them both to the opposite side of the room. She held his hand, trembling with fear.

"You came after my family and left me no choice."

"You have no idea what you're dealing with," he sneered, rolling his head in a circle and rubbing the back of his neck. "You think you—"

"I don't think. I know!" Jade interrupted. "I already told you, you could have ended this and kept me out of it."

Nathan's head was hanging low, and he shifted his eyes to her hand and what it held. He finally saw it. The cursed drive he'd spent months trying to locate was within reach.

"Give it to me," Nathan demanded.

"No."

"Jade, just give it to me, and all of this goes away."

"If I give this to you, you will use that untraceable gun you have holstered to your side to send a message to the people who are losing faith in your command," she declared. "I won't lie and say I'm not terrified, but giving up this drive is not something I can do."

"How is it you know everything going on in my life!" he shouted.

"Nathan," Daniel intervened, "you want the drive; we want to get out of this problem. Why don't we find a way that works for everyone?"

"Because I can't," Nathan bellowed. "The people that need this back can't have witnesses."

Jade glanced at Daniel. "I know who wants this drive gone," she said. "And based on their political position, they will make a deal, if you suggest the right one."

Nathan glared at her. "Just give me the drive, Jade." He suddenly hurled his laptop across the room, slamming it into the wall, then pulled out his loaded gun. He pointed it to the ground—for now.

A loud slam came from outside Jade's office, and Amber's voice rang through the space, shouting for Jade. Fearful that her sister might walk into Nathan's furious fit, Jade shouted a warning.

"Oh, no, no, no," Nathan hissed as he shook his head. "You said your biggest weakness is your greatest strength. Let's see just how strong you are."

Nathan demanded Amber join him, or her sister would be shot. Amber slowly stepped around the corner along with Mr. Porter. Jade shook her head, silently pleading for Amber to leave, but just as she could never walk out on Amber, neither could Amber abandon her sister.

"Now, maybe you can talk some sense into this stubborn, annoying, entitled little bitch," Nathan screamed. Jade shivered as he pointed the gun at her. "Amber, tell her to give me the drive."

"Please, Jade, you know he'll do it." Amber's voice broke as tears poured down her face. "Please, just give it to him."

Jade glared at Nathan and knew he was planning on using that gun on her and her sister. In that moment, she had one job: to find a way to spare Amber. Every Elliot witch in her family from Uporia had been in the same position Jade was. Once again, someone had to be put ahead of her.

Jade looked into her sister's shattered face and slowly shook her head.

"You know that I *know* what he'll do after he gets this drive."

"I'll learn more about Avania," Amber sobbed. "I'll use it and get better. Whatever we need to stop him, I promise, Jade." Her knees trembled, and she took a step back to the wall behind her. "He'll kill you."

Jade knew what she needed to do. Determined to live up to her family's legacy of keeping the sixth daughter safe, she needed to make Nathan believe he had the drive even though he would never get it.

"Okay," she said. "You will get the drive, *after* my sister and Mr. Porter are outside."

"Jade!" Amber cried out but was held back by Mr. Porter.

"Amber, I'll be okay," Jade assured her, holding Daniel's arm, which he still held protectively in front of her. "You and Mr. Porter need to go outside."

"No one is going anywhere."

Chapter Forty-Eight

As Nathan stalked toward Jade, Amber yanked her arm free from Mr. Porter's grip and lunged closer, but Nathan swung the gun on her.

"No!" Jade shouted. "Don't point that at her."

Nathan immediately lowered the weapon, then stared at his arm in distracted confusion. He quickly brushed it aside, demanding once again that she hand over the drive. This was the now-or-never point. Jade stepped toward Nathan—and the loud echo of sirens in the distance interrupted her stride.

"You called the police?" he barked, spinning his gaze around the room, too busy to see the girls denying it. "You can't call the police. I am the police!"

He was growing unhinged as he whipped the gun back and forth between Jade and Amber. Jade once again shouted at him, causing him to lower the gun; then he grunted with frustration. He'd had his fill of the Parker sisters.

Mr. Porter pulled Amber back, but she resisted. Nathan's eye remained on Jade's hand for an intense split second, and Jade moved her head to the side, pulling her ear.

Shifting his weight between his feet, his desperation growing, he grunted to himself, "Why did I let the bitch get a job! I should've just made her stay in that house like she was supposed to."

As the sirens grew closer, sweat poured from Nathan's temple, shining under the bright fluorescent lighting.

"I'm taking that drive!" he finally shrieked, diving toward Jade as an ear-shattering bang erupted, followed immediately by another.

Jade hurtled to the ground instinctively, acknowledging the sound of falling objects around her. She eventually peeked up from her curled position to see that Nathan had run off, though the drive was still in her hand and the computer lay where it had landed.

"What was that?" Jade gasped, pulling herself up and staring at the cardboard mess surrounding her. "Amber?"

"I'm fine, Jade," Amber weakly responded from the other side of the room.

Relieved that Nathan had finally gone, Jade turned to Daniel.

"Daniel," Jade whispered, gaping at her only friend in disbelief. Daniel lay on the ground, face up, grasping his chest. It was bleeding profusely. He looked around in bewilderment, his other hand absently reaching for something to pull himself up. Jade crawled over to him.

"No," she gasped, her eyes filling with tears. "No. Daniel, no."

He grabbed her hands, staring into her eyes, struggling to breathe and begging for help without saying a word.

"Daniel, I'll get help." Jade turned to search for her phone, but he would not let her hands go. His blood poured over his clothing. She pulled a hand free to press it to his chest, trying to stop the gaping hole from releasing any more of his precious blood, but to no avail.

The more she pressed down, the more blood gushed out.

"Daniel, please, I need to get my phone. I need to get help." Jade sobbed and wept in complete denial, watching him give in to a battle he couldn't win. "Daniel, no."

His eyes remained locked onto hers, blood oozing from his mouth and bubbling with every straining breath.

"Daniel, I can't," she begged. "Not you." Her tears landed on his face as his eyes started to drift away. "No!"

His grip lessened, his eyes rolled back, and his head fell. His hands, which had been holding hers so tightly, fell to his soaked chest.

Jade wept hysterically with him motionless in her lap.

She seemed to sit there for an eternity.

Eventually, the tears stopped. She felt dried up. Coming to her senses, Jade turned to see Amber bending over something obscured by the boxes, calling out Mr. Porter's name. Everything in her went numb. Her power had betrayed her. While she'd made it clear that Nathan was not to shoot Amber, he'd shot the two other people in the room she would have taken a bullet for.

Glaring down at Daniel's lifeless body, Jade knew what she was going to do.

Chapter Forty-Nine

Jade raced past Amber and Mr. Porter, unable to confront another death. While she had played with the idea of seeking revenge against the thing that had killed her parents, she was going to make sure Nathan Carlisle suffered for killing Daniel and Mr. Porter.

Bereaved, she tumbled out into the street, spotting Katherine waving in the emergency vehicles from the sidewalk. She wiped her face with the back of her sleeve, retreating into the shadows, away from Syndicate and all who knew her.

The reality of what had happened sank in as she circled the building, streaks of sunrise painting the dark sky on the horizon.

Mr. Porter, her remaining father figure, and Daniel were gone because Jade did not have the skill to control Nathan. Her mind filled with self-recrimination as she homed in on her power. Despite her failure, her power was her best weapon against Nathan, and she was prepared to make it a worthy battle.

She stood on the sidewalk and closed her eyes. She played back Daniel gasping as he held her hand, his blood pooling over his chest, then pushed through the invisible walls she felt around her. She heard the thoughts of countless people, quickly distinguishing one that focused on Nathan. She concentrated on that voice and threw psychic strings around it, tying the voice to her mind.

Once she'd captured the voice, she made it speak. It wasn't long before she heard a man repeating, "Here I am" until she walked right up to him. In front of a car stood the two men she knew to be the officers responsible for following her.

She marched to them without breaking eye contact, pushing the one under her control onto the hood of the sedan behind them.

"I will give you one chance and one chance only!" she screamed, shoving her hair out of her face. "Where is Nathan!"

The man stuttered and shook his hands in front of his face, but it was too late. His mind had turned against him. She stomped away, tapping on her phone to order a car service, then placed the phone in the pocket of the blood-soaked hoodie.

Before she got too far away from the wretched creatures that served Nathan, she turned back, blood still dripping from her sleeves, and narrowed her eyes at the two dumbfounded men.

"When I'm done with Nathan," she gritted out, "and I will be the one to end him, I'm coming back for you."

While the driver would have attempted to engage in civil conversation, Jade made him drive silently. And when she left the car, she rid the driver's memory of the bloodstains. She planned to murder Nathan, after all, and did not want witnesses.

She calmly approached a warehouse with a substantial lock on the main door. She laughed at the notion that such a trivial thing could stop her. In a way, Nathan was the person who'd ignited the flame she had burning—the flame that boosted her power beyond limitations.

She screamed, "Nathan!"

The beaming sunrise distracted her for a split second as she recalled a conversation with Daniel; his favorite time of day was sunrise, and he believed the most majestic sunrise was one over the ocean. That memory gave Jade even more power, and she reached out with her mind until she heard Nathan's trembling and terrified thoughts.

"Open this door, now," Jade demanded tersely, projecting the words psychically so that they were the only thing left in his head.

A clang from the other side came soon after, and he opened the door, his eyes wild.

"What is going on?" Nathan slurred. "It's like I have no control over myself. Did you drug me?"

"Shut up!" Jade shoved the door open, pushing inside.

Nathan grunted as he lifted his hand but then stopped. "Why—"

"You can't do anything without my say-so, Nathan," she announced, aggressively throwing him to the ground.

"What the hell is going on? What did you do to me?" he croaked from his back.

"I think you mean what did *you* do to *you*." Jade stalked closer to the squirming man, who crawled away in terror, scrambling to make sense of what was happening to him. "You filth! You truly have no respect for anything other than yourself. No." Jade stopped. "Not respect, value. The *only* person you value is yourself."

"You'd be a fool to think anyone is any different than me."

"Daniel was different," she shouted, failing to hold back her tears. "He was a man you can't even dream of becoming." Her voice broke as she remembered. "Mr. Porter . . ."

Then anger suffused her once again.

"Look," Nathan grunted, trying to stand.

"No!" Jade yelled. "You look!" She stomped him back down with her heel. "Do you know what it's like to have a person to connect to?" Her tears hit the ground beside him. "Do you know what it's like to go through life broken and messed up and have someone who *likes* that you're broken and messed up, who thinks that being broken and messed up is what makes you the best person you could be?"

Nathan struggled to speak, gawking at her, feeling his demise upon him.

"Do you know what it's like to talk to someone about absolutely nothing, and they think it's the most amazing conversation ever?" Jade recalled talking to Mr. Porter and Daniel, then glanced down at her bloodstained sleeves. "Do you know what it's like knowing you don't have to worry about yourself because someone else is watching your back?"

Crouching, Jade got closer to Nathan. "Do you know who *you* took away from me?" she whispered, seeing him shake as he stared into her fiery, manic eyes.

"No," he finally panted. "I don't think I've ever known anyone like that, and I don't think I ever will."

"You're going to wish you never met me, Nathan," she divulged, standing back up. "Even more than you already do."

Chapter Fifty

"Jade!" Amber shouted across the warehouse, grunting from the pain of using her power to find her sister. She came across Jade towering over Nathan, who shook on the ground, helpless and terrified in a way Amber had never before witnessed from anyone.

Amber approached her sister. "What happened?"

Nathan bellowed, "She's attacking me!"

Jade shrieked as she threw her leg out and kicked him in the chest. "He killed Daniel!" she sobbed. "And Mr. Porter."

Amber knew better than to physically hold Jade in this state and simply stood in front of her, breaking her contact with Nathan. "Jade, Jade. Look at me."

"No!" Jade yelled. "He killed them!" Jade held her hands over her mouth in utter devastation at the words she spoke. "They're gone."

She cried weakly, sinking against the wall behind her. Meanwhile, Nathan seemed to struggle against invisible chains.

"*You* aren't going anywhere," Jade spat as she pulled herself up. "You're gonna pay for—"

"Jade, pay for what?" Amber pleaded. "Tell me."

Jade did not reply.

"We've been here before, Jade," Amber announced. "You know for a fact that nothing will bring Daniel back." She slowly approached her sister. "There is no price that can do that."

Jade glared at her sister with rage in her eyes. "I can see why you don't like me psychoanalyzing you," she remarked. "It's infuriating."

Knowing she'd crossed a line, Amber took a step back.

"No, please, Amber," Jade sarcastically added, "tell me you know what I feel. Tell me how, because we both share the loss of our parents, it's somehow okay that Daniel died with his blood covering me." She gestured wildly. With her grief masked as anger, she whimpered, "Mr. Porter! There isn't a punishment known to man that's enough for killing Mr. Porter, but I am going to thoroughly test them all."

"Mr. Porter is fine!" Amber interrupted, taking a chance and grabbing Jade's hands. "He's hurt but he's fine. I promise."

Jade stared at her sister. "Is he hurt or is he fine?"

"He fell down when the gun went off, but I *swear* that's it," Amber assured her. "An ambulance took him to the hospital, and Aunt Katherine's with him." She pulled out her phone, showing Jade the conversation with their aunt. "Mr. Porter is gonna be fine."

The bittersweet moment seemed to throw Jade into more emotional turmoil. Then her eyes went almost blank. She moved Amber to the side and glared down at Nathan, who was exhaling heavily, holding his side.

"Amber, if you don't approve, then leave."

"Jade," Amber calmly said, "right now, you're hurting, and you don't care. But you will care. At some point down the line, you will. I'm here for *that*."

"Amber." Jade looked directly at her sister and repeated herself. "If you disapprove, leave."

"Yeah, Amber," Nathan laughed, then grunted in pain. "Leave so she can stand there and do nothing like the whiny, crying little baby she is."

That was a mistake.

Amber very slowly turned to face him. "What did you say?"

"Everyone here knows she ain't gonna do squat!" He hobbled to a kneeling position. "You're too spoiled to do anything that'll get your hands dirty."

Amber's face went hot. She remembered him attacking her in the hospital. She played back her visions of Al's murder, all for the sake of that ridiculous drive. She played out what he would have done to Amy if he'd found her. She thought about what he'd planned to do to Oscar before Jade took action. Amber turned to her sister.

"What do you want to do?"

"I want him to hurt. I want him to just *hurt*," Jade replied, focused on Nathan.

"No, what do *you* want to do?"

Jade looked at her sister, frowning with uncertainty.

"If you want to kill him, say the word. I'll help you kill him, and no one will find the body," Amber promised. "If you want to tie him to an anchor and drop him to the bottom of the ocean, I'll get the rope. Tell me, what do you want to do?"

"I want to make him suffer," Jade stated, contemplating her options. "The kind of mental suffering that only he would feel—the kind of suffering that would make him beg."

Amber stood beside her sister, staring down at Nathan. "Do it."

"Do what?" Nathan laughed derisively.

Amber stepped forward. "Nathan, you done messed with the wrong spoiled brats."

"Oh really?" he huffed.

"Did you know that our family records are sealed, Nathan?" Jade said as she nudged her sister aside. "Let me introduce myself." She cleared her throat. "I am Jade Elliot Parker, the fifth daughter of Annalise Elliot of the sixth-daughter witches and James Parker of the seventh-son wizards. I was born with the ability to know people's thoughts, and recently, thanks to you, I have learned how to control them.

"You unleashed rage and hatred I never thought I could feel when you took Daniel's life, and in return"—she turned her head to the side with a borderline evil smile—"I will wreak havoc on your life by bringing every one of your fears to life and making you live through it."

"Empty words," Nathan said with a sneer. But as Jade held her gaze on him, as she sent helpful reminders of what she'd already done to him, Amber saw a sense of horror suffuse him. Jade stood silently, not breaking eye contact; then he stood and started walking to her.

"What the hell?" he protested. "What is happening?!"

Jade called to her sister, "Amber, there's a camera over there. I want video footage of him walking of his own accord."

"You bitches better—"

"Not a word," Jade hissed.

His face crinkled as he struggled to speak, yet his lips remained shut behind the invisible tape Jade had put over his mouth.

Amber did as her sister asked, and the group crossed in front of the camera, then continued to Nathan's car.

Chapter Fifty-One

WEEKS HAD PASSED since Daniel's death, but everyone in the Parker household still suffered the aftershock. As far as the press knew, Nathan went into hiding after a case was opened against him and several other officers. The people who benefitted from his criminal activities of course offered no help—to their ultimate detriment. Meanwhile, Amy returned to her family safe and sound, providing evidence against her ex-husband.

Two weeks after Nathan's disappearance, he was discovered gassing up his car at a station not far outside of Solas and was brought in forcefully, making a scene for all to witness on video at his trial. Pained by his son's death, Martin Prescott, Daniel's stepfather, spared no expense or effort going after the scum.

Though no one blamed her for Daniel's death, Jade cloistered herself in her room, sitting by her window almost every day while Syndicate remained closed for the duration of the trial. It was almost a blessing that the company hadn't been doing any actual business for years.

Jade spoke when spoken to and not a word more, bringing the house to a standstill. She left only for Nathan's trial, where she stood proud and strong at Amber's side, watching him from the back of the courtroom, forcing him to act and behave in ways that were counterintuitive and against his lawyers' wishes—all to guarantee that he got the strictest possible sentence. At one point, she had him attempt to flee. He was a puppet, and she held the strings.

Only Amber knew of the mental anguish Jade had inflicted upon him in those two weeks he'd been missing, coupled with some hardcore beatings to give him a taste of Amy's suffering.

The high-profile politicians in Nathan's drug operation had professed strong public opposition to drug use before being exposed. The focal point of the trial was a couple who had abused their power and exploited their son's tragic death to influence the laws around certain drugs. The woman's affair with Nathan had been documented on the drive, along with her connections to the gangs hauling drugs throughout the region.

Their plan seemed ingenious. The gangs would carry large amounts of illegal contraband across the area and purposely get caught. After the police took the drugs and built a solid anti-drug reputation, they would slowly release them back to the gangs for a price—essentially just a more widespread money-for-protection scheme.

The web of crime spread far. It spilled into medication prescribed in copious amounts, using the names of doctors who were either no longer practicing medicine or had passed away. With the narcotics department completely under Nathan's control, he trafficked millions of dollars to the real powerhouse of the city, the politicians running the show.

Although the information on the drive and the computer was monumental, it meant nothing to Jade. She handed everything over to Amber after the family reviewed the contents together, then excused herself to be alone, as always.

Her family gave her the space she needed and only spoke to her when necessary.

After the verdict and Nathan's attempted escape, he was sent to a maximum-security facility. Jade no longer had control over his mind and actions, but she had another's mind to consider.

Katherine was surprised to hear the doorbell chime after Jade's return from the courthouse. Amber glanced through the window, then back to Mr. Porter.

"It's Daniel's dad!" Amber whispered, hesitating to answer the door.

"I'll get it," Mr. Porter offered, then went to take care of the unexpected guest.

Amber remained in the sunroom, listening as Katherine joined Mr. Porter in greeting Daniel's stepfather. After politely offering Mr. Prescott refreshments, Katherine inquired if he would like to come in.

"I'd like to speak with Jade," Mr. Prescott announced, "if that's not too much trouble."

"Mr. Prescott has some documents for Jade," Mr. Porter told Katherine.

"Jade isn't seeing anyone," Amber announced, bursting from behind Mr. Porter. "Maybe I can help with the documents."

"Unfortunately," Mr. Prescott said sadly, "this is a matter only Jade can attend to, and I'd like to have this taken care of before the funeral."

Amber took a step back when she heard the word "funeral" and recalled the man's insistence on having the service only after his stepson's murderer had been brought to justice.

"Mr. Prescott, as Amber said, Jade hasn't been taking guests lately. Perhaps you can join us for some lemonade while Amber checks to see if Jade's awake," Mr. Porter suggested.

Amber took the hint, rushing upstairs to Jade's bedroom. But she hesitated at the door, not daring to knock, and instead she texted her older sister.

HE CAN COME UP was all Jade replied. Disheartened, Amber made her way downstairs, offering to show Mr. Prescott the way to Jade's room. As Amber led him back upstairs, she received another text from her sister. Jade did not mind if Amber or anyone else wanted to be present while Mr. Prescott spoke to her.

The door was unlocked when Amber turned the knob to let Daniel's stepfather in. Katherine did not come up, but Mr. Porter wanted to be around, expressing worry that Mr. Prescott might not be considerate of Jade's situation.

Amber and Mr. Porter stood by the door as Mr. Prescott hesitantly crossed over to the bay window where Jade sat. Her hair was pulled back, so she had nothing to hide the dark circles around her eyes. She held a stuffed toy shark tightly to her chest as she regarded Mr. Prescott with shiny eyes.

"Hello, Jade," Mr. Prescott said, sounding empty. "I can't tell you how I wish this were under any other circumstance."

Jade did not reply but nodded.

"My lawyer shared this with me, now that the trial is over and Daniel can be laid to rest."

"Will he be buried beside his mother and father?" Jade asked quietly.

"I couldn't find it in my heart to do it any other way."

She nodded again, turning away to hide her tears, and stared out the window at the setting sun.

"I regret never telling him how proud I was to be his dad."

Jade slowly turned back, her expression startled.

"He really was the best son anyone could ask for." Mr. Prescott wiped his eyes, then proceeded, "I wanted to have this done before we saw you at the funeral."

Jade struggled to speak, finally saying, "I wasn't sure you wanted me there, Mr. Prescott."

"Why wouldn't I want you there?"

"Because if it weren't for me," Jade admitted with her voice breaking, "you probably wouldn't be planning Daniel's funeral."

"I'm content with the outcome of the investigation, Jade."

"I'm not content with this outcome," Jade replied, dropping her head.

Mr. Prescott cleared his throat and took a single step closer. "I have here the official documents from Daniel's will," he said, prompting Mr.

Porter to enter the room and stand near the bed. "Daniel essentially left everything he owned in this world to . . . to you."

Jade gawked at him. "What?"

"His portion of my estate, his late mother's estate, and all of his legal authority over his foundation—everything."

"I don't understand, Mr. Prescott."

"This was completed weeks ago, a little before . . . before the shooting." Mr. Prescott handed her a folder. "It's what he wanted, and I will honor his wishes. There won't be any issues from our end, not even from Lucy."

Jade held the folder but did not respond. With her mouth half-open in shock, she looked pleadingly at Mr. Porter.

"Please excuse me," Mr. Prescott said, patting his chest. "There are several things I must attend to before tomorrow."

Courteous to their guest, Amber walked Daniel's father out.

He grabbed her forearm at the front door. "I have one more thing for Jade," he whispered. "I just didn't think it was appropriate to give her, not now."

Amber stood still. "What is it, Mr. Prescott?"

Placing his hand in his right breast pocket, he pulled out a small, black-velvet jewelry box. "This belonged to his mother," Mr. Prescott stated, opening the box to show a breathtaking diamond ring. "Daniel's father was killed when Daniel was very young," he explained. "When I proposed to his mother, she kept the ring Daniel's father gave her."

"His mother's ring!" Amber whispered, her sorrow for her sister compounded by the fact that what she had seen of Jade and Daniel's future all those weeks ago would never come to pass.

"He planned on giving it to Jade," Mr. Prescott admitted, wiping away more tears. "Please, give it to her when she's ready."

✼

The next day seemed to come in two blinks of an eye. With Al prepped to drive the family to Daniel's funeral, Katherine and Amber waited for Jade at the bottom of the staircase.

Nervous they would be late, Katherine suggested that Amber see if Jade needed help. Amber dragged her feet up the stairs. Considering the Elliot family's history, Katherine's stoic views on losing someone might not be what Jade needed to hear, so Amber accepted her duty as the sister and quietly knocked on the door.

Jade had not answered the door since the day Mr. Porter returned from the hospital. Amber could have knocked and waited for a million years; Jade would not answer. So she pushed the door open instead, announcing her entry.

Soft music played, and Jade sat by her window—silent, bereft—as she had every day for weeks. Ready to leave in body, but her spirits were as shattered as ever.

Amber stopped by the foot of the bed, making out the song as Ed Sheeran's "Supermarket Flowers."

"Jade, we're downstairs and ready when you are," Amber said gently.

Jade remained where she was, peering through the glass. Amber recognized that look of desperation: Jade was fervently wishing none of this were real.

"You don't have to go if you don't feel up to it," Amber said.

Jade turned abruptly.

"I think Daniel of all people would agree that what I feel isn't something we should depend on," she stated angrily. "I *am* representing our family in public as I *always* do, so"—she plastered on an insincere smile—"let's go."

Jade marched out of the room, not checking whether Amber followed her, then walked straight to the waiting car without acknowledging her aunt or replying to Al as she got in.

Amber was the last to join the group before the long, dreary drive to Daniel's funeral. With Jade's eyes fixated on the window, the others in the car carried on mundane, mind-numbing conversation until they reached their destination.

Jade was the first to step out of the car, and again walked on, not waiting for her family to join her before disappearing amid the crowd at the front of the funeral home.

Amber managed to locate Mr. Prescott before the memorial service began, pretending to have only recently been separated from her sister. When Amber took her seat beside Katherine and Mr. Porter, she searched around the hall for Jade, unable to find her.

"Was Jade expected to say something?" Amber asked Katherine, pondering why she could not find Jade.

Katherine shrugged as Daniel's father began to speak.

Amber elected not to use her power to find Jade. She released a breath she'd held in for longer than she should, wiping her tears before they could escape as she rose with the crowd.

Feeling out of place, she left during the latter part of the service, when it was time for those closest to Daniel to say their final goodbyes. Later, Amber stood beside a large tree, away from everyone, observing Mr. Prescott and Lucy lay flowers over Daniel's casket before it was lowered into the ground.

"Isn't it the most moronic thing people do?" Jade declared, emerging from behind Amber.

"Some might say it's poetic," Amber replied, trying to keep her grief contained.

"A final goodbye," Jade said. She stood by her sister and unexpectedly locked her arm into Amber's. "I think it's a way to make people feel better about not being able to say goodbye."

"Sometimes people do a lot of things just to feel better about a sad situation."

"Do they *really* feel better?" Jade posed. "Does feeling better even matter?"

"I think for them, for Mr. Prescott, it matters that he does something."

"I was there at the one time that saying goodbye would have mattered. If anything, I was the only one who could have said goodbye."

Amber held her sister's arm tighter, not knowing what to say. Jade seemed to be finally embracing her feelings.

"And what did I do?" Jade choked out. "I was in complete denial of what was happening." She pulled her arm back and took a step away. "He was there because of me," she said, looking at Amber with glassy eyes. "He's in that box going into the ground because he pulled me aside. He's dead now, because of me."

Amber reached out, but Jade turned and walked away, muttering, "Goodbyes don't matter when only one person says them."

Wanting to take the pain her sister felt and let it blow away with the wind, Amber only stood helplessly. People had begun to drift away and back to their cars when she made her way back to the grave site.

Amber met Katherine to give their final condolences to the family before returning home. Mr. Porter was talking to Daniel's father, probably offering him words of solace or comfort, assuming there were any.

Lucy walked over to Amber, holding a small bouquet of daisies. Amber hoped to avoid conversation with the girl, but Lucy did not respect any type of boundary.

"It's so hard to believe," Lucy softly said, pulling up beside Katherine and Amber as though they were old family friends. "I know it's been weeks, months, but still, it feels like it didn't happen at all."

Amber shrugged, not saying a word as she shifted to and fro on her feet, waiting for Mr. Porter.

"Well," Katherine scoffed, showing her disdain for Lucy's comment, "if it didn't happen, someone has a lot of explaining to do."

Amber pushed her aunt's arm, coughing.

"Can you believe the last conversation we had was actually at your house?" Lucy commented, either completely ignoring Katherine's remark or just so self-involved that she didn't feel the need to acknowledge it.

"That *is* strange," Amber said, looking at her aunt, annoyed by the conversation.

"Yeah, if I knew telling Daniel about Jade meeting up with that Nathan guy would make him so jealous that he went after him, I never would have called him."

"I beg your pardon," Katherine demanded, turning to Lucy.

"Yeah, I overheard Jade saying she had some drive for work or something, but this Nathan guy wanted to see her," Lucy rambled.

"*That's* what you told your brother?" Amber shrieked, hunching a little when the gazes of lingering mourners turned her way.

"Well, I don't remember exactly," Lucy replied.

"You eavesdropped, Lucy!" Amber said finally, confronting her. "You think we don't know you were hiding behind our house?"

"I wouldn't say hiding." Lucy waved her hand dismissively. "I was just waiting for the right time to talk to Jade since she didn't get my texts."

"You're insane!" Amber announced. "Jade—"

"Not the time, not the place," Katherine whispered.

"Hey," Lucy whined as she edged away, "I don't care if Jade was dating that guy. Anyway, I tried to tell Daniel not to get too close."

"She wasn't—" Katherine began to shout.

This time it was Amber whispering, "Not the time, not the place."

"Oh, I hope you don't think I blame Jade," Lucy added. "Oh, no. That nutjob killed Daniel, and I hope he rots in hell for it." She casually looked at her phone. "Sometimes we don't know the guy we're dating is a bad guy until he shows us."

"Lucy, I think you should go by your father now," Amber gritted out as she pointed at Mr. Prescott. "If you keep talking, this funeral will have an ending no one wants to have. Or maybe they do. Who knows."

Chapter Fifty-Two

"Knock knock, kiddo," Mr. Porter announced, standing by Jade's door. "Can I come in?"

Nodding and pulling her feet under her, still covered by the blanket, Jade moved the folder she'd received from Mr. Prescott, along with the small black box on top of it.

"I wanted to check on you. Amber told me about Lucy, and the ring," Mr. Porter said softly.

"Lucy crawled behind the house determined to prove Daniel wrong when he told her I was willing to be acquaintances, not friends."

"I heard."

"She overheard us talking about going to Syndicate and told Daniel her convoluted version of it, making it sound like I was going to meet Nathan with the drive." Jade caved in on herself, heavy with grief. "She called Daniel as she passed Nathan's men, and they heard her. That's how he knew to go to Syndicate."

"She's a special girl," Mr. Porter said sarcastically.

Jade rolled her eyes, too exhausted to generate true anger, then stared at the box.

"That's his mother's ring."

"I was told."

"He was going to give it to me, Mr. Porter."

Mr. Porter sat beside her, not responding.

"What do I do now?" Jade asked, holding on to her guilt, her remorse, but more importantly, her grief.

"I wish I had something to make this better, Jade." He squeezed her hand.

Jade leaned forward, moving her hand over her stomach and letting out a deep breath.

"This isn't your fault, Mr. Porter," Jade said. "He would've killed you too."

"It isn't your fault either, little gem," he assured her.

Jade shrugged, pulling the blanket over her shoulders and tugging her feet even closer to herself.

"Are you okay?"

"Just a little nausea, upset stomach. Aunt Katherine said our Elliot power was born out of pain and grew from pain." Jade glanced at Mr. Porter. "That's kinda cruel. I mastered my power going after Nathan," she confessed, not mentioning the time she'd spent torturing him. "It's terrible that I have this amazing ability, I have power, but I don't want it. I'd rather be weak and not deal with this."

Mr. Porter glimpsed a folder on the windowsill—containing the sum total of the information she'd ripped out of Nathan's mind to replace the smoking guns in the destroyed laptop. He sighed.

"I'd keep that away from your sister and aunt," he advised. "I would have done a few things to the monster that killed my sweet wife and precious daughter, but I also would've had a hard time explaining it."

"Justifying . . ." Jade trailed off.

"Explaining," he said, meeting her gaze and sharing an unspoken thought.

He stood to leave the room, wishing her a good night, but paused by the foot of her bed and looked back at her.

"I know you were planning on making Nathan confess publicly after the verdict," Mr. Porter told her. "You were going to make him tell the details that would have ruined his life more than it already was. I know that's why you went there every day and why you helped the prosecution with that evidence."

Jade simply stared with watery eyes, neither admitting nor denying anything.

"Why didn't you, little gem?" he whispered.

"Daniel's father," she replied. "He was there; he's in pain. He raised Daniel and has a love for him he never planned to have. He feels more toward Daniel than Lucy, even though he'd never admit it. He . . ." She cleared her throat, steadying her breaking voice. "He was the only person in the room who was hurting as much as I was. I couldn't make the trial about Nathan's other crimes; it was Daniel's murder."

Mr. Porter regarded her fondly and then shared an unexpected sentiment. "I know from experience that the feelings you face will grow and change every day. My heart breaks for you, but it is also filled with pride for your compassion and loyalty, and your bravery. Just know that you have a great support system in myself, your sister, and your aunt. I hope we can all be there for you the same way your parents were for me."

www.ingramcontent.com/pod-product-compliance
Lightning Source LLC
LaVergne TN
LVHW041752060526
838201LV00046B/978